Beautifully
BROKEN REDEMPTION

THE
SUTTER LAKE
SERIES

CATHERINE
COWLES

Editor: Susan Barnes
Copy Editor: Chelle Olson
Proofreading: Julie Deaton and Janice Owen
Paperback Formatting: Stacey Blake, Champagne Book Design
Cover Design: Hang Le

Beautifully

BROKEN REDEMPTION

Prologue

Anna
PAST

DEREK'S VOICE CUT THROUGH THE CAR AT A DECIBEL that endangered our eardrums.

"D, noooooo," I begged.

He only cast his gaze in my direction, belting out lyrics I could barely make out about wanting to know what love was.

I couldn't help the laughter that escaped. Even on the worst days, the ones where I thought I might drown with the weight balanced on my shoulders, he could always make me laugh.

I reached over and took the hand currently drumming a beat on his thigh. A hand I knew better than any other. Each callus and scar. Every bump and ridge. The familiarity brought a sense of comfort I couldn't find anywhere else. I linked my fingers with his.

"Love you, D."

His singing trailed off, and he gripped my hand tighter. "I'd do anything for you, Angel."

"I know." That kind of gift for someone like me…it was everything.

Lights flashed behind us, and Derek's gaze snapped to the rear-view mirror.

I swiveled to look. The cop car definitely had us in its sights. I glanced at the odometer. He was only five over the limit. "They probably just want to give you a warning."

Derek didn't say a word, and he didn't pull over.

"Derek?"

"Can't get pulled over."

My heart picked up its pace. "Why not?"

He didn't look away from the road in front of us as he pressed his foot down on the gas pedal. "I'm sorry, Anna."

Cascading red and blue. I concentrated on the way the colors blended from one into the next. As my vision went unfocused, the two almost melded into purple. I wanted to fall into that new color, hoping it would take me somewhere else. Anywhere but here.

I found myself leaning towards it, but the bite of the handcuffs around my wrists brought me out of the haze. The little bit of numbness that meant blessed relief from the panic fled with it. The thrum of my pulse picked up again.

"Anna," Derek hissed.

I didn't turn to look at him. Couldn't. Not when I watched as three police officers unloaded an array of what I knew had to be drugs from the trunk of his car. A car that had been the scene of so many firsts for me: Date. Kiss. Whispered "I love you." A car that had been my refuge from a home I would've given anything to escape.

How did the same ton of metal I'd once seen as a lifeline now seem like the weight that would drag me under? I swallowed against the burn rising in my throat as one of the cops lifted another bag and pointed at me. It was the rocker Hello Kitty makeup bag I'd left at Derek's a few months ago. I'd brought over some toiletries to have on hand after he finally got an apartment.

My parents didn't know that he had his own place now. But they knew almost nothing about me and hated what they *could* see. Perhaps they had been right to feel that way. Maybe I was reckless. And now, I was going to add moron on top of it. Because inside that makeup bag with the skulls I had thought were so cute were little baggies filled with pills.

"What did you do?" The words ripped out of me without my permission.

"I'm so sorry," he whispered. "I needed money to get the apartment. We needed it, Angel."

"Quiet," one of the cops barked, moving closer to cut off any conversation.

That was for the best. Because no excuse I heard from the boy I loved would cut it. The boy who had always been my safe place. Who now was anything but.

"Get them loaded up. Separate cars. I don't want them talking," an older cop told the one standing between us.

The younger one bent, grabbed hold of my arm, and tugged me to my feet. "Come on."

I went without argument or complaint. I didn't say a word as he forced my head down and shoved me into the back of the squad car. I didn't cry out when the metal of the cuffs bit into my skin, tearing at it. I stared straight ahead as we pulled away, and I didn't once look back at the boy I loved with everything I had.

"Do you really think the cuffs need to stay on?" A man dressed in khakis and a button-down scowled at the officer standing next to my chair.

"Do you want to see photos of the stash we pulled from her

and her boyfriend's car? They could've kept the whole county high for weeks."

"Uncuff her, McAdams," the older man ordered.

The cop grumbled something under his breath but did as he was told. I felt blessed relief as the metal dropped away from my wrists. I brought my arms around, rubbing at the red marks.

The older man scowled as he took in the abraded skin. "You're done here, McAdams."

"Happy to be," the officer spat as he left the interrogation room.

The man eased himself into a chair opposite me. He folded his hands, letting them rest on the table. The gold of his wedding band glinted against the dark brown of his skin. "Would you like some water?"

"No, thank you."

"You let me know if that changes. I'm Detective Markum. You're in some pretty serious trouble. But I'd like to help you as much as I can."

The burn was back in my throat. And no amount of swallowing alleviated the pain. "Did you call my parents?"

"I did. They weren't home, but I left a message with your sister for them to call me as soon as they return."

Date night. Their ritual where they left their cell phones at home and went out together. I glanced at the clock on the wall. I had at least another thirty minutes of respite before they returned. Thirty minutes before the hammer came down.

I could already feel the sting of the slap. The burn of the punch that would land somewhere on my torso—anywhere clothing would cover. Never on the face. The one time he'd been overzealous and had broken several ribs, my mother had invented a story about me jumping on my bed and taking a tumble. The hospital had believed it hook, line, and sinker.

"Anna, did you hear me?"

Detective Markum's voice brought me out of the memory. "Sorry, what?"

"You can wait until you've spoken with them to talk to me."

I shook my head. I didn't want to wait. I wanted to hurry up and get this over with. The conversation. The punishment that would come after my parents picked me up. Everything. "I'll tell you anything you want. But I don't think I know much."

Markum nodded slowly. "That's not what Derek is saying."

I stiffened at the way the detective said my boyfriend's name. As if it were a bomb just waiting to go off. "What did he say?"

"He said the drugs were yours. Said he was just holding them for you."

"What?!" The word came out on a panicked shriek. "I've never even done drugs." Sure, I drank at parties, but every time Derek smoked pot or took a pill, I always declined.

"Evidence is pointing to you both being involved."

My breaths started coming faster, one after the other. Each one seemed to tumble over the last with the urge to get out and be free. "I-I'm not. I didn't." My fingers began to tingle as I struggled to suck in air.

Markum rose, coming around the table. "Easy now. Just breathe. Nice and slow. Follow me."

He took a long, slow breath, raising his hand with his inhale and lowering it with his exhale. I tried to follow him, but it took several tries before I could. After a few minutes, the tingling in my hands started to retreat. "Sorry," I mumbled.

He patted my shoulder. "No need to apologize. We're going to figure this out. We just have to take it one step at a time."

"Test me." I straightened at the genius of the thought. "You guys can do that, right? I can pee in a cup or give you some of my hair."

"We'll do that. And if it's negative—"

"It will be."

"Then that will be in your favor." Markum pulled out a little notepad and pen from his pocket. "But right now, I need you to tell me about Derek. Did you know he was involved in drugs?"

I stared down at the table as if it held all the answers in the world.

"I can't help you if you don't tell me the truth."

I looked up at the detective. "Pot and some pills. I don't know what they were. Usually, just at parties…at least, that's what I thought." But apparently there were all sorts of things I didn't know about my boyfriend.

"How long have you been together?"

"Since I was fourteen, and he was sixteen." A lifetime in teenage years. Longer than any of our friends. We were simply waiting for my eighteenth birthday so I could move in with him. So that I could be free. I had the two-and-a-half-year countdown on my calendar at home.

Markum jotted down something on his notepad. "And when did he start using?"

"I think he always smoked pot. I mean, he started before I met him." He'd hidden it from me for a while, and then one night at a get-together with some friends, he'd taken the joint someone offered him. He hadn't even asked me if I wanted it. He knew better. But that was how everything had gone. A slow evolution. Before I knew it, the parties were more frequent, and there was pressure for me to join him on the ride.

"Have you ever seen him dealing?"

"Never. I—" My words cut off as I thought about all of the times he'd had to drop something off at friends' houses when we were out and about. Friends that I didn't know or recognize. Times when he kissed me and told me he'd be right back. "Oh, God. I'm such an idiot."

I could hear my father's voice in my head. *"I don't know how you're my daughter. Insolent and stupid. Why can't you be more like Chelsea?"* My sister broke her back to make sure she never displeased our dad. She rarely found herself on the receiving end of his fists. But his cruelty only made me want to rebel more.

Markum bent to meet my gaze. "You're not an idiot. You put your trust in someone you shouldn't have."

"What's going to happen to me?"

"That's what we're going to figure out. I'm going to talk to the district attorney and your parents. If you cooperate like you are now, I'm hoping the charges will be minimal."

Charges. That meant court. Maybe jail. Some sort of juvenile facility? My breaths started coming quicker again.

A knock sounded on the door, and a female officer poked her head in. "You've got a call, Markum."

He looked at me. "I'll be right back. Officer Stapleton will wait with you."

Thankfully, she didn't try to make conversation. I closed my eyes and pictured the way Detective Markum had breathed. I counted to five as I inhaled and then out to five with the exhale. Any time I saw Derek's face in my mind, felt the way his arms had always made me feel so safe, I shoved it out. Any time I began to panic about judges and jails, I counted my breaths.

The door squeaked as it swung into the room, and my eyes flew open. Markum had a pretty good poker face, but I could still see the lines of concern. I dug my fingers into my thighs. "What is it?"

"I spoke with your father."

My nails bit into the denim. "What did he say?"

"He and your mother declined to come down to the station or to get you a lawyer."

My eyes shut again for the briefest of moments. I had expected a silently seething father and a mother with disappointment in her eyes. But still, parents with a lawyer in tow. "They're not coming?"

"No."

"So, what happens to me now?"

Markum shifted on his feet. "I can call a court-appointed lawyer for you, but unless you have someone who can post bail, I'm afraid you'll have to stay in holding for tonight, at least."

Derek. He was the person I would've called. The one I could

always count on. Yet he was sitting a few rooms over, betraying me to anyone who would listen. Selling our love in hopes of getting off scot-free.

"Is there someone else I can call? A grandparent or aunt?"

I stared down at my hands, saw the red marks from the handcuffs, my peeling purple nail polish, the fraying tear in the knee of my jeans. "No, there's no one you can call." Because I was completely and totally alone.

CHAPTER
One

Anna
PRESENT

"**A**RE YOU WEARING YOUR MESH GLOVE, KENZ? I DON'T want you to lose a finger."

Kennedy let out an exasperated sigh. "I'm not going to chop off a finger."

I set my knife down on the cutting board and turned to face my friend. "Do you not remember that hot man of yours gluing your finger closed after you sliced it open?"

"That was *one* time. I swear, neither of you will let me live it down."

I couldn't help the laugh that bubbled out of me. "You're lucky we let you back here after all the near disasters you've had." But I had to admit it was nice to have her here again. Being the head honcho of the Community Center meant she was in charge of all the big-picture stuff and had less time to be in the trenches with me. So, when we got afternoons like this one where we cooked for the shelter's thirty or so residents, I soaked them up.

"Traitors," she grumbled under her breath.

"Traitors who care about keeping all of your fingers and toes firmly attached."

"Yeah, yeah. You're just lucky I love you both."

"Good thing because you're stuck with me for life."

My phone buzzed in my back pocket. I quickly wiped my hands on a towel and pulled it out. Being permanently attached to my phone was just one of the requirements of being head of Hope House. The shelter could have any number of emergencies pop up at any time, and I had to be ready to put out the fires.

The corners of my mouth tipped up as I saw my sister's name on the screen.

Chelsea: *How are the hooligans? Making you pull out your hair yet?*

Me: *I bribed them with beer and cigarettes. That seemed to do the trick.*

There was a pause for at least thirty seconds, and I started to question if we were ready for those kinds of jokes. It had taken us a long time to get back to a place where we could be in each other's lives, where Chelsea believed my truth about what had really happened all of those years ago. The fact that she was moving to Sutter Lake and trusting me with her kids while she wrapped up her life in Portland was a huge step.

Chelsea: *Don't waste the good stuff on them. Natty Light is all they need.*

A laugh burst out of me, startling Kennedy. She let out a rather creative curse. "If you don't want me to lose a finger, don't scare me like that."

"Sorry."

"Who is it, anyway? New boyfriend?" She waggled her eyebrows in my direction.

I rolled my eyes and shoved my phone back into my pocket. Boyfriends had not been on the docket for me. Not since my first and last had landed me in juvenile detention for two and a half years. I'd gone on dates here and there, but it never quite seemed worth the risk. And I'd had other things to worry about—like staying alive.

"It was Chelsea, checking on Lyla and Justin."

"Where are they, anyway?"

"They're helping watch the younger ones on the playground." There was little that made me happier than seeing my niece and nephew fall in love with the shelter. From the first time they'd visited with Chelsea, staying in my small cottage at the back of the property, they had simply understood the special nature of Hope House. And they always wanted to help.

Kennedy dumped a pile of carrots into the pot that would be beef stew in a few hours. "They have a way with them. It's not typical for an eleven-year-old boy to be so eager to play babysitter."

"Justin has a tender heart under that preteen bravado."

A gentle smile stretched across Kennedy's face. "You're right there. And Lyla is the sister all the little girls wish they had."

I chuckled as I remembered the *gymnastics camp* my niece had held yesterday afternoon. She'd taught cartwheels, handstands, and other things I didn't know the names of. "The gymnastics teacher over in the rec center asked if she could hire her."

"It's not a bad idea. She's got the touch."

I poured my pile of veggies into the pot and turned down the heat. "Okay, this just needs to simmer for a few hours. Want to go find the munchkins, or do you need to get home to Cain?"

Kennedy took off her apron, hanging it on a peg. "I'm with you this afternoon."

I hung my apron up by hers and headed for the door. "How is Mr. Tall-Dark-and-Handsome?"

The goofy smile that stretched across Kennedy's face had me averting my gaze. "He's good. Busy. They're about to start on a big new project."

Kennedy's husband had built a second headquarters for his security company in Sutter Lake. Halo was one of the best in the business and had brought a lot of new jobs into the community. "That's exciting."

"I don't understand a word he says when he's talking about it, but it's adorable how excited he gets."

I snickered as I pulled open one of the double doors that led to a massive outdoor space with a playground, sports fields, and a picnic area. "Somehow, I don't think Cain would appreciate being called 'adorable.'"

Kennedy bit her lip. "Probably not. Better to only call him that behind his back."

"Smart woman." My steps faltered as I took in the scene on the playground. Kids ran around screaming and laughing, a whirling flash of limbs as Justin chased them. But in the center of it all, a tall man held Lyla and another little girl upside down by one ankle each as they cackled. "What's he thinking?" I asked as I started towards the fray.

Kennedy caught my arm. "Mason?"

"Yes, Mason. That's dangerous. One of them could fall and get seriously hurt." I could only imagine how injuring one of her children would halt the progress of my slowly mending relationship with Chelsea.

Kennedy's lips twitched. "He's like six-foot-four and has muscles for days. I'm pretty sure Mase isn't going to drop them."

My cheeks heated. I knew what he looked like. It was the kind of size that was hard to ignore. But he was always gentle and unassuming as he moved through the shelter, as if he understood that his size could be intimidating to the women and children there—people who had fled situations where size had been used to terrorize. "It doesn't matter how many muscles he has. Accidents happen."

She sobered, studying my face. "What is it with you and him?"

I clamped my mouth shut. It was impossible to explain just how or why Mason Decker got on every last nerve I had. "He... he's too nice."

A laugh bubbled up out of Kennedy, building on itself until she had to brace an arm on my shoulder to hold herself upright. "I'm sorry, did you say he's too nice?"

I scowled in her direction. "No one's that nice all the time. It's weird."

She patted my shoulder. "Oh, my paranoid friend. It's no wonder you and Cain get along so well. You both think everyone is a potential serial killer."

"Hey, if you would listen to those true crime podcasts I keep sending you, you would, too." I kept my tone light, but pain lit a path along my sternum. A sensation carved by all the stories I'd heard in juvie. All of the things I'd seen. Hellish nightmares that would never leave. I knew that the worst of humanity could hide under a pleasant expression. Worse, it could hide under a face you'd always trusted.

Kennedy wrapped an arm around my shoulders. "I think it might be time for a breather from the creepy podcasts."

"One woman's creepy is another woman's Zen."

"That's really messed up."

"Anna! Anna! Did you see? I was upside down, and Mase made me fly." Lyla ran at me, crashing into my middle and wrapping her arms around me with an oomph.

"I did see. Looked like…fun." Incredibly dangerous fun, but at least she'd have a high before her concussion.

"Hey, Kenz. Anna."

I looked up from my niece's face to meet swirling hazel eyes. Something about the dance between gold and green was hypnotizing, which only annoyed me more.

"Hey, Mason," Kennedy greeted.

I nodded in his direction. "Mason."

The corner of his mouth quirked. "I've told you time and again, call me Mase."

"Sure." But something about using his nickname was simply too familiar, too comfortable. I wanted clear boundaries. Those had been hard to come by since Mason had started volunteering here. Cain had a program where he encouraged his employees to get involved with organizations in the community for a certain number of hours a month while still getting paid as if they were working at their desks. As vice-president and chief operations officer of the company, Mason led by example and worked every single one of his hours at Hope House.

"I need to head back to Halo. But, Anna, the kids want to come over and go fishing in the lake this weekend. They're welcome anytime. Just text me."

I ground my back teeth together. "If we have time."

"Pleeeeeeease," Lyla begged. "I want to catch a fish."

Justin appeared next to Mason. "Yeah, it would be fun. Can't we go?"

"How about Sunday? I'll even provide the lunch," Mason offered.

I heard a soft laugh coming from Kennedy's direction. I studiously ignored it and did my best not to bite Mason's head off for offering this outing to Justin and Lyla without running it by me first. "Sure. That would be nice. Just tell me what I need to bring, and what time to be there."

"You don't need to bring a thing. And how about eleven?"

"Sure, just text me your address." All of the shelter volunteers had my phone number in case they ever needed to change shifts or ran into an emergency. But having Mason text me for personal reasons made me twitchy.

"See you then." He gave Justin a knuckle bump and Lyla a high-five and then headed for the parking lot.

Justin gave me a pleading look. "Can I have a snack?"

My eyes bugged. "Are you about to have a growth spurt? I swear you need to be fed every hour."

He grinned. "Mom says I'm definitely going to be over six feet."

He was already well on his way. I waved them inside. "Come on. Can't have you wasting away on my watch."

The kids ran ahead, and Kennedy fell into step beside me, bumping her shoulder against mine. "I see what you mean. He's scary-friendly. Definite serial killer vibes."

"Shut up."

She wrapped an arm around my shoulder. "Love you, Anna. But at some point, you're going to have to realize that there are good people out there. Ones who simply want to help or make a difference."

I knew she was right. I'd seen it in the group of friends I'd started to build here. In the way the town supported our work at the shelter and the community center. But I couldn't simply turn off the little voice inside me that told me to be on guard. And if I felt chemistry with someone? That alert was on in full force.

CHAPTER
Two

Mason

"How was everything at the center?" Cain asked as I slid into a chair opposite his desk.

"Good. Sorry I'm late getting back. I got caught up."

"You never have to apologize about that." He leaned back in his chair. "Anna tear you a new one this time?"

The corner of my mouth kicked up as I pictured Anna's annoyed expression. "I've never known a woman who got so frustrated by me trying to be helpful."

"What's even more interesting is why you find that so compelling."

He had a point. I had no idea why Anna was so fascinating to me, but she had been from the first day I started volunteering at the shelter. And the pricklier she was with me, the more I wanted to know what lay beneath that spiny exterior. "I admire her."

That much was true. She ran Hope House with a mixture of drill-sergeant exactness and empathetic kindness. I'd seen her put a burly man three times her size in his place and hold a young mother as she cried after leaving an abusive marriage. It was a heady combination.

Cain arched a brow. "Admire her? Attraction has nothing to do with it?"

Heat crept up the back of my neck. The fact that I could imagine just how well Anna's petite, curvy form would fit against me might have a little to do with it. "Can we get back to the business at hand?"

Cain chuckled. "All the answer I need." He sobered. "Just tread carefully there. I don't know her whole story, but I don't think it's an easy one."

I swallowed against the burn in my throat. I'd gotten the same feeling. Anna hadn't shared anything about her past around me. Not even where she'd grown up. All I knew was that she'd been a shelter resident for years before taking on a managerial role. Justin and Lyla had let a few things slip, but it wasn't anything that helped me put together the pieces of who Anna really was.

"I'm just trying to get her to see I'm not an ax murderer."

Cain barked out a laugh. "That's where Anna and I are of the same mind. Suspect everyone. Maybe if I showed her your extensive background check, she'd let up a little."

"It's not a bad idea. I'll sign off on you taking it public."

"I'll find a way to slip it onto her desk."

"You're a true friend." I slid my phone out of my pocket and opened my notes app. "Now, let's talk about phase two."

My role at Halo was the dream job. A blend of business and tech, working for someone who I truly respected and who treated me as more of a partner than a second-in-command. Cain and I worked effortlessly together, brainstorming ways to take the company to the next level.

For the next hour, we talked through a new version of our home security line. How we would bring it to market and at what price point. It was important to both of us that a feeling of safety be affordable to all who might need it. Each new incarnation of our systems had varied levels and expenses to ensure it could be in everyone's hands.

I'd even started a program where we gave out our personal alarms at no cost to people who might not be able to afford one or had been the victim of a crime. Pocket devices that let out an ear-splitting scream when you pulled the pin. We'd distributed thousands so far, including one to any resident of the shelter who wanted one.

Cain flipped his laptop closed and checked his watch. "I think that does it for today. I need to get home before Kenz decides to burn down the kitchen."

"I thought she was getting better."

He grimaced. "She is. Until she decides to try some fancy something or other. Sunday, there were literal flames coming out of the oven."

I tried to stifle my laughter and failed. "Well, she's got Funfetti cake down."

The smile that came to Cain's face was one that had me wanting to look away. One that spoke of contentment and peace and having everything you could ever want. "That she does." He pushed to his feet and slipped his laptop into a messenger bag. "You heading out?"

There was no risk of anyone burning down *my* kitchen. No one waiting on dinner until I got home. "I think I'll put in another hour or so. I want to go over our plan one more time. See if I'm overlooking anything."

Cain clapped me on the shoulder as I stood. "Don't work too hard. Oh, and Saturday, barbeque at the lake house. We'll get started around noon."

"I'll be there. Need me to bring anything?"

"Nope. We've got it covered."

"See you then." I headed for my office just down the hall. The place was mostly empty, the vast majority of employees already having gone home to their families. The sound of my boots hitting the hardwood echoed through the halls.

I pushed open one of the double doors to my office. I would never get tired of the view that greeted me. Expanses of green forests that met up with craggy mountains capped with snow, even as we moved into summer. The views from my place in San Francisco hadn't been anything to sneeze at, but this view spoke to me more.

When I arrived in Sutter Lake to interview for the V.P. position, I'd felt a sense of peace I hadn't experienced since…a much simpler time. Before my childhood had been blown apart. I eased into the chair behind my desk, letting my gaze settle on the two photos. One of my mother and me. In the picture, she held my hands as she helped me to balance while I learned to walk. And one of my sister at her college graduation, her bright smile beaming at the camera.

My phone buzzed in my hand, and I glanced down at the screen. *Juliette* flashed on the display. I hit accept. "Think of the devil…"

"Careful who you're calling devil, big brother."

I grinned, leaning back in my chair. "If the shoe fits…"

"I'm an angel."

I nearly choked on my cough. Juliette was the reason I had salt and pepper at my temples at the age of thirty-six. "Keep telling yourself that. How are you? How are classes?"

Juliette sighed, and I could picture her curling up in her favorite chair in her apartment off campus. "Killing me. Remind me why I thought it was a good idea to go to Stanford again?"

"Because you're going to be the most kick-ass lawyer I've ever known."

"I really hope so. But I'm starting to think I shouldn't have taken a summer class. I need a break."

I leaned forward in my chair. "Why don't you come up here for a week? You said this one's online, right?" I wanted to lay eyes on my baby sister. Make sure she wasn't pushing herself too hard.

"So you can make sure I'm eating properly and taking my vitamins?"

"Maybe."

"Don't be a worrywart. I'm fine. I just wanted to whine."

I picked up a pen from my desk and twirled it between my fingers. "You know you can always whine to me."

"And I love you for it." She was quiet for a moment. "I was actually thinking about heading to Cabo for a long weekend with some girlfriends. Beaches and a few margaritas. What do you say, big brother?"

"Is that an invitation?"

She choked on a laugh. "You might be a bit of a buzzkill…"

"Let me guess, you want me to foot the bill."

"You love me, right? And you know how hard I'm working."

I did, and Juliette deserved a break to blow off some steam. "Fine, put it on my credit card. But no presidential suites, Jules."

I'd learned the hard way that I had to give that disclaimer.

"A suite might be fun…" She let the words dangle.

"Jules," I warned.

"Oh, all right. We'll stay in one of the tiny regular rooms." Her voice got faraway for a moment. "Hey, I've got another call, I need to jump."

"A boy?"

She groaned. "Mason…"

"Tell him if he hurts you, I'll kill him."

"I'll be sure to relay exactly that to my study buddy."

"He might say he wants to study, but really—"

"Mason!" Juliette cut me off. "I do not want to have this conversation with you. The first time was awkward enough."

My twenty-something-self trying to talk to sixteen-year-old Juliette about birth control and safe sex had been painful, to say the least. "Trust me, I have zero desire to repeat that."

"Thank God. Talk to you later, brother bear."

She hung up before I could tell her I loved her. I stared at the photos on my desk. Two. It seemed empty. Despite the dream job and amazing friends, I felt so damn alone sometimes. I'd spent most of my dating years raising Jules, and I'd missed the train on finding someone. I didn't regret it for a moment. But it didn't change the fact that things simply felt lonely now.

CHAPTER
Three

Anna

LYLA RAN OUT OF THE LAKE, MAKING A BEELINE FOR ME. She threw her arms around me. I shrieked as the freezing-cold water dripped off her and onto my bare legs. "You little monster." I went for her sides, tickling her.

She dissolved into giggles, falling into my lap. "I love it here. I'm so happy we moved."

Her words were music to my ears. I'd been nervous when Chelsea had first broached the subject. Sutter Lake was different from Portland, and I wasn't sure if she and the kids would love it as much as I did. I couldn't have been more wrong. The last two weeks I'd spent taking care of my niece and nephew, they'd bloomed in this slower pace of life. They'd also fallen right into my group of friends.

I blew a raspberry on Lyla's neck. "I'm so glad."

She leapt from my lap and ran back to the water, swimming out towards the massive inflatable trampoline Kennedy and Cain had installed this year. She made it to the ladder in under two minutes.

"She swims like a fish," Kennedy said, adjusting her sunglasses.

"I don't know how. She's barely had lessons."

Our friend Taylor looked up from the little girl in her arms. "She's got a gift. You should get her in lessons at the center. She might be a good candidate for the swim team. I help out a couple of times a week and can put you in touch with the coach."

"That would be great." School didn't start for months, but the kids needed ways to meet friends and stay active. I typed out a quick text to Chelsea.

Me: *What do you think about swim team for Lyla? I can sign her up.*

I dropped the phone back into my lap as Jensen let out a loud catcall whistle.

Tessa covered her ears. "Are you trying to make me lose my hearing?"

J shrugged. "I want those sexy men to know they're appreciated."

"That's my girl," Jensen's grandmother, Irma, said as she looked up from her book. "And a fine bunch of specimens they are. We should make ourselves a calendar."

"Mom," Sarah chastised as she handed her a glass of lemonade.

"What? I'm old, not dead. I can appreciate those abs of steel. And those v-things. Those are my favorite."

Sarah let out an exasperated sigh. "One of those men is your grandson."

"I'm not looking at him. I'm looking at the others."

A laugh bubbled up as I glanced out at the trampoline. But that sound died in my throat. I knew the other guys were there, tossing laughing kids off the floating structure, some in life jackets, others only in swimsuits. But my eyes seemed to be pulled to only one form. Lightly tanned skin and lean muscle. Mason's head tipped back as he laughed. So damn carefree as if he'd never had a worry in the world.

"You've got a little drool there," Kennedy whispered.

I snapped my gaze away. "Sorry, I spaced."

"Mm-hmm. You know, you could always try talking to him."

"I do talk to him."

She rolled her eyes. "To bark orders at him or scowl in his direction. Try not looking like you want to murder him and ask him something normal, like how it's been settling into Sutter Lake."

"You know I don't do normal well."

Kennedy laid a hand on my forearm. "*Normal* was a bad word choice. Normal is overrated and boring."

I couldn't help looking out at the trampoline again. Mason launched Lyla into the air as she shrieked in delight. That man screamed: *normal*. He would want a wife who baked cookies and gave him two-point-five kids and adopted a golden retriever. He wouldn't want someone who had a permanent record and countless demons.

Kenz squeezed my arm. "You have a messed-up idea of who you are and what you're worth. Your past doesn't determine who you are now."

I wished I could believe that, but I knew the truth. The past determined everything. It haunted and taunted, popping up when you least expected it with a sucker punch to the solar plexus. "I'm happy as I am. I don't need anything more than what I have."

"Just because you're content doesn't mean you can't reach for more. You deserve mind-blowing happiness."

A yell from Jensen broke off our conversation. "Tucker Harris, you put me down right now. That water is freezing."

He gave Jensen a playful swat on the butt. "Oh, I'll put you down, Wilder…"

"Tuck—"

Her words were cut off as he launched her into the lake water. Their son, Noah, hooted and hollered. "She's gonna kill you for that."

Tuck gave him a high-five and then picked up their other son, Drew, hoisting him on top of his shoulders. "Did you see Mommy fly?"

The little boy nodded. "She went far."

Jensen burst out of the water, spluttering. "You. Are going to pay for that."

"Aw, come on, Wilder, I just wanted to see you all wet."

I choked on a laugh. Tessa turned bright red and bent to cover Taylor's daughter's ears. "They're all going to get sent home from school on their first day for saying inappropriate things."

Taylor rolled her eyes. "First day of kindergarten, I got called into the office because Cooper said s-h-i-t. I almost murdered Walker."

Kennedy sent me a wavering smile before turning back to our group. I reached out and gave her hand a squeeze. She and Cain had been going through the foster-to-adopt program and had gotten their hearts broken more times than I could count. "At least we know we'll never be bored."

As my gaze traveled around the group, I couldn't help but think about how my friendship bucket overflowed. I'd landed in this amazing community. Yet, I still felt unsettled. As if I were waiting for the other shoe to drop. Countless years had passed, and I was still waiting. Maybe I always would be.

"I told Kenz I would take over for her on dishes."

I jolted at the deep timbre of Mason's voice, almost dropping the dish I was putting into the dishwasher. "Hasn't anyone told you that sneaking up on a woman is a bad idea? You could've gotten a knee to the junk."

The corner of his mouth kicked up. "I wasn't sneaking, but I'll keep that warning in mind."

I bit the inside of my cheek. I didn't need my mouth running away from me any more than it already had.

"I'll rinse. You put in the dishwasher?"

He looked so damn hopeful. Like a puppy I couldn't bear to kick. *Nice. Normal.* I repeated the words in my mind. "Sure."

"You would've thought I'd asked for a kidney, not to help with the dishes."

"I had a system down."

"And I'm forever messing up your systems."

He was, damn it. Messing up my carefully boundaried life with his smiles and offers of help. With his ideas for the shelter. And, even more infuriatingly, they were usually good ones. The personal alarms he'd offered to the tenants had given them an extra sense of safety I hadn't seen coming.

I slid the plate I was holding into its appropriate slot. "You are kind of an interfering bastard."

Mason barked out a laugh. "At least, you're honest."

"But I think your heart is in the right place."

He turned to face me, clutching at his chest. "Anna, was that a compliment?"

My face heated, and I grabbed a bowl from his other hand. "I'll take it back if you keep this up."

"Okay, I'll shut up. I just wish I'd had a recorder running. It might be the only one I get from you."

God, I could be a bitch. But it was only when something hammered against my defenses. And this man, he was a threat to them all. "At this rate, it will be."

He chuckled and pulled another dish from the stack, washing off the excess food before handing it to me. "Just you wait. I'm going to win you over with my wit and charm."

I blinked up at him. "Charm? Wit? Are you talking about Tuck?"

"You wound me."

I couldn't help the curve of my lips as I put the dish in the washer. "I'm sure I'm the only one." I knew plenty of women in town had their eyes on the bachelor. From what I'd heard, Mason had been on a handful of dates, but nothing had ever gotten serious. I wanted to know why. Did he have some crazy standards that no one could possibly live up to? Was he intent on being a bachelor forever? As I studied him out of the corner of my eye, I didn't feel that either scenario really fit.

"The only one who what?"

"Wounds you."

His brows pulled together. "You certainly seem to be my toughest critic."

Shit. I'd been harder on him than I'd intended. Time to rein it in. My phone buzzed in my back pocket, and I slid it out. I didn't recognize the number or area code, but I answered anyway. It wouldn't have been the first time I'd gotten a call asking if we could place a resident from somewhere out of state.

"Hello, this is Anna."

A female voice cut across the line. "Anna Foley?"

"Yes, this is she."

"I'm Detective Johnson with the Las Vegas Police Department."

I leaned a hip against the counter, waiting for her to say more. She didn't. "Do you have someone who needs to be placed at Hope House?"

"I'm sorry, Hope House?"

"The shelter in Sutter Lake. I assumed that's why you were calling."

"No, it's not regarding that."

I stiffened, my fingers curling tighter around the phone. Flashes of memories danced in my mind. Images that were dark enough to take me under. I focused on my breathing, keeping my voice even. "What can I help you with?"

"You were in Chelsea Foley's phone as her emergency contact."

Everything in me seized. "Yes, that's my sister. Is she okay? Was she hurt?"

Mason shut off the water and moved in closer. I didn't have the energy or focus to move away.

"I'm so sorry, but your sister was found dead early this morning."

"What? N-no. That's impossible. Chelsea wasn't even in Las

Vegas. She was in Portland." My legs began to tremble. I had no control over them—as if they had suddenly turned to mush.

Mason caught me just as I was about to go down, half guiding, half carrying me over to a chair at the kitchen table. I hardly noticed that either. I could barely hear the detective over the blood rushing in my ears.

"Your sister's fingerprints were on file from when she was a child. It's a program a lot of schools have in case a student ever goes missing. Between that and the match to her identification, we know it's her."

My fingers began to tingle, and I realized I wasn't breathing. "How?"

"Do you know if your sister struggled with depression or addiction?"

"What? No. Neither of those." The question gave me a jolt of adrenaline that my system desperately needed. "She's one of the healthiest people I know." Chelsea wouldn't even let herself or her kids drink soda, saying it was poison.

"Sometimes, people can hide that kind of thing from the ones they love the most."

Derek's face flashed in my mind. I knew all about the things people could hide. I knew how those lives could rip apart your existence. But I also knew without a shadow of a doubt that this wasn't a lie Chelsea would've been wrapped up in. It had taken almost a decade for my sister to even speak to me again. Another year before she believed that I was telling the truth, that Derek had lied to the police about my involvement in his operation.

I'd missed so much. Her wedding. The birth of her babies. I'd missed supporting her when her marriage fell apart just weeks after Lyla was born. I'd missed Thanksgivings and Christmases and birthdays. The only thing I hadn't regretted missing out on was seeing my so-called parents. They had been something I'd been happy to leave in my past.

"She wouldn't." I said the words with finality. "She'd never do that to her kids. To me. To herself." My voice cracked on the last word, but I refused to let the tears come.

Mason wove his fingers through mine, squeezing tightly. I didn't have the heart to pull away. In that moment, it felt like he was the only thing tethering me to this Earth.

"She had a lethal dose of methamphetamine in her system when she was discovered at a motel just off the Strip."

My hand clamped down on Mason's, squeezing hard. "There's been a mistake. You have the wrong person."

"Ms. Foley, there's been no mistake. I'm sorry, but your sister is gone. I know this has likely been a shock for you, but I do need to ask you some questions."

I could barely comprehend what Detective Johnson was saying. I tried my best to answer what she asked. No, I didn't know what Chelsea had been doing in Vegas. Yes, I had her children with me. I told her that she was in the process of moving from Portland to Sutter Lake. My eyes burned as I remembered how happy she'd been the day we registered the kids for school next year. How happy I'd been that I was getting a fresh start with the only family I had left.

The click of a pen sounded over the line. "I think that's everything. You have my number if you need anything. I've left a message for your parents, but if you'd like to call them instead—"

Her words cut off in my mind. Just the mention of them sent me hurtling back. I could feel the sting of a slap. The loss of air when an especially vicious punch landed just below my ribs. The physical scars of my father's anger had long since faded, but the emotional scars would never leave.

Mason seemed to understand that I was losing it and pulled the phone from my grasp. "This is Mason Decker. I'm a friend of Anna's. She's understandably upset right now. Can we call you back?"

There was a pause.

"Thank you. We'll be in touch."

He hung up and set the phone down on the kitchen table. Without a word, he pulled me up and into his arms. I didn't resist. I simply held on. As if gripping his t-shirt and feeling his strong arms around me could solve all of my problems.

"I'm so sorry, Anna."

I wanted to break then. So badly wanted to let the sob tear out of my chest and cut through the air. To scream and rage. But I swallowed it all down. My pain didn't matter. There were kids in the other room who would be destroyed by this.

But that wasn't what scared me the most. What terrified me down to my bones was that my parents could get their hands on Lyla and Justin. I couldn't let that happen. Refused. Those little ones who held my whole heart would not be subjected to what I had been growing up. I'd do whatever I had to do to protect them. Even if that meant running.

CHAPTER
Four

Mason

NONE OF US SAID A WORD AS WE SAT CROWDED INTO THE small living area of Anna's cottage. Cain and Kennedy squeezed together on an oversized armchair, Cain's arm wrapped protectively around his wife, whose eyes were rimmed in red. Walker perched on a barstool, his jaw tight. As Sutter Lake's chief of police, he'd already reached out to the detective in charge of Anna's sister's case to see if he could glean any additional information. So far, there wasn't much.

I leaned back against the small couch, looking up the stairs, straining to see or hear any signs of life. Little Lyla's broken sobs from an hour ago had quieted. Now, there was only silence.

But Anna's voice still rang in my ears. Her words about an overdose. Justin and Lyla being left without a mother. Images flashed in my mind. Ones I desperately tried to burn out of my brain but never seemed to succeed at. Our SUV crashing through the fence on the side of the road. Slamming into the water. Juliette's wails.

"Those poor kids," Kennedy whispered, bringing me out of my freefall.

I moved my jaw from side to side, trying in vain to loosen some of the tension there.

Walker looked up from his phone. "Does anyone know if their father is in the picture?"

"I don't think so." I hadn't heard Justin or Lyla mention him once. Anna, either.

"He's not. He signed over his rights when he left my sister."

All of our heads turned as Anna appeared at the bottom of the stairs. There was only one word to describe her. Ravaged. She had always hidden her emotions so well, so it was startling to see them displayed so clearly on her face. As if they were carved into her bones, never to leave again.

"Oh, Anna." Kennedy pushed to her feet and pulled her friend into a tight hug, rubbing a hand up and down her back.

I fisted and flexed my hands, my fingers itching to comfort her. It was stupid. Anna didn't know me. Not really. She certainly didn't trust me. Yet, I still wanted to be the one pulling her into my arms.

Kennedy ushered Anna over to the couch. "Here, sit. Do you want some tea? Something to eat?"

Anna sank down next to me, just a foot away. "No. Thank you. I'm sorry you guys hung around so long. You can go. Really."

Cain scowled. "We're not going anywhere until we know what you need."

The corner of Anna's mouth twitched. As if she wanted to smile but couldn't quite get there. "Good to know the bossy streak doesn't go away, even in a crisis."

Kennedy rolled her eyes. "It's even worse in a crisis."

Walker tapped a few things on his phone. "I've made contact with Detective Johnson. She seems more than capable and is taking the case seriously—"

"My sister didn't do drugs. I would've known."

Kennedy's expression softened. "You two were just getting close again. Maybe she hid it from you."

"No." Anna's face fell. "She has always been incredibly against drugs of any kind. I could barely get her to take an ibuprofen if she needed it."

Walker cleared his throat. "Detective Johnson is going to do everything she can to figure out the what and the how of it. She still hasn't been able to get ahold of your parents. Do you have another number for them?"

Anna went ramrod straight next to me. "No, and I'd appreciate it if you didn't help them find it."

Walker's gaze narrowed on Anna, assessing. "And why's that?"

"Justin and Lyla…they can't go to my parents." Her hands fisted at her sides. "Do you know what I need to do to petition for custody?"

"Why can't they go with their grandparents?" Walker asked slowly.

Anna's mouth clamped closed. Everyone was quiet for a long beat. Waiting and watching.

Kennedy eased down next to Cain. "If you don't tell us, we can't help. Whatever you say won't leave this room unless you want it to."

Anna's gaze swept around, stopping on me. It killed me, the fact that I was the one she trusted the least. But I swallowed down that hit and cleared my throat. "I can leave if that makes you more comfortable, but I do have a law degree that might come in handy as you're figuring things out."

"You do?"

"I never practiced, moved into programming and tech before I had a chance, but I went to a good school. I know more than the basics."

She looked down at her hands as if her fingernails were suddenly the most important things in the world. "My father doesn't accept anything less than perfection. And he makes his displeasure known with his fists."

The rage that swept through me caught me off guard. "Is that why you ended up at the shelter?"

"It's more complicated than that…" Anna let her words trail off.

The mask Walker had perfected over the years on the job slipped into place. You'd never know that, under it all, he wanted to level Anna's father. "Were reports ever filed?"

Anna shook her head. "He was good at hiding it. And it was the worst for me. Chelsea was incredibly good at toeing the line, doing exactly what he expected of her."

"Do Justin and Lyla have a relationship with their grandparents?" I couldn't imagine exposing my children to someone I knew could be violent. But I also knew that family ties were the ones hardest to sever.

Anna tugged at a thread on her denim shorts. "Chelsea said she'd never left them alone with our parents. But they see them once a month for a family dinner."

Just saying the words seemed to be a struggle. I could understand why. The pain of seeing someone you loved returning to an abuser. Because as much as Chelsea might've thought she had put boundaries in place to keep herself and her children safe, just putting the kids in the orbit of those people would have a steep emotional toll.

"Do you know if your sister had a will?" Walker asked.

"She didn't. When we were signing the kids up for school, she mentioned needing to find a lawyer in town to get all that squared away. But I'm on file as the emergency contact with the school. Will that help?"

Anna's words came out faster and faster until they almost tripped over each other. I laid a hand over hers, stilling her movements. "I have some contacts I can call. We'll find you a lawyer who knows all the ins and outs of custody cases and family court."

She stared down at our joined hands, but I didn't pull away. Her fingers spasmed in mine. "I can't ask you to do that. I can do some research—"

I squeezed her fingers. "Let me do this. Please."

Anna's cheeks heated. "I don't have a lot of money in savings, but I have some—"

"You don't need to worry about that," Cain cut in.

Her head snapped up. "No. I'm not taking your money."

"It's just money, Anna. I happen to have a lot of it. Luck of the draw. But it will really piss me off if you don't let me use it to help someone I care about."

She swallowed visibly, her eyes falling closed. "Okay."

I gave her hand another squeeze. "I'll call my contacts on the way home. I'll have a name tomorrow."

"Thank you." Her gaze circled the room. "All of you. I'm sorry you had to step in—"

Kennedy leaned forward in her seat. "You're not alone. We've got your back, whatever you need."

I knew every single person in the room would do anything for Anna. I just hoped she knew that. Because I had a feeling the road to come would be rocky.

CHAPTER
Five

Anna

I WATCHED THE KIDS RUN AROUND THE PLAYGROUND THROUGH my office window. I couldn't quite figure out what game they were playing, some kind of freeze-tag, maybe. Everything in my body hurt. Ached in a way I wasn't sure would ever go away. Not just for me but also for them.

Justin grinned as he tapped a little boy on the shoulder. But I could see beneath the mask—the pain a living and breathing thing inside him. Lyla had shut it off, pretending yesterday hadn't happened at all. When I'd asked how she was feeling this morning, she'd snapped at me that she was fine.

I wasn't sure how to proceed. I needed to find the name of a therapist in town. Someone who could tell me what steps to take. Someone who could assure me that I wasn't messing these kids up beyond repair.

I let my eyes fall closed, sending up a prayer to God or the Universe or whoever might be listening. All I wanted was to keep the kids safe. To make sure they were loved and had everything they needed.

I winced at the last thought, my eyes opening. My salary for running Hope House was generous. Especially for someone who'd barely graduated high school, but I would have to rework my budget—and my living arrangements.

The cottage only had two bedrooms. I'd bought two twin beds for the guest room when Chelsea and the kids had started to visit, but Justin and Lyla would only be content with sharing a room for so long.

I rubbed at my temples, the pressure thrumming there in a steady beat. My cell phone rang, cutting through my panic. I swiped it up, barely glancing at the unknown number before answering.

"Hello, this is Anna."

"Hello, Ms. Foley. This is Keisha Williams. I believe Mason Decker told you I'd be calling."

He had. I'd woken from a rocky sleep at seven this morning to a long text from him on my phone. Mason hadn't delayed in finding me help. He told me that Ms. Williams was one of the best lawyers in the state when it came to custody cases, and she only lived an hour away.

"Please, call me Anna. Thank you so much for taking my case."

"And call me Keisha. I'm happy to help any friend of Mase's."

Mase's. The fondness in Keisha's tone had my breakfast souring in my stomach. "How do you two know each other?"

She chuckled. "He and my husband got into all sorts of trouble together in law school."

Why did I feel such relief at the word *husband* falling from Keisha's mouth? *Dumb, dumb, dumb.* I forced some levity into my voice. "Sounds like you have some good stories."

"Anna, I've got all the dirt. Just stick with me."

The warmth and kindness in her voice was a balm I hadn't realized I needed. "Can't wait to hear them."

"All right. What do you say we get down to business so I can do my best to file today or tomorrow?"

Everything inside me seemed to twist at her words. "That would be good."

"Your sister, Chelsea Foley, left her children in your care while she was away?"

"Yes. She was supposed to be wrapping things up in Portland because they were in the process of moving here. I'm honestly not sure what she was doing in Las Vegas."

Her location, everything surrounding Chelsea's death…none of it made sense. The questions had circled my brain for most of the night as I tossed and turned. But, most of all, why had she lied? Both of us had made a conscious effort for brutal honesty as we'd reconnected these past few years. We hadn't held anything back, knowing that lies and deceptions had forced us apart all those years ago.

The sound of typing came over the line. "That piece of things is less important right now. We need to establish you as the caregiver she left her children with. Has that happened in the past, as well?"

"Yes, the kids have stayed with me for a week the last two summers."

"Good. And had Chelsea found a home in Sutter Lake yet? Anything that would give us proof she intended to make her home there?"

My throat constricted as I struggled to get the words out. All I could see was the bright future we'd planned. All of the things I'd wanted to share with her and the kids about this place. The birthdays and holidays we'd never have. "She was staying with me while she looked for a place. But we registered the kids for school here a few weeks ago."

More typing sounded. "That's good. It means if it goes to court, we'll be able to do that here."

I breathed a sigh of relief at that. I would've gone to hell and back for Justin and Lyla, but having to trek to Portland for court dates, to be in the vicinity of my parents, to be forced to drown in all of my memories there, it would've been rough. "Great news."

"Now, is there a chance your parents might be willing to handle this in mediation? Or that they may simply let you take custody of the children?"

"No. There's no chance." Each word seemed to rip at my throat. The razor's edge of the hatred I knew they felt for me, slicing.

"I need the full backstory there. We'll get into every detail when I come out to Sutter Lake tomorrow, but for now, I need the broad strokes. Remember, I'm on your side. But if I don't have the full picture, I won't be equipped to help you."

I stared at one of the half-dozen photos on my desk. Before Chelsea, Justin, and Lyla came back into my life, there'd only been one. A picture of Kennedy and me the day she'd broken ground on the new center. Now, they crowded my desk. So many memories in just a couple of years.

"My father was physically abusive, and my mother covered for him."

There was a pause on the line and then typing. "I'm incredibly sorry you went through that."

"I won't let the same happen to my niece and nephew."

"We'll do everything we can to prevent them from being placed with your parents. I have to ask you—is there anything they could use as ammunition against you?"

I squeezed my eyes closed, gripping the phone tighter. I'd regretted getting involved with Derek countless times. Trusting him. Giving him everything I had. But I'd never regretted it more than in this moment. "Yes."

There was no typing now. "Tell me. And remember, this is a safe space. We've all made mistakes, Anna."

Except mine would haunt me for the rest of my life. If it sent Justin and Lyla into my parents' care, I'd never recover. But that wouldn't happen. I would take the kids and run first. "When I was fifteen, my boyfriend and I were arrested for possession with intent to distribute. The drugs weren't mine, but he cut a deal first. It got put on me. My lawyer took a plea deal that sent me to juvie for thirty months for possession. They dropped the distribution charges."

Keisha was quiet. I couldn't read her silence. Doubt, like anyone else I'd tried to plead my case to? Judgement for my stupidity? "I swear to you, I've never done drugs in my life. My tests were clean then, and I'll take any test you want me to now. And my fingerprints were only found on one bag. An old makeup bag I'd left at my boyfriend's house."

"I'm sorry that happened to you. It sounds like your attorney didn't know what the hell they were doing."

I gripped the edge of my desk. "It was a court-appointed lawyer, who seemed to be in a rush."

"Your family couldn't afford private counsel?"

It was my turn to be quiet. Why did this feel like the greatest shame of all? "My parents didn't even come to the police station when I was arrested. They told the detective they were done with me."

My eyes burned as I pictured the pity in Detective Markum's eyes. He'd never forgotten me. Visited me at least once a month while I was in juvie. He had been the one to pick me up the day I was released. The one who found Hope House when my situation in Portland only got worse. He had been my only glimmer of light in years.

"I'm going to be honest. Your parents sound like real assholes."

I barked out a laugh. I hadn't realized just how much I needed that release of pressure. "Understatement of the century."

"You need to be prepared, Anna. I have a feeling this is going to get ugly."

Every millimeter of breathing room the laugh had given me disappeared in a flash. "I do, too."

Keisha's chair squeaked, and I could hear her shoes clicking across a hard floor as if she were pacing. "We're going to need every single piece of dirt we can find on your parents, and every good thing you've ever done on your side. Cain has already rec-ommended a private investigator we can use to help."

I could see the case mounting in my mind. A retired couple who was home all day and could devote every moment to two children. Pillars of their community. Dad, a deacon at the church. Mom heading up a volunteer group that crocheted blankets for people undergoing cancer treatments.

And then there was me. Barely a high school education. Spent my eighteenth birthday in jail. Had called a shelter home for more than ten years. It didn't take a genius to figure out who the courts would award custody to.

My ribs tightened around my lungs, and my throat constricted. I couldn't seem to pull air in, no matter how hard I tried. I heard Keisha's voice in the background, but it sounded far away.

Then, someone was in front of me. Turning my desk chair. Mason's face filled my vision, too beautiful for his own good. He tugged the phone from my hand, speaking into it briefly before setting it down.

"Look at me, Anna. Breathe with me, nice and easy."

His hands came to my face, tipping my head back. The feel of those palms, rougher than I would've imagined, knocked me out of my panic. Air slowly filled my lungs.

"That's it. Keep it slow."

I followed his instructions until oxygen made its way back to my brain. As it did, I realized his hands still cupped my jaw. I pushed my chair back, and they fell away. The absence made me feel so incredibly alone. "Sorry about that."

Mason frowned as he straightened. "You don't have to apologize."

"I just…" I searched for something, any excuse for my freak-out that would allow me to keep my boundaries intact. I'd already broken them once last night, letting a whole room of people know about something I'd never told anyone but Derek. I couldn't take any more.

Mason's jaw hardened as if he knew I was preparing to lie to him. But I couldn't do it. I couldn't weave some excuse to a man who'd been so incredibly kind to me over the past twenty-four hours.

"I went to prison. Juvenile detention. For almost three years. Drug possession. I never did drugs, and they weren't mine, but that didn't matter. You may not believe me, and that's okay. I lived in a shelter almost every day since, until I moved into the director's cottage. My parents will use all of that to try to take Justin and Lyla."

My voice cracked, a sob breaking free, but I forced the tears down. "I can't let my parents take them."

Instead of seeing disgust or disbelief, I saw only understanding. Mason didn't turn to leave or make an excuse. He didn't slowly back away like I thought he would. He stayed. "We won't let them take Justin and Lyla."

"You can't promise that. I'm running through everything in my head, and they're the perfect parents on paper. All they ever wanted was for me to be the perfect daughter. And I couldn't do it. Now, they're going to use all of that against me. You don't know them. You don't know how good they are at manipulating everything and everyone around them. You'll probably believe them, too." My ribs began to ache as the muscles tightened again. "What am I going to do?"

I looked at Mason as if he could actually answer that. As if he could give me the path out of this nightmare of my making. He stared directly into my eyes. "It's simple. Marry me."

CHAPTER
Six

Mason

WHAT IN THE EVER-LOVING HELL HAD I JUST SAID? Had those words really come out of my mouth? They had. Because Anna was sitting here, desperate and panicked and broken. In the two years I'd been coming to the shelter, I'd never seen any of those emotions cross her face. And I would've done anything to take them away.

"Are you insane?"

One side of my mouth curved up. "Probably."

"You can't marry me."

"Why not? I don't have a wife. I'm not seeing anyone."

She pushed up from her chair and began pacing on the opposite side of her office. This frazzled side to her was almost amusing. Or it would've been if the stakes weren't so high. "You don't even know me."

"I know you better than you think." As much as Anna had tried to keep her walls of defense firmly in place around me, she'd let them down for others, and I'd been there to see behind them.

"I-I don't fit with you."

"What the hell does that mean?"

"You have this beautiful, perfect life. You're this catch that I swear every woman in Sutter Lake has her eye on. You should marry some Sunday school teacher who bakes muffins, not someone whose only real home has been a shelter."

A muscle in my cheek ticked. "No one's life is perfect."

Anna scoffed. "Sure."

"I'm only trying to help."

Her expression completely blanked. "Of course. Sorry. I know you don't have any actual interest in me. I was just trying to make a point that marrying me, even for show, could ruin your chances with the person you're truly meant to be with."

I muttered a curse under my breath. "That's not how I meant it."

Anna sighed, scrubbing her hands over her face. The dark circles were stark against her pale skin. It seemed as if she'd lost some of that early summer glow overnight. "It doesn't matter. There has to be another way."

I'd been racking my brain, but I couldn't think of one. "It's complete crap, but I have pull. No record. Plenty of money. A great job. And enough community service projects to put your so-called-perfect parents to shame. And while things are changing, courts still look favorably on two-parent households."

She turned away from me, looking out the window to where the kids were running around the playground. Her eyes tracked Justin and Lyla, searching their expressions in a way that told me she already read them better than most in their lives. "We can find something else. Some dirt on them."

Cain already had his P.I. searching. If there was dirt to find, Dante would get the proof. "We can. Just do me one favor."

She turned back to face me. "What's that?"

"Don't tell Keisha you're single. If she asks, evade."

Anna's brows pulled together. "Why?"

"She can't knowingly deceive the court. If we decide we need a marriage to pull this off, we're gonna want that to be an option."

She bit down on the side of her thumbnail. "Okay."

"Good. Now, tell me what I can do around here today to take some stuff off your shoulders."

I dumped the soccer balls out onto the field. As I straightened, I stretched my back. A few hours, and these little Energizer bunnies had me beat.

Anna had started a summer camp of sorts for the kids from Hope House and had opened it up to any other parents in the community who needed care for their kids while they worked during the summer. Even with ten volunteers today, things had been madness.

"All right. We're going to practice passing." I'd taken on the task of a three-times-a-week soccer workshop with the help of a few others. It had been a long time since I'd played intermural in college, but with the help of a few online videos, it had mostly come back. "Everyone pair up."

The kids ran around, finding buddies to pass with. My eyes searched out Justin, who'd grabbed Lyla. Normally, he paired up with Noah, who came to the camp a few times a week to hang with his friends. But Justin knew his little sister needed him today.

Pulling air into my lungs became a little more difficult as I watched him send Lyla a gentle pass. She stopped it with her foot and grinned at her brother. It didn't quite reach her eyes, but it was something.

Cain came up alongside me. He'd been the one to suggest that a few of us from the company handle some sports aspect of the camp a few days a week. I'd worked for several companies over the years and had consulted with even more. No one ran their ship quite like Cain did. And his generosity paid off in spades. His employees were happier and worked harder because they genuinely cared about Halo.

"How are they holding up?"

I twisted the cord of my whistle, wrapping it around my hand. "I'm not sure. Anna said they wanted to be here today. She planned to keep them home, but they insisted on coming in."

He nodded, watching the siblings pass the ball back and forth. "Maybe it's better if they're busy."

"Maybe." I glanced over at him. "Any word from your P.I. yet?"

"Dante sent me a text telling me he's in Portland now. He's doing the boots-on-the-ground piece first. Talking to neighbors, old co-workers, everyone he can. He found out the Foleys are away for a few days for their anniversary. Had some car trouble on their way home. He's trying to talk to as many people as he can before they get back tomorrow."

I pulled the cord tighter, picturing the shame and fear that had engulfed Anna's face when she talked about her parents. "That's good. It gives Keisha a chance to file the paperwork."

"As soon as that happens, social workers will get involved."

The whistle's lanyard groaned as I pulled it a little too hard. I forced myself to unravel it from around my hand, but I needed something else to ground me. A long run or a sparring session with Cain. I needed a little dose of pain to keep me in the here and now.

The little sleep I'd gotten last night had been dogged with nightmares. It had been a long time since I'd had one. I'd thought I had banished them for good, but the past twenty-four hours had brought it all to the forefront again.

I focused on the two-dozen kids trading soccer balls back and forth. Forcing myself into the present. "What does Walker say?"

A muscle in Cain's cheek ticked. "He says there's a good chance she'll get custody until things play out in court. What happens in front of a judge is anyone's guess."

I studied Cain carefully. Worry and frustration lined his face. "You know about her past?"

His head snapped in my direction, eyes narrowing. "Know what?"

Of course, he did. Kennedy wouldn't have let anyone run Hope House without a comprehensive background check. Jail time, even juvie, would be the first thing that popped. "You ran her background."

Cain chose his words carefully. "I run everyone who works here. I wouldn't put anyone at risk by having someone around here whose history is an unknown."

"Smart. Anna told me about juvie." It was the truth, but it felt like a lie. She hadn't shared the information because she trusted me. She'd shared it because she was in freefall. Anna had been desperate and reaching out for anything that she could hold onto.

Cain's eyes widened. "She did?"

"She was scared. Freaking out after talking to Keisha. I was there."

"Your lawyer friend thinks it's going to be a tough case?"

I'd called Keisha as soon as I left Anna's office, but she hadn't told me a damn thing. "I don't know. Attorney-client privilege."

Cain scrubbed a hand over his jaw. "I've got a bad feeling, man."

"You and me both." I knew what it was like to live with a family where everyone pretended to be perfect. It usually meant you were dying on the inside. But there was someone who was doing the killing.

Justin gave the soccer ball a little more heat this time, and when Lyla went to kick it, she missed. The force of her attempt threw her off balance, and she landed on her butt.

I moved towards her. "Here you go." I reached out a hand, but she didn't take. Lyla's lip began to tremble, and tears welled in her eyes. I crouched low. "Did you hurt yourself?" She shook her head as the tears spilled over. "Scared you?" She nodded. "Happens to me all the time. The wind got knocked out of you. I've got you."

I reached out both hands to help her up. But instead of taking them, she launched herself at me and broke into sobs. *Shit.* I rubbed a hand up and down her back as I lifted her.

"I-I want my mom."

The tremble and pain in her voice nearly brought me to my knees. "I know you do. I'd give anything for you to have her right now." I would've traded places with Chelsea Foley in a heartbeat if it meant this little girl wouldn't be hurting.

Justin jogged over, a panicked look in his eyes. "I'm sorry. I didn't mean to kick it so hard."

I squeezed his shoulder, balancing a crying Lyla in my other arm. "Not your fault. It's a hard day."

Justin bit his lip and nodded, but his eyes were red.

"Let's go find your aunt."

Cain waved us off. "I've got this. Take all the time you need."

We headed for Anna's office, Lyla in my arms and Justin at my side. As the girl's little body shook against mine, and Justin fought back tears, I knew down to my bones that I'd do whatever it took to keep these kids safe.

CHAPTER
Seven

Anna

I HEARD THE TEARS BEFORE I SAW THEM—THE SOUNDS OF Lyla's broken sobs echoing through the hallway. I pushed to my feet, my desk chair slamming into the wall. I met them at the entrance to my office, Lyla wrapped in Mason's arms and Justin trailing behind, looking worried.

"What happened? Is she okay? Was she hurt?" Oh, God, my first day with the kids truly in my care alone, and something bad had happened.

"I want Mom!" Lyla hurled herself from Mason to me.

I caught her with an oomph, and Mason's hands went to my shoulders, steadying me. "Oh, Lyla." Tears burned the backs of my eyes, but I shoved them down. Lyla and Justin didn't need me losing it right now.

"I'm s-sorry," she said between hiccupped sobs.

"You never have to be sorry for saying how you feel. You should always let that out." These kids would never be forced to toe some invisible line, never free to truly live.

"I want her back."

"I do, too." I didn't know what else to say. I simply stood there, holding her. Mason's hands didn't leave my shoulders. And it somehow felt as if he were the one keeping me upright. I shoved that thought from my mind as soon as it entered and forced myself to step away. "What do you say we go back to the cottage, curl up on the couch, and order some pizza?"

"Pepperoni?" Lyla sniffed.

"As much as you can fit into that belly of yours."

Justin tried to force a smile. "She can eat more than you think. Pepperoni's her favorite."

"What about you? What's your favorite?"

He ducked his head. "Pepperoni's fine."

"Justin…" I gave him an I-mean-business look.

"Hawaiian."

I made exaggerated gagging noises as I slowly lowered Lyla to the floor. "Pineapple on pizza? Ick."

Justin shrugged. "Don't knock it till you try it."

"I'll just have to take your word for it." I glanced over at Mason. "Thank you. For bringing them to me." I fought the urge to shuffle my feet.

"Of course." He looked around at all three of us, and I almost thought I saw a flash of pain in his eyes. "Call me if you need anything. Even if it's just a grocery run."

"Thanks, but I think we'll be okay." Lies. We were as far from *okay* as possible. But Mason wasn't the person I should be leaning on. He'd helped more than enough already.

Yet as he headed out the door, his words from this morning echoed in my head. *Marry me.*

Lyla twisted in her spot on the couch as the credits to *The Parent Trap* rolled. The three of us were crammed onto my tiny sofa and had watched two movies back-to-back as we stuffed ourselves silly with pizza. She looked up at me. "What's going to happen to me and Justin?"

The slight waver in her voice was a knife to the heart. "Well, I'm hoping you'll want to stay with me. What do you think?"

She nodded slowly. "I don't want to go back to Portland. I like it here."

"What about Grandma and Grandpa?" Justin asked.

I did my best to keep my expression blank. "They are probably going to want you, too. But I need to ask you something, and I want you to tell me the one-hundred-percent truth, okay?" They both nodded. "Do you like spending time with your grandparents?"

I didn't know how to ask the question without leading them in any way. I knew the lawyers and social workers would ask more pointed questions, but I wanted to get a general feel first.

Lyla's face scrunched up. "They're not very nice."

"What do you mean?" Every muscle in my body tightened as I struggled to keep my breathing even.

"They say nasty stuff to Mom that makes her cry, and they tell me I have to get better grades. Grandpa got really mad when Justin said he didn't want to play football. Sometimes, he yells."

My fingers dug into the blanket covering all three of us. "Has your grandpa ever hit you?"

Lyla's eyes widened. "No. He just says Mom needs to punish us more, so we learn our manners."

The pizza I'd eaten a couple of hours ago felt as if it might come up. I swallowed and turned to Justin. "What about you?"

He shook his head and looked away. "Can they make us go with them?"

I took a slow breath. I wasn't going to lie to these kids. That wasn't the kind of relationship I wanted to build with them. And this wasn't something I could shield them from entirely. "I don't know. That's what I'm trying to figure out. I've got a lawyer, and she already filed the paperwork to request custody."

Lyla gripped my arm. "I want to stay with you."

I pressed a kiss to the top of her head. "I'm going to do absolutely everything I can to make sure that happens."

We sat there, quiet until the credits ran out. I glanced at the clock and saw that it was after nine. "I think it's time to start moving in the direction of bed."

Both Justin and Lyla were too lost in their thoughts to argue. I waited on Lyla's bed until she'd brushed her teeth and then tucked her under the covers, kissing her forehead. "Love you, Lyla Bean."

"Love you, too. Thanks for my pizza."

"I think Fridays should be pizza nights from here on out."

Her mouth curved. "I like it."

Justin wandered in from the bathroom. "I'll never say no to pizza." He eyed me as I stood. "I do say no to being tucked in, though."

I chuckled and held up both hands. "I promise, no tucking. I'll be downstairs if you guys need me."

I couldn't resist leaving the door open a crack so I could hear Lyla if she cried or Justin if he had a nightmare. I quietly made my way down the steps to the living area. It was a disaster. Blankets and pillows. Pizza boxes and paper towels. I wrapped up the leftovers, put them in the fridge, and then stacked the boxes with the recycling.

As I moved to fold the blankets, my gaze caught on a figure at the bottom of the stairs. "What's wrong, Jus? Can't sleep?"

He looked down at his hands, his fingers twisted together. "I lied."

"Okay. Why don't you come over here and tell me what you lied about? We can figure it out together." I sank onto the couch and patted the seat next to me.

He slowly made his way over and sat. But he stayed quiet. I didn't say a word, giving him whatever time he needed to find his words. He studied his twining fingers. "Grandpa hit me. Just once. Right before we came here. He was mad about peewee football and said I talked back."

I sucked in a sharp breath. "Did your mom see?"

He shook his head. "No one did. I didn't tell her. I didn't know what to say."

I took Justin's hands in mine, bending down so he could see my face. "I'm so sorry that happened. It wasn't your fault. Your grandfather is a sick man who doesn't know what to do with his anger."

Tears welled in Justin's eyes. "We can't live with them. It would be so bad."

"You won't." My words held a finality that had a bit of hope flaring to life in Justin's eyes. "I will do whatever it takes. But you are not going to live with them."

He tugged his hands from mine and threw his arms around me. "Thank you."

"Love you, Jus."

"Love you, too," he mumbled as he released me.

"Think you'll be able to sleep?"

He nodded.

I waited thirty minutes and then tiptoed upstairs. Justin and Lyla were both dead to the world. I pulled my phone out of my back pocket and hit the first contact on my favorites list. Kennedy answered on the second ring.

"Is everything okay?"

I normally didn't call her this late unless we'd had an incident at the shelter. "Everything's fine." Lies. "I just need to run out for a minute and wondered if you could come over to be with the kids. They're asleep, but—"

"I'll be there in ten."

God, I didn't deserve Kennedy. But I was so grateful I had her. "Thank you."

"See you soon." She hung up without another word.

I paced the small room, straightening blankets and putting everything back into its correct place. I straightened the box on the coffee table where I put the remotes and other odds and ends, adjusting it until it was at the perfect ninety-degree angle. Then

I moved on to the kitchen. I wiped down every surface, paying special attention to a spot where some pizza sauce had landed. I scrubbed until long after it had disappeared.

A soft knock sounded at the door. I hurried to open it. Kennedy stood there with a small bag slung over her shoulder.

I ushered her inside. "Thanks again for coming. I'm so sorry I had to make you come all the way back here and—"

"Anna," she cut me off. "I'm glad you called. I've leaned on you so much over the years, but I think this is the first time you've actually asked me for help. I'm glad you trust me enough to watch them."

I swallowed against the burn at the back of my throat. "I'm not used to leaning on others."

"I know. But you'll get there eventually, and we'll all be here when you do." She inclined her head to the sponge in my hands. "Stress cleaning?"

My mouth wanted to curve into a smile, but I couldn't quite get it there. Justin's words still echoed in my mind. "You know me. I like to take out my anxiety on any surface."

Kenz reached out and squeezed my hand. "You're going to get through this."

God, I hoped she was right.

"Where are you going, anyway? I brought an overnight bag just in case."

"I shouldn't be that long. Less than an hour."

She studied me carefully, not missing the fact that I hadn't shared where I was headed. "Okay, but be careful. Text me or Cain if you need something."

I pulled her into a quick hug. "You're the best. You know that, right?"

"I am pretty awesome," she joked.

"I'll be back soon." I grabbed my purse and keys from their hook by the door and headed outside. The cottage was at the back of the community center property and had a separate access road that gave me some additional privacy. It had taken me months to get used to the quiet after years of living in the hustle and bustle of Hope House. There was never true quiet there.

I beeped the locks on my hatchback, suddenly thankful I'd gone with this model instead of a sedan. I'd need the extra space if I had two kids in tow. My stomach cramped. Two children that I was responsible for keeping safe.

I slid my phone out of my pocket as I eased into my vehicle. Tapping on my contacts, I pulled up the one I needed and checked the address. It only took a couple of seconds to plug it into my GPS, and then I was off. I did a solid five miles per hour below the speed limit. The last thing I needed was to get into an accident because a deer or elk jumped in front of me.

I took one of the several roads that ran out of town. As pavement turned to gravel, my nerves kicked up a notch. I tightened my fingers around the wheel. I was doing the right thing. The only thing.

I turned off onto a smaller road that read: *Private*. God, I was really out in the middle of nowhere. If you had told my fifteen-year-old self that this was where I would end up, I would've said that you were crazy. I'd thought I would make my home in a city, getting lost in the swarm of people and endless energy.

But that was before. Now, I craved the peace of Sutter Lake. When I first smelled the air here, I'd felt clean for the first time in years. And, even now, when old demons threatened to take hold, I would take in a lungful of that air. It always helped me fight them back.

I slowed my hatchback as I muttered a curse. The gate in front of me was almost artistic, its rustic beauty melding with the landscape. But it was imposing, too. No one would get through it or over it without the owner of the property knowing.

I sank my teeth into my bottom lip as I rolled down my window. The little speaker box seemed to taunt me. I took a deep breath, hoping the air I loved would give me the strength I needed for the next step. I pressed the button.

I heard a whirring sound as the camera adjusted its direction, followed by a buzz. The gates slowly opened. I guessed that was my answer. I slowly took my foot off the brake and switched it to the accelerator.

Aspen trees with low lights at their bases lined the long drive. It created a glow. Just enough to guide someone's path but not so much that it distracted from the stars overhead. I followed the curving drive until a house came into view.

House was the wrong word. Mansion? But that wasn't right either. Because as large as the home was, it fit with the property in the same way the gate did. As if whoever had designed it wanted the structure to feel like it had simply sprung from the earth around it.

But when it had, it had created something massive. I didn't even want to think about how many bedrooms the home contained. And I really didn't want to think about how much the thing had cost. This was the kind of money that came from more than a cushy job. This was *wealth*.

I suddenly regretted my decision. Maybe I could just turn around and head home. Just as I was considering making a break for the gate, the front door opened. A tall figure with broad shoulders appeared, backlit from the glow inside.

I closed my eyes for a brief moment, trying to channel all of the strength inside me. I opened my eyes and turned off my vehicle. The walk up the front path and climbing the stairs to the house seemed to take both an eternity and a single breath. I came to a stop in front of Mason.

Concern lined the planes of his face. "Is everything okay?"

"No. It's not." Things were as far from okay as they could be.

"What can I do?"

It was that simple for Mason. I'd never trusted it before, the instinct he had to simply jump in and help. I never understood what was in it for him. But maybe, just maybe, that was who Mason Decker was. I tamped down that little glimmer of hope and focused on the man in front of me. Hopefully, he was the answer to my worst fears and nothing more. "If the offer still stands, I'd like to marry you."

CHAPTER
Eight

Mason

"COME INSIDE." THEY WERE THE ONLY WORDS I COULD manage to get out. Something had changed in the past twelve hours, and it couldn't be anything good.

"It's okay if you changed your mind. I can think of something else." Anna shivered. The thin, long-sleeved t-shirt she wore slipped off one shoulder and did nothing to fight off the chill in the air.

I stepped back, motioning her in. "That's not what I meant. But there are a lot of details to discuss, don't you think?"

Her fingers tightened around the strap of her purse, knuckles bleaching white. "Of course."

She slowly stepped inside, taking in the wide entryway with its two staircases that led to the second level. I tried to see it through her eyes, the expanse and the details. Juliette had rolled her eyes when she saw the plans for the house, thinking it was over the top for one man. But I'd always hoped that a family would fill the space someday. It looked as if that might happen, just not in the way I had planned.

"How about some tea? I have some from Jensen's shop. Or hot cocoa?"

Anna's mouth curved the barest amount. "Hot cocoa?"

I shrugged. "I hate coffee, and I've got a sweet tooth."

"Hot cocoa would be good."

I inclined my head in the direction of the kitchen. The lower level of the house was open-concept. A large family room to the left of the stairs spilled into a kitchen at the back, which led to a dining area. The rear of the house had as many windows as possible to take advantage of the view of the mountains. But none of that was visible in the dark.

"Your home is beautiful," Anna murmured.

I glanced over my shoulder as I hit the kitchen. I couldn't quite read her expression. It was almost as if the space made her nervous somehow. Or maybe it was simply the subject we were about to broach. "Thanks. It took a long time to design, and even longer to build. I feel like I'm still not all that settled."

"You had this place built?"

I nodded as I pulled a pot from under the sink. "I've always loved the idea of getting to choose everything about the place you call home, but it never made sense until I moved here."

"It's quite the place."

I chuckled and poured milk into the pot, turning on the heat. "My sister says it's ridiculous."

Anna leaned against the counter. "I didn't know you had a sister."

Because she hadn't asked. From the moment I'd made my way through the doors of Hope House, Anna had kept her distance. I just couldn't figure out why. Over the past two years, I'd seen her with other volunteers, both new and old. She might have an eagle eye until a newcomer proved to be trustworthy, but then she was warm. Welcoming. I'd never gotten that kind of treatment.

"Yup. She's in law school at Stanford right now."

Anna let out a low whistle. "Smart cookie."

"That she is, and she uses it to beat up on her big brother."

"It sounds like you two are close. That's really nice."

I muttered a curse under my breath. "I'm sorry. I didn't mean—"

Anna waved me off. "Don't apologize. I meant it. I'm glad you have her."

"Me, too." But I hated that Anna had lost her chance at that. I scooped out some chocolate mix from my favorite shop in San Francisco. I still ordered the stuff by the crate to be shipped here now that I couldn't pick it up in person. Carefully, I poured the milk on top, swirling it around with a spoon.

I moved past Anna to the massive fridge and pulled out a canister of whipped cream. "A little, a lot, or somewhere in the middle."

Anna stared at the canister. "A lot," she whispered.

I heaped it on top of hers and then handed her the mug.

"Thank you."

"Anytime." I sprayed some on mine and then stuck the can back in the fridge. "Stools or couch?" I wanted Anna to be wherever she felt the most comfortable.

"Stools. I don't want to spill on your couch."

"Trust me, it wouldn't be the first time. I usually end up eating my dinner in front of the TV."

She slid onto a stool. "I think the countertop still feels a little safer."

I eased onto the seat one down from hers. Close but not right next to her. "Want to tell me what happened?"

She stared down at her hot chocolate, stirring it with a spoon.

I knew it wasn't easy for her to open up, and I wished I could've given her time, but we simply didn't have it. "If we're going to do this, we have to be honest with each other. That's the only way we'll pull it off."

"You're right." Anna lifted her chin, meeting my gaze, but her grip on the handle of the mug was iron. "My father hit Justin a few weeks before they came here."

My back teeth ground together as I did my best to keep the anger from my face. The fury. A grown man laying hands on an eleven-year-old boy. Justin. A kid who had the best heart. He always looked out for the little ones at camp, making sure they never felt left out. He stayed late to help the volunteers pick up. And he always kept a protective eye on his sister.

"Did your sister file a report?" If she had, that would be a point in our column when we made it to court.

"Justin didn't tell her. That's the thing about my parents. They have an uncanny ability to make you think that no one will believe you."

So many abusers had that skill. They stole every ounce of power their victim had until they believed that their current circumstances were normal. That their life would be like that forever. "Do you think he'll be able to tell Walker or a social worker now?"

Anna stirred her drink. "I think so. He knows what's at stake. Mason, I can't let them have Justin and Lyla. I don't care what it takes, I'll run if I have to."

I sucked in a sharp breath, the air almost burning. The vision that filled my mind of Anna on her own with those two kids, trying to hide from everyone, was a sucker punch to the gut. "We're going to make it so you don't have to do that."

She looked me dead in the eyes. "Do you honestly think this will work?"

"Yes." Because I would use every resource at my disposal. And I had more than a few of them. The references I could pull would make any judge think twice about taking the kids away from us.

"You sound sure."

I released my hold on my mug, flexing my fingers. "I've got some strings I can pull." Anna's eyes narrowed on me. "Nothing illegal. But I know people in positions of power who will be happy to write letters of reference to any judge. We've already got one of the best lawyers in the state on the case. Now, we just have to get married."

A laugh bubbled out of Anna, and she clamped her lips together. "Sorry. You just sounded so matter-of-fact about it."

"Not exactly how I imagined my first proposal going, but…"

"I swore I'd never get married."

That shocked me. I'd always thought Anna would be one for a husband and a whole horde of kids. "Why not?"

She froze for a moment before answering, seeming to choose her words carefully. "The one person I thought was my forever stole everything from me. I promised myself I'd never put myself in that position again."

Her tone was so unemotional that it twisted the phantom knife in my gut deeper. Trust would be a long, winding road for us. But better I knew that now. I met her gaze and didn't look away. "I promise I'll always be honest with you, even if the truth is inconvenient. If there's ever anything you want to know, you only have to ask."

Anna cleared her throat and looked away. "Thank you." She took a sip of the hot chocolate, and her eyes widened. "This is amazing."

"It's from a little shop near my old condo. Best I've ever had."

"Me, too."

We sat in silence for a few minutes before Anna spoke again. "So, when should we do this? And where? I don't know what we need."

"We'll have to file for a marriage license, and then we can do the ceremony at the courthouse. Unless you want something in a church." I realized I had no idea if Anna was religious or a million other things I'd thought I would know about my wife-to-be.

"Courthouse is fine."

"We should dress up. Have someone take pictures in case the courts get suspicious."

"That's smart. I can find a dress tomorrow." She took another sip of her drink. "Our friends are going to suspect something."

"They'll know what we're doing. But all we need to do is give them a plausible story. They'll go along for the ride." They weren't stupid, but if they had an excuse to give the world, none of that mattered.

"And what story is that?"

I grinned. "We've been keeping our relationship under wraps for months. You didn't want to have things get awkward since I'm a volunteer at Hope House. But losing your sister put things into perspective. We didn't want to waste another day without each other."

She blinked a few times. "That's a good story."

"What can I say? I'm a hopeless romantic."

Anna nibbled on her bottom lip. "I hope I don't ruin that for you."

I reached across the island and took her hand. Anna's fingers twitched in my hold, but I didn't let go. "We're doing the right thing. And, who knows? Maybe you'll end up with a friend at the end of all of this."

"Okay."

"We're doing this?"

She nodded. "Thank you. I'll never be able to repay—"

I squeezed her hand. "I want to help."

Anna stared into my eyes, searching. "Why?"

I didn't look away. "I know what it's like to have no power. I don't want that for them."

CHAPTER
Nine

Anna

"SMELLS GOOD DOWN HERE," LYLA mumbled as she shuffled down the stairs and through the living room.

My niece was not one to wake up quickly. She needed at least an hour to finally get with the program. And it was adorable.

Justin jumped over the bottom three stairs, the opposite of his sister in the mornings. "She's right. It smells awesome."

I chuckled as I bent to pull the egg bake concoction out of the oven. Sleep hadn't happened for me last night. At four a.m., I'd finally given up and come downstairs to read. Reading had been a failure, so I'd turned to cleaning and organizing again. By six, nothing in the downstairs had even a speck of dust, and I'd turned my attention to creating a breakfast feast.

"We've got biscuits, breakfast casserole, and hot chocolate." The hot chocolate wasn't nearly as good as what Mason had made me last night, but it would do the trick.

Justin raised an eyebrow. "Hot chocolate? It's going to be like eighty degrees today."

"But it's still a little chilly this morning." That was the thing about living so close to the mountains, temperatures could swing fifty degrees within any given day.

"Quiet," Lyla hissed. "I want the chocolate."

I slid a mug over to her. "No one's going to steal your cocoa."

She wrapped her hands around the mug and sighed. Justin and I looked at each other and burst out laughing. Lyla didn't even flinch, she simply inhaled the chocolatey goodness.

I plated slices of the casserole and biscuits, handing them to the kids. Then I made a plate for myself. As we ate, I kept a close eye on them, trying to see beneath the surface for any clue of how they were truly doing. As we finished eating, I straightened. "How are you guys feeling? Do you want to hang out here today? Go to Hope House? Do something else?"

Justin stiffened. "We're fine."

"I want to go to Hope House. Can we play soccer with Mason again?" Lyla asked.

Just the sound of his name made my stomach churn. And the hopeful look in Lyla's eyes told me she'd already grown attached to the man. Maybe this was a horrible idea. I would be bringing someone into the kids' lives who I knew wouldn't be permanent. It would likely break their hearts when it didn't last.

"Mason's working today. He only comes to the shelter a few days a week." Yet I found myself wishing he was going to be there today. He'd somehow become a touchstone over the past few days, and that was dangerous.

Lyla popped the last piece of biscuit into her mouth. "I still wanna go. I like camp."

"What about you?" I asked Justin.

"It's cool. I like hanging out with Noah."

"Then camp it is." I met both of their gazes. "But if you're feeling overwhelmed or sad or scared, just come find me. We can take a break or go home, whatever you need."

Lyla looked down at her plate. "Sorry about yesterday."

I moved in close, pulling her to me. "You never, ever have to apologize for what you're feeling. I want to know what's going on in that amazing brain and heart of yours. Always."

She pressed into me. "Love you, Anna."

"Love you, too, Lyla Bean."

I met Justin's gaze over Lyla's head. "That goes for you, too. You don't have to hide how you're feeling. We can talk about it or just sit together as you process."

He nodded slowly. "Thanks."

That was all I would get from Justin. He was a preteen boy— the world didn't exactly encourage them to lean into their feelings. But I would. I didn't want him stuffing things down until he exploded.

"All right. Let's get cleaned up, get our bags, and head over to the center."

The kids helped me with the dishes, and then we all gathered our belongings. Lyla chattered about a girl she'd met who would be in her class next year. But I could only half listen. My mind swirled with a million different questions about how everything would work with Mason. This marriage.

Just the word had me feeling a little queasy. As I watched Lyla skip across the field in front of us, I couldn't help but see those same hopeful eyes as she asked about Mason. I pulled out my phone and typed out a text.

Me: *Do you have a few minutes to chat today? There are some details we need to discuss.*

I stared at my phone, waiting for a reply. I figured vague was best. I had no idea if a court could subpoena our phone records in an effort to figure out if our marriage was a sham, but better safe than sorry.

Mason: *Sure. I can stop by over lunch. That work?*

Me: *Yup. Thanks.*

Mason: *Have a good day. Call if you need anything.*

I stared down at my screen. Was that for show? What was I

supposed to say back? I started and deleted three different texts before landing on one.

Me: *Thanks. You, too.*

I waited, but there was no response. My message hadn't required one. So, why did I want my phone to ding one more time?

I rested my head in my hands. The steady pulse of a tension headache banded around my skull. The numbers on my computer screen had all started to blur together. Spreadsheets, my least favorite part of my job, but one of the most vital. Thankfully, Kennedy had sprung for me to take a few business and non-profit classes before I took over as head of Hope House. But crunching numbers would never be one of my greatest strengths.

A knock sounded on my open door, and I looked up. Mason stood there, little worry lines creasing his brow.

"Are you okay?"

I leaned back in my chair. "Spreadsheets."

The corner of his mouth kicked up as he moved into the room, shutting the door behind him. "Never one of my favorites, either." He eased into one of the chairs opposite my desk. "But I'm guessing that's not why you texted."

"No. I…" I wasn't sure how to finish my sentence. The urge to word-vomit all of my fears and worries was so strong.

Mason leaned forward, so I had to look him in the eyes. "Anna. Talk to me. If this is going to work, we can't hold things back."

Hadn't I been encouraging Justin and Lyla to do the same thing this morning? Maybe if we could all talk it out, we'd make it through the coming months. "I'm worried what marrying you is going to mean for the kids. I mean, are we going to move into your house? Are you going to move into the cottage?"

A hysterical laugh bubbled out of me. "The cottage only has two bedrooms and one bathroom. How would that work? But the kids… They already love you. Lyla was asking if you were going to play soccer with her again today. What happens when this is over, and we get a divorce? Are you going to disappear from their lives? That would kill them."

"No." Mason cut me off as he stood from his chair and rounded my desk. Leaning against it, he took my hand and squeezed. "This marriage might be a temporary thing, but I'll always be there for you guys. Justin and Lyla are so damn special, it's not exactly a hardship to hang out with them. I promise you. I'll never disappear from their lives. Yours, either."

I swallowed as tears burned the backs of my eyes. God, I wanted to believe that. To lean into Mason's promise. But I knew some promises weren't worth a damn. "Okay."

He released his hold on my hand but stayed leaning against my desk—so close I could feel the heat from his body. "In terms of where we live, I think it makes the most sense for you guys to move in with me. There's plenty of space. And, honestly, I think people would find it a little odd if you didn't."

He was right. Choosing to forego a massive estate in favor of a miniscule cottage would definitely raise alarm bells. And I knew I would have to let go of the cottage anyway. It wasn't big enough for me and two kids. But there was pain in doing that. A swift pang, squeezing my chest. Because that had been the first home I'd been able to make mine. A place that had always felt safe. Somewhere I was free. The burn behind my eyes intensified.

"Hey." Mason leaned in closer. "If you want to stay in the cottage, we can. We'll figure it out."

"No. You're right. Your place makes more sense. I just—the idea of leaving it is harder than I thought."

Mason's expression gentled. "It was your first real home, wasn't it?"

How he understood that with what little I had told him was beyond me. But I was starting to suspect there was more beyond the easygoing exterior Mason showed the world. I'd never pushed for more because he was everything I'd avoided since I was fifteen. The spark I felt every time our eyes met meant I needed to run in the opposite direction. But that running and avoiding meant I hadn't had a chance to truly get to know the man in front of me.

Somehow, knowing there was an understanding there made me want to give Mason a little more. It was reckless, but I couldn't resist. "It's been my safe place."

"I hope my house will be your safe place, too."

There was so much hope in his eyes, I couldn't tell him that it would never be that. Because it would never be mine. It would be like Mason was: on loan for a short period. "Thank you. It's incredibly generous—"

"You don't have to thank me—"

It was my turn to cut him off. "You want to help."

"Already finishing each other's sentences. Practically an old married couple."

I barked out a laugh. But the sound of raised voices coming from down the hall cut it off.

"I'm sorry. I'm going to have to ask you to leave. You're not on the approved visitors list," our daytime security guard, Jefferson, said in a calm but firm tone.

"Our daughter works here, and we need to have a word."

The voice I hadn't heard in over a decade had ice sliding through my veins and all of the blood draining from my head. My father.

"Anna?"

My head turned towards Mason's voice, but I couldn't seem

to get my eyes to focus on him as memories slammed into me as hard as my father's fists once had.

Hands came to my face. "Breathe. Just breathe. He can't hurt you. But I need you to concentrate. Where are Justin and Lyla?"

Their names snapped me out of my haze. I moved without a word, picking up my phone and hitting one of our staff member's numbers. Kristin picked up on the third ring. "Hey, Anna. What's up?"

I did my best to keep my voice even. "I need you to take Justin and Lyla to the cottage right now. Try not to worry them, but don't leave until I call or come to get them."

"Sure…is everything okay?"

"Not really. I'll call when I can."

"All right. Don't worry. I've got them."

My fingers tightened around my phone. "Thank you."

As soon as I hung up, I pushed to my feet, taking a deep breath. My parents didn't get to do this. They weren't allowed to sully the place that had been my refuge for so long. They didn't get to win. Not this time.

Mason stood, too. "You okay?"

I nodded. But as I met his stare, worry gnawed at my resolve. My parents were expert manipulators. It was why Chelsea had stayed away for so long. They'd convinced her that I was an addict and dangerous. That I'd abandoned her, choosing drugs over her. They could color Mason's view of me, too. "They're very convincing."

His expression hardened. "I know a wolf in sheep's clothing when I see one."

The anger pouring off Mason told me there was more to that statement than I had knowledge of. But now wasn't the time to push or prod. I had to face the last two people I ever wanted to see again. "Let's go."

I moved down the hallway, the voices echoing from the main room of the shelter. Jefferson stood, muscular arms crossed, blocking their path. He caught my movement out of the corner of his eye. "Sorry about this, Anna. I've already called the station. They've got officers en route."

My eyes were solely trained on the two people who had once been my parents. No, that was wrong. They had never been what a parent should be. They were simply two halves of my genetic makeup. I lifted my chin, refusing to be intimidated by my father's stare. "You'll have to leave. This is private property. If you choose not to, the police will remove you."

"Now, Anna," my father began, his voice deceptively gentle. But that softness hid a threat. One his family knew all too well. "This is unnecessary. We simply want to talk with you. I know you were too ashamed to return to us after what you did, but that's no reason to push us away now."

It took everything in me to keep my face a blank mask, digging my nails into my palms for some outlet for the pain and rage flowing unchecked through me. "I have nothing to say to you. Please, leave."

My mother stepped forward. "If that's what you want, we'll be happy to do so. Bring us Justin and Lyla, and we'll leave for Portland."

My heart hammered against my ribs in a painful beat. "No."

My father gave me a sickly, sympathetic smile. "I'm afraid the courts will have something to say about that."

Boots sounded on the linoleum as Walker strode towards us. "Mr. and Mrs. Foley, you'll need to vacate the premises."

Mom's hands began fluttering the way they always did when she panicked that she wouldn't be able to fix something she knew would make Dad angry. "We just want to see our grandchildren. Anna isn't equipped to care for them."

A muscle in Walker's cheek ticked. "You may believe that, but Chelsea put Justin and Lyla in Anna's care. That's where they'll stay until a court decides otherwise."

Cain and Kennedy hurried through the front doors, their attention going straight to my parents.

My father straightened to his full height. I remembered how terrifying that used to be to me. Now, it seemed pathetic. A small man doing everything he could to intimidate. "Are you aware that Anna has a record? Would you honestly put two innocent children in the care of someone who has spent time in prison?"

"Yes, he would."

It was Mason who spoke, sliding an arm around my shoulders and pulling me close. He'd hung back this entire time as if knowing I needed to fight this battle alone, to prove to myself that I could do it. But he'd clearly had enough.

Dad's eyes narrowed, assessing the new player entering his game. "And you are?"

"Mason Decker. Anna's fiancé."

CHAPTER
Ten

Mason

KENNEDY LET OUT A LITTLE GASP AT MY WORDS, QUICKLY covering them with a cough. Cain wrapped an arm around her, his eyes tracking from me to Anna, settling on her bare ring finger. Shit. I needed to remedy that if we were going to make this believable.

Anna's father surveyed me carefully, his gaze sharp. "Fiancé." He seemed to mull over the word as if it were impossible to believe.

I pulled Anna a little tighter against me. "That's correct. Now, I believe multiple people have asked you to vacate the premises. I think it's best you do that."

I saw it then, the flare of rage in Mr. Foley's eyes. He didn't take kindly to someone telling him what to do. He wasn't in control of the world outside his home, so he'd done everything he could to force absolute tyranny inside it.

"This is a mistake, Anna. I'd hate to have to bring everything we know about you up in court. There's no way a judge would give you custody. You have to know that."

Anna stiffened in my hold. I could practically feel the waves of anger and fear rolling off her. I brushed my thumb back and forth across her shoulder, trying to bring some sort of comfort. But I didn't take my eyes off Mr. Foley. "Us. We'll be asking the court to grant *us* custody."

A light dawned as he put the pieces together, suddenly realizing that this wouldn't be as much of a slam dunk as he'd thought. "Elise, let's go back to the hotel and call our lawyer."

Walker motioned towards the doors. "I think that's best. I'll also have to ask that you not return to Hope House. This is private property."

Elise stiffened as she walked. "This is ridiculous. I want my grandchildren. John, they can't do this."

"Elise," John said softly. "Quiet."

She snapped her mouth closed. As if that soft tone were something else entirely. Not gentle at all, but the most severe threat.

John met Walker's stare as they paused before the doors, Jefferson behind them. "Is it really wise for the police department to so clearly take sides in a matter like this one? Some courts wouldn't look favorably on that."

Anna tensed at my side, drawing in a sharp breath.

Walker gave John an easy smile. "I work for the people of this town. And I'm simply carrying out the law as it stands. Anna has custody right now."

"I just hope you're prepared to carry out that same law when a judge awards us custody."

Walker shrugged. "We'll just have to see what the courts say. Have a good afternoon."

John and Elise turned and headed out the door. As John put his hand on Elise's lower back, she flinched.

The doors shut, the bang of the action seeming to echo in the silent entryway. Jefferson moved quickly to lock them. "I think this is best for now," he said.

Kennedy moved to help him. "You're right. Just in case."

Anna stepped out of my hold. "I'm so sorry."

I felt the loss of her warmth instantly. I wanted to pull her back, to shield her from all of the ugliness I knew was coming her way. "This isn't your fault."

"I brought this here. Hope House is supposed to be a haven. A place where people feel safe. Not somewhere strangers barge in and create a scene. How did they even know where I was?"

Kennedy moved to her friend, pulling Anna into a hug. "Mase is right. None of this is on you. And we've had far worse scenes than this one. That's why we have security and the police department on speed dial."

She was right. I'd seen a handful of incidents that were far worse than what we'd just encountered. Ex-husbands looking for wives who had left them, a dealer looking for someone who owed them money, even a fight between two residents. But those were few and far between. Kennedy and Anna had worked hard to make this place into exactly what Anna had called it: a haven. And one dustup wasn't going to change that.

Anna straightened from Kennedy's hug and looked at Walker. "He's going to cause trouble for you. He'll probably contact the mayor and the city council. Maybe even some higher-ups in the county."

Walker shook his head. "Let them try. I've had far worse thrown my way."

Anna braided her fingers together, squeezing tightly. "You don't understand. Today was nothing. My dad thought he'd be able to simply show up, and Justin and Lyla would be given to him. He didn't think he'd even have to try. Now that he knows there are people who have my back…you don't know what he's capable of."

My fingers itched to pull Anna to me again. As if that would make it all better. "We aren't taking this lightly. We'll do whatever it takes to keep Justin and Lyla safe."

She glanced over her shoulder towards the doors. I could see the panic racing through her body. The pull to simply grab the kids and run. I moved in closer, slipping a hand under her hair and giving the back of her neck a squeeze. "We've got this. I promise you."

Anna looked at me, her eyes dull and dead, none of that fire I normally saw in the blue depths. "I hope you're right. But even if you are, I'll have to go through hell first. And my dad will drag you all along for the ride, simply for supporting me."

I brushed my thumb back and forth across the nape of her neck. "We can take it. No one's leaving your side. You're not alone in this."

Cain stepped forward, wrapping an arm around Kennedy's shoulders. "He's right. We're not going anywhere."

Anna blinked a few times as if forcing back tears. "Thank you. But if it gets to be too much—"

"It won't," I cut in.

"If it does, it's okay if any of you needs to walk away."

Kennedy gave her a serious look. "You know, it's a little insulting that you think we're so wimpy. We can handle your ass of a father."

Anna was quiet for a moment, and then her mouth curved the barest amount. "I didn't mean to insult you."

"Good. Apology accepted. Now, where are Justin and Lyla?"

"At the cottage with Kristin. I need to get over there because they're probably freaking out."

Kennedy motioned her friend towards the back hall. "Come on, I'll go with you."

Anna looked up at me, and I was frozen for a moment, not wanting to let her go. "Thank you," she whispered.

"Anytime." I forced my hand to leave the back of her neck and then stepped away. But I couldn't keep myself from watching her walk off, not turning around until she'd disappeared out the back doors.

Walker let out a low whistle. "Fiancé?"

Hell. This would be the tricky part. "That's right."

He looked between Cain and me. "As much as I want the full story on that one, I think it's best if I'm in the dark. Fill me in with the official line when you're ready. And call if you need anything. Hopefully, those two won't be back."

God, I hoped so. But the fact that they'd mentioned a hotel in town gave me pause. "Thanks, Walker."

He saluted and headed for the front doors, walking out into the summer sunshine. Cain cleared his throat. "Do you know what you're doing?"

I focused on him. Cain had become more than a business partner over the past two years. He was a friend. And our histories meant that he should understand exactly why I was doing this. "John Foley hit Justin just before they moved to Sutter Lake."

A muscle in Cain's jaw ticked. "Reported?"

"No."

"Fuck."

"Exactly." I flexed my fingers and then cracked my knuckles, trying to relieve some of the phantom pressure there. "Wouldn't you do anything to save those kids from that?"

Cain was quiet for a moment. "I hope you know what you're doing. That's giving up a chunk of your life for something you might not even be able to pull off."

But I didn't see it that way. The only things I would be giving up were lonely evenings and a ghostly quiet house. It wouldn't be a sacrifice to have Anna, Justin, and Lyla there. And I wouldn't be able to live with myself if I could do something to help and simply didn't. "Failing at this isn't an option, Cain."

"Then let's make sure you don't fail."

CHAPTER
Eleven

Anna

I PUSHED OPEN THE DOOR TO THE COTTAGE, KENNEDY ON MY heels. I'd done the fastest power walk I could manage from Hope House. I knew if I ran, people would worry there was an emergency, so I'd opted for an almost comical walk instead. But there was no hint of laughter inside me. Only a desperate need to lay eyes on Justin and Lyla.

Justin was pacing the living area but froze mid-step at the sound of the door, then whirled around. "What is it? What happened?"

I took in a shaky breath. I'd promised I wouldn't lie to them. But I didn't want to scare them unnecessarily, either. I looked over to where Kristin sat on the couch with Lyla, clearly playing some sort of game on her phone. "Thank you so much for bringing them over here."

She pushed to her feet, giving me a kind but concerned smile. "Anytime." She squeezed my arm as she made her way to the door. "Just let me know if you need anything."

"Thank you."

As soon as the door shut, Justin asked again. "What happened?"

"Your grandparents are in town."

Lyla's eyes went wide. "We don't have to go with them, do we? I don't want to."

I crossed to the couch, sinking down onto it and pulling her into a hug. "No. They can't take you anywhere."

"Not yet," Justin muttered. I looked at him, and he shrugged. "I looked some stuff up on my tablet last night."

Kennedy cleared her throat. "How about I make everyone a snack while you guys talk?"

"Thanks, Kenz." It wasn't like she wouldn't be able to hear everything we said from the kitchen, but it gave some semblance of privacy. "Come here, Jus."

He moved slowly and opted for a tufted footstool instead of sitting next to me and Lyla on the couch. "I read that the judge will ask us who we want to go with. We'll say you. Right, Lyla?"

She bobbed her head up and down, holding onto me tighter. "We want to be with you."

"I want you guys with me, too." I took a deep breath. "How would you feel if we went to live with Mason?"

Justin looked confused, but Lyla was excited. She straightened, eyes shining. "That would be awesome. He has that lake at his house. He was going to teach us to fish before…"

Her words trailed off. I'd completely forgotten about his invitation to go fishing with him before Chelsea had died. It felt like a lifetime ago.

Justin's eyes narrowed. "Are you guys boyfriend and girlfriend?"

I chose my words carefully, trying to avoid a lie. "We're planning on getting married. But only if you're okay with it." If they weren't, I'd find another way. Running. Hiding. I didn't care.

"Married?" Lyla asked in a reverent whisper. "With a big dress?"

"Probably not a big dress. Mason and I don't want a big, fancy wedding. It'll probably just be the two of us."

Lyla's shoulders slumped. "That sucks."

"Lyla," I chastised. Chelsea had not been a fan of *sucks* or *shut up* or any form of cursing.

"I mean it stinks."

I sighed. "Maybe we can have our own little party after. But what I want to know is if you guys would be okay with that. I know there are a lot of changes happening right now."

"Mase is really fun. I think he'll be a good husband. Does that mean he'd be our uncle?" Lyla asked.

"Yes, he would be your uncle." It was a struggle to get the words out. I was tying Mason to the kids, possibly forever. I struggled to keep my breathing even as I looked at Justin. "What about you?"

He studied me carefully. "I like Mase. And the judge would probably like it if we had two guardians."

It might be time to take Justin's tablet away for a while. "You don't need to worry about that piece of things. I only need to know if you'd be happy living at Mason's."

His jaw hardened. "I'm happy living anywhere that isn't with Grandma and Grandpa."

My chest gave a painful squeeze, and I reached out to take his hand. "I'm doing everything I can to make sure that doesn't happen."

Justin's eyes met mine, and I saw understanding beyond his years there. "Thanks, Anna."

Kennedy bustled into the living room with a tray. "I've got crackers and cheese, grapes, and some lemonade."

I gave her a grateful smile. "Thank you."

Lyla bounced on the couch as she reached for a cracker. "Did you know Mase is gonna be my uncle?"

Kennedy took a seat in the empty chair next to the couch. "I heard something about that."

"I didn't even know they were boyfriend and girlfriend," Lyla said around a mouthful of food.

"Your aunt is pretty good at keeping secrets."

Heat crept up the back of my neck. "You know I'm a private

person." That much wasn't a lie. Everything I'd had to bring out into the open this past week had almost been more than I could take.

Kennedy's lips twitched. "And you probably didn't want anyone at the shelter getting the wrong idea or thinking Mase was getting favorable treatment."

Justin popped a grape into his mouth. "He is kind of bossy on the soccer field. Probably because he has an in with the boss."

Kennedy chuckled, and my face only got hotter as I squirmed in my seat. It would take a while for me to get used to this kind of attention.

I smoothed my hands down the sides of my dress. I'd spent too much money on it, but after Mason's warning that this needed to look as real as possible, I'd panicked. I hadn't wanted to look like I'd thrown on something from the back of my closet. I wanted it to look special.

But now, I regretted going all out. I could've picked something less fancy and still looked nice. This wasn't a real wedding. It was a life jacket. An emergency ladder. But here I was, playing dress-up.

I surveyed my reflection in the mirror. I'd curled my blond hair so that it hung in loose waves around my face. And had spent far too long creating a shimmery eye-makeup look. The dress had a strapless bodice that hugged my curves. A full tulle skirt flowed out from my waist. The pale blush tone complemented my complexion perfectly. I'd fallen in love with the piece the moment I walked in the door. And when I tried it on, I'd felt…beautiful. But standing in front of the mirror now, I felt foolish.

"Oh, well." It was too late now. I glanced at the clock on my bedside table and cursed. The last thing I needed was to miss my own wedding.

Mason had arranged for a judge to do the ceremony at City

Hall. So, we didn't have to make the drive to the courthouse a few towns over. However, I was sure judges were busy people and couldn't wait around for tardy brides. I snatched up my clutch and headed downstairs and outside.

The sun shone extra brightly as I slipped behind the wheel of my hatchback. I resisted the urge to text Justin for the fourth time today. He and Lyla had been invited over to Jensen and Tuck's to have a sleepover. Lyla had been beside herself with excitement to spend the night at a wild horse rescue, and Jensen had promised to take her for a ride. But that didn't stop my worrying.

I gripped the steering wheel a little tighter as I guided my vehicle off the property and onto the road into town. The drive was short, only a couple of minutes, but my stomach still managed to knit itself into intricate knots. I slid into an empty space in front of City Hall and caught sight of Mason's Range Rover a few spots down.

I took a deep breath. "You can do this. It's just for a little while." We hadn't even settled on how long—so many significant details still to figure out.

I pushed open my door and stood, brushing out invisible wrinkles in the skirt of my dress. I closed the door and started towards the building that looked like a modern reincarnation of something from Old West times. My heels clicked on the asphalt, making the man on the sidewalk turn around.

Taking him in, my steps faltered. The navy-blue suit had to be custom-made, it fit him so well. Highlighting broad shoulders and a narrow waist. And the color of the material only made the gold in his irises seem to glow. His thick scruff was neatly trimmed and I had the sudden urge to know what it would feel like against my fingertips.

Mason swallowed, his Adam's apple bobbing. "You look… amazing."

My fingers itched to smooth my dress again. "It might be a little much—"

"It's perfect." He held out his arm for me to take. "Ready to do this?"

A wave of nerves swept through me. "Are you?" This wasn't a sacrifice for me. I had no plans of marrying…ever, so I wasn't giving anything up. But Mason? He practically had *wife and family* tattooed on his forehead.

"Anna. I want to do this."

The *why* dangled in my mind again. Something in his past had led him here, and I still didn't know what that was. But it was unfair of me to push when I wasn't ready to unpack so many things for him, either. So, instead, I slipped my arm through his. "Here we go."

"Wait." He handed me a gold band. "Thought rings would help."

I hadn't even thought about that detail. "Oh." It was all I could muster.

Mason gave me a reassuring smile. "Now, we're ready."

The walk up the steps to City Hall seemed to take forever and be done in a flash at the same time. Mason pulled open the door and held it for me. My hand shook as my arm slipped from his steady hold. I flexed my fingers. I wouldn't tremble. Not for anyone, not anymore. I'd been through hell and had come out the other side. I wouldn't let anyone take the beautiful life I'd built from me, and that included having my niece and nephew safe and cared for. They would never experience what I had.

"Anna, you look gorgeous." Kennedy beamed as she hurried over to me, pulling me into a tight hug. "Are you sure about this?"

There were a million questions contained in her simple query. But I appreciated that she didn't voice them. I hugged her back. "I'm sure."

Her eyes bounced from me to Mason and back again as she released me. "You two make quite the pair."

"She's not wrong," Cain said as he wrapped an arm around his wife's shoulders.

A woman who looked familiar but whose name I didn't know, bustled up to our group. "Mr. Decker? The judge is ready for you."

Mason threaded his fingers through mine. "Thank you."

The heat of his palm against mine was more comforting than I wanted to admit. The first time his fingers had locked with mine had been a jolt to the system. It had been forever since I'd had the simple contact of holding someone's hand. There was an innocent intimacy in the gesture. More so than even sex in a way. It was claiming. And I liked it too much.

We followed the woman down the hall to what looked like a conference room. A man waited outside with a camera. When he saw us, he lifted the lens in our direction, snapping a few shots. I did my best to make sure there was a pleasant expression on my face but worried it might look more like a grimace.

Mason read my anxiety and gave my hand a couple of quick squeezes. "You're doing great. This will be over in just a few minutes."

It would be over, and we would be husband and wife—on paper, at least. We hadn't discussed what that meant. Would Mason have to take his dates a few counties over? My stomach hollowed out at the idea of him with another woman.

I shoved the feeling down. I had no rights to this man. He was only doing me a favor—the greatest one anyone would ever do for me. I could live with the rest, whatever it might be.

A woman with silver threaded through her blond hair stood as we entered. "Mason, it's so good to see you."

Mason reached out a hand to shake hers. "Angela, thank you so much for officiating. This is Anna, my fiancée."

Angela gave me a warm smile as she shook my hand. "It's lovely to meet you. You've got yourself a good one with Mason."

Hysterical laughter wanted to bubble out of me. I had no real idea if Mason was a good one. He seemed to be, but I'd been so deadly wrong about that kind of thing before. "It's nice to meet you, too. Thank you for marrying us."

My voice gave a little hitch on the M-word, but Angela didn't seem to notice. Or, if she did, she passed it off as nerves. She clasped her hands together. "Well, let's get you two hitched." She inclined her head towards Cain and Kennedy. "These are your witnesses?"

"They are," Mason answered.

"Perfect."

We stood at the end of the conference room that had a little space. Large windows looked out over a sea of forest. I almost zoned out as Angela recited traditional vows for us to repeat. The only sound that interrupted our voices was that of a clicking camera.

I promised to love, honor, and cherish Mason for all the days of my life. And I would, in a way. I would love, honor, and cherish him for saving Justin and Lyla. And that would never go away. Not when we signed divorce papers. Not when he met the love of his life and married her. Never.

"Mason, you may now kiss your bride."

Those words snapped me out of my musings as panic took hold. I hadn't even considered that we would need to kiss. Oh, God. The first kiss was usually awkward. You didn't know how the other person moved yet. Which way would he turn his head? Would he use tongue?

Mason squeezed my hands as he dipped his head towards mine. His lips melded to mine in a way that felt much more practiced than it was. I couldn't describe it any other way than to say it felt like coming home. Even as my heart rattled my ribs, a peace settled in my bones. A feeling of warmth and comfort. But one that sparked something fiercer in me. A fire low in my belly. Before it could fully flame, Mason pulled away.

I blinked up at him a few times, trying to get my senses back. He grinned down at me. Heat flamed my cheeks. Mason knew he affected me, and that was enough to send me running from the room. Instead, I kept my smile wide and bright as Angela congratulated us.

I barely heard the rest of her words and hoped I responded appropriately. I was in a daze while the photographer took more photos of us both in the conference room and outside in a field. By the time we were done, I was exhausted. Anxiety had burned through all of my energy reserves.

Cain clapped Mason on the shoulder. "Well, we're going to head home and leave you two to celebrate."

"What are you guys doing anyway?" Kennedy asked, curiosity lighting her eyes.

I looked up at Mason, a little panic lighting through me. We hadn't planned anything. Mason, of course, met the question with ease. "Pizza and packing. They're moving into my place tomorrow, so I told Anna I'd help her box everything up tonight."

Amusement flickered across Kennedy's expression. "Maybe you two can take a honeymoon later."

"When everything's settled," he assured her.

With a round of goodbyes, we watched as they headed down the street to Cain's SUV. I let out a long breath. "That was…"

"Something," Mason finished for me.

"Not exactly the word I was going for, but a more appropriate one."

He chuckled. "How about I pick up pizza and meet you back at the cottage? What toppings do you like?"

This time, I couldn't stop the hysterical laughter that burst out of me. Concern flashed across Mason's face. "Are you okay?"

"Sorry." I sucked in air, trying to stop the laughter. "It's just… we're married, and you don't even know what I like on my pizza."

His lips twitched. "You have a point there. But I'll learn that kind of stuff."

"I like just about anything. No anchovies. No pineapple."

"You really should give pineapple a shot."

I scrunched up my face. "You and Justin. At least, you guys will have someone to share your gross pineapple pizza with."

"Okay, no pineapple for you."

I toyed with the clasp on my clutch, locking and unlocking it. "You don't really have to help me pack."

He shrugged. "I'd like to. I don't have anything else to do."

"Okay. I'll see you in a bit?"

"As soon as I've got the pizza."

I wasn't sure how to say goodbye. Should I hug him? I couldn't take another one of those kisses. I settled on an awkward half-wave.

But Mason didn't. He pulled me into a tight hug, pressing his lips to my hair. "Everything's going to be okay. You'll see."

Everything about the moment was a wash of reassurance. The strength of his hold. The warmth of his body. The feel of his words. And all of it was dangerous for me to sink into. But I was stupid when it came to men. So, I sank into the comfort anyway.

CHAPTER
Twelve

Mason

I CHECKED MY WATCH FOR WHAT SEEMED LIKE THE HUNDREDTH time. They were late. Movers were rarely on time, and the whole process always took longer than you thought it would, but it didn't stop worry from gnawing at me. I should've met them at the cottage instead of waiting for them here. A million what-ifs ran rampant in my brain. The Foleys showing up and wreaking havoc. A car accident.

An alert on my phone dinged, and I pulled it out of my pocket. I'd left the gate open, but the security system would still notify me if there was movement. I pulled up one of the video feeds just in time to see a familiar blue hatchback drive slowly by.

I headed down the stairs. I already had one of the bays on my garage open for Anna, but I wasn't sure if they had stuff they needed to unload first. She rounded the circular drive, rolling down the passenger window. Justin stuck his head out. "Your house is sick!"

The corner of my mouth kicked up. "Is that a compliment or an insult?"

"Total compliment."

"Glad you like it since you'll be living here."

His eyes widened as if just remembering that fact. "This is gonna be awesome."

I hoped he was right. There were a lot of balls in play right now, and this transition would take time. But no matter what hurdles we encountered; it would be worth it to keep the kids safe.

Anna leaned forward. "Where should I park?"

I reached through the window and held out a garage door opener. "I left a bay open for you. Here's the remote that goes to it. That'll be yours."

"Thanks." She slowly pulled forward, heading for the garage, and I followed.

There was more than enough room in the five bays. Only two had truly been used. One with the SUV I drove most often, and another for a truck I used around the property if I was working on a project. A couple of ATVs and a snowmobile were stored in the bonus space.

Doors slammed as everyone got out. Justin's gaze immediately cut to the toys. "Are those yours?"

"Yup. Have you driven an ATV before?"

"No, but I've always wanted to."

"Maybe we can take them out tomorrow once you're all settled." I glanced at Anna, who was scowling at the vehicles. "But you have to wear a helmet."

"I don't know if he's old enough, and those don't exactly look safe," she argued.

The cage-like covering for the four-wheelers didn't exactly inspire confidence. "I promise they are. I got the safest ones on the market. You could roll it a dozen times and not get a scratch."

Anna's eyes narrowed in my direction. "I don't want him rolling anything."

Justin leaned into his aunt with a grin. "I'll be super careful, promise."

"Sure, you will," she grumbled.

I motioned them towards the garage's entrance to the house.

"Come on, let's head inside." I looked at Lyla, who seemed more nervous than I'd ever seen her. "You ready?"

She nodded but didn't say anything. I waited while she caught up to me. "I know this is a new place, and new can sometimes be scary, but we can do whatever we need to make this feel like home, okay?"

"Are me and Justin gonna share a room?"

I paused. I hadn't thought they would want to, but maybe I'd miscalculated. "I have you in rooms right next to each other, but we can change that."

"No way," Justin cut in. "Having our own rooms is great." He seemed to catch himself as he took in his sister's worried expression. "But you can come get me if you get scared, Ly."

"Me, too," Anna assured as she pulled the little girl to her side.

"There's an extra bed in your room, too, if you want someone to sleep in there with you tonight." I'd begged an emergency with a local interior designer to have her pull together the kids' rooms in under a week. I remembered that Juliette had always wanted to have sleepovers when she was Lyla's age, and I hoped having an extra bed in the girl's room would make it that much easier for her to have friends over.

Lyla looked up at Anna. "Will you stay with me tonight?"

She grinned down at her niece. "Only if we can stay up past our bedtimes and eat cookies till we can't move."

Lyla's mouth curved into a smile. "Snickerdoodles?"

"We'll make them after dinner," Anna assured her.

The tightness in my chest abated at that first glimpse of a smile from Lyla, and I started inside. "The kitchen's stocked, so we should have everything we need for cookies. But if we're missing anything, there's a list on the counter by the fridge. If you add something to that, Jessie, my housekeeper, will pick it up at the store."

"That doesn't mean you can put twelve kinds of candy on the list," Anna warned.

Justin threw up his hands. "Aw, Anna. Why'd you have to go and ruin it?"

"So you don't end up in a diabetic coma. That's why."

Sounded like Justin was going to be my partner in crime for both pizza and sugar. I bent down and whispered to him, "I've got your back."

"Heard that," Anna called.

Justin shook his head. "She's got ears like a freaking bat."

We made our way through the large mudroom. "You guys can each claim a cubby to put your school stuff in if you want. And there's plenty of room for muddy shoes when the weather turns."

Lyla looked up at Anna. "Will there be enough snow for sledding?"

"You bet."

I mentally added sleds and tubes to a list of things I'd need to get. That list was growing by the second. I'd already given my credit card a workout, but damn, it had been a blast. As much as I'd looked out for Juliette growing up, I hadn't started to make real money until I sold my first video game on a lark. So being able to spoil these kids was too much fun.

"How about a tour?" I asked.

Anna kept an arm around Lyla but gave me a shaky smile. "That would be great."

She didn't even know her way around the house yet. Hopefully, that wouldn't be evident to the kids. I led them into the kitchen where Lyla gasped. "You have a pool?"

"I do. And a hot tub."

It had been so dark when Anna had been here the one time before, she probably hadn't seen it, either. And the idea of her laying out there in her bikini wasn't exactly unappealing. I guided our crew through the lower level of the living space, including the library and my office. We made a quick trip down to the basement so I could show them the gym and the screening room.

"Definitely need a movie night," Justin muttered.

"Anytime you want," I offered.

Then we headed to the second level where the majority of the bedrooms were located. I led them to the end of the hall to Justin's and Lyla's rooms. We made it to Lyla's first. There was muted lavender on the walls, a color I'd noticed she wore a lot, so I hoped it was a favorite. Two built-in bookcases I'd had the designer fill with books and movies she thought a nine-year-old might like bracketed a window seat.

Two twin beds rested against the far wall, the comforters covered in shimmery stars. And above each were illustrations of constellations. She also had a walk-in closet, and her own bathroom I'd had the designer kit out with supplies.

Lyla walked through the space, her jaw hanging open. "This is mine?"

The look of awe on her face had me biting back a chuckle. "It's all yours, but we can change anything you want."

She flew at me, throwing her arms around my waist. "It's perfect. How'd you know purple's my favorite color?"

I tugged on a bow in her hair with the same color. "Just a lucky guess."

She released me and made a beeline for the bookcases, surveying the contents. Anna came up alongside me. "You didn't have to do all of this."

I looked down at her. "I wanted to. And they deserve a little spoiling right now."

She pressed her lips together. "I guess you're right. Lyla Bean, are you going to keep on the tour with us?"

"Can I stay here? I want to look at my new books."

"Sure, we'll come back and get you when we're done."

Justin might've been a too-cool-for-school teenager, but he couldn't disguise the look of excitement in his eyes. "Can we see my room?"

"You're up next," I assured.

We headed out of Lyla's room and into the room next door. The designer had gone straight ahead in this room since I didn't have the first clue what Justin's favorite colors were. The walls were a pale gray. But the furniture had industrial accents that made the space a bit more unique. She'd also worked in Justin's love of soccer with prints over the bed and a few signed soccer balls from nearby professional teams dotting his bookshelves. There was also a sitting area where he could have friends over and a full gaming setup.

"This is sick," he said as he explored the space.

"That's the good sick, right?"

Justin grinned. "Totally good." He sobered a bit. "Thank you, Mase."

"Happy to do it." They deserved more than this after everything they'd been through. They deserved everything.

Justin moved to the gaming system, checking out the games I'd stocked for him. Anna moved a little closer to me. "I think we've lost him, too."

"Well, I can show you the rest of the house."

She paused for a moment as if not sure she wanted to be alone with me. "Okay."

"We'll be back," I called to Justin. He just nodded absentmindedly and waved us off.

I motioned towards another set of stairs at the end of the hall. "It's really just my bedroom up here." My architect had designed a suite that stretched the length of the third story. But I honestly didn't spend much time up there unless I was asleep.

Anna's steps faltered. "Are we—? We have to share a bedroom, don't we?"

It was something I hadn't been able to stop thinking about since starting the project of Justin's and Lyla's rooms. There simply wasn't a workaround. "Unless you want to bring the kids in on what's going on—"

"No. I won't put them in that position. They need to think this is real."

We reached the top of the stairs that opened into a sitting

area lined with built-in bookshelves. Two overstuffed chairs and a small table were tucked into the space. Anna sucked in a breath. "This is beautiful."

The window looked out over the property, the pool, the lake, forests, and then those gorgeous mountains. "It doesn't get used nearly enough."

Anna sent me a tentative smile. "Maybe I'll have to remedy that."

"It's all yours." I liked thinking about her curled up in one of those chairs, reading or relaxing. It fit somehow. As if I'd designed the space for her, even though we hadn't met yet.

I motioned to the open double doors. "Here we are."

Anna started inside, but her steps were hesitant as if she were checking for landmines as she walked. "It's a great room."

The bed was against the far wall, with a view of the massive windows looking out on that gorgeous view. And there was another sitting area in front of the windows, including a large couch. I gestured to it. "I can sleep there."

She shook her head. "No. I'll sleep on the couch."

"Anna. I'm not making you sleep on the couch for a year or however long this takes."

Her jaw tightened, a surefire sign that she was about to get stubborn. "You've already done more than anyone will ever do for me. I'm not stealing your bed."

I blew out a long breath. "There's one other solution."

"And that is?"

"It's a California King. We make a pillow barrier, and both sleep in the damn bed."

Her perfect bow-lips twitched. "A pillow barrier."

I pointed to the bed. "My interior designer insisted on about thirty pillows, so we've got plenty." I held up a hand in a pledge gesture. "I solemnly swear not to violate the pillow barrier." Unless I was invited to. But I kept that thought to myself.

"I always did love making a good pillow fort."

"They're the best."

Anna's gaze locked with mine, and all humor fled from her face. "Thank you, Mason. I'll never be able to repay—"

"I don't need repayment. I just want you, Justin, and Lyla safe."

"Then just take my gratitude."

"That, I can do." I grinned. "That and maybe some of those double fudge brownies you made for the Christmas party this year."

She barked out a laugh. "I solemnly swear to keep you in brownies for as long as I'm living here."

I rubbed my hands together. "And that was my evil plan all along."

I closed the door behind me as I stepped onto the back patio. Anna had music going while she and the kids prepped chicken fajitas for dinner. I'd offered to pick up something in town, but Anna had said she wanted to cook for their first night here. It was smart, getting the kids into a routine right off the bat.

As much as I wanted to be in there with them, I had a call to make. One I'd been putting off. I stared down at the contact in my phone. I tapped the number before I could think of an excuse to put it off again.

"Hey, big brother."

"Hi, Jules. How was Cabo?"

"A blast, but way too short. Hitting the books felt especially painful this morning. What are you up to?"

I looked out over my property, the sun hanging low in the sky, casting a pink hue. "I'm watching a stellar sunset."

"Not a bad way to end a day."

"Not at all." I walked to the end of the patio and out onto the lawn, the urge to move too strong. "Listen. I need to tell you something."

The other end of the line was quiet for a moment. "Things that start like that are never good."

"Well, this one is." I'd considered telling Juliette the truth. Spilling and asking her to keep our secret. But Jules was protective. Too much so. And I couldn't trust that she wouldn't blow this whole thing sky-high. I'd tell her the truth later. When the dust had settled, and Lyla and Justin were safe. "I got married."

"What?"

The single word was more of a screech than anything else. I winced, pulling the phone away from my ear. "Tone it down to decibels that won't burst my eardrum, would you?"

"Mason Decker. You weren't even dating anyone. And how could you get married without me?"

I strode around the pool and towards the woods. "I've known her since I moved here. We've been seeing each other, and we had a scare. Something that made us realize we didn't want to waste any more time."

"Did she fake being knocked up?"

"Jules," I warned.

"What? Women do that. Especially when a guy has money like you do. Please tell me you had her sign a prenup."

I hadn't. The thought had barely crossed my mind. Because I trusted Anna. I'd grown to know her character over the years, and there wasn't anyone I respected more. "She's not pregnant. Her sister died, so we're taking custody of Anna's niece and nephew."

"Mason..." Juliette let my name hang. "Your heart is too good. You get suckered into helping all sorts of people that you shouldn't. How do you know she's not taking advantage of the situation?"

Because Anna would never take advantage of anyone. I knew now that it was because people had betrayed her in the worst way, abandoning her when she'd needed them the most. "She's not like that."

"You don't see it, Mase. You always see the best in people."

"I see their potential. But I also see the truth. You know that."

I wasn't blind to the darkness in our world. I'd seen too much of it up close and personal.

"Are you sure her sister even died? I wouldn't be surprised if this was some con."

I pulled the phone away from my ear reflexively. I had to see if it was still my sister I was talking to. "Anna and these kids just lost the person they love the most. I can't believe you'd say that."

She was quiet again. "I'm sorry for them. But I care about *you* most. Someone has to look out for you when you won't protect yourself."

I pinched the bridge of my nose. Jules had always had a fierce streak. It was impossible for her to hold her tongue any time she thought I was being wronged. And she had never once thought a woman I'd dated was good enough for me. "I'm perfectly capable of defending myself. And once you meet Anna, you'll see there's nothing to worry about." I could only hope.

"Anna. That name is familiar…"

I'd told Juliette plenty about the shelter, and I was sure the woman who ran it had slipped into our conversations. "She's the head of Hope House."

Jules made a humming sound in the back of her throat.

"She's spent her entire career helping people who need it."

"People can put on a convincing act."

I sighed. I couldn't deny that people had tried to take advantage of me before, and Jules had dealt with more than one friend trying to make a move on me behind her back, but it didn't warrant this kind of response. "Promise me you'll try to keep an open mind."

"Only if you promise *me* you'll watch your back."

I grimaced at the grass. She might take more convincing than I'd hoped.

CHAPTER
Thirteen

Anna

A FLICKER OF MOVEMENT CAUGHT MY ATTENTION AS THE door to the back patio opened. Mason stepped inside, shooting the kids and me a smile. But something about his grin rang false to me. A flicker of alarm ran up my spine.

"This is my favorite part, Mase. Come watch," Lyla urged.

He strode over to the stove. "Can't miss your favorite part."

I studied his face. Beneath the easy expression were lines of concern. All I could wonder was if he'd heard from Keisha or someone else. "Everything okay?"

Mason's eyes darted to mine. "Yup." I didn't look away. He shook his head, true amusement curving his mouth. "I swear, there's nothing to worry about. I'll fill you in later."

Lyla pushed the platter of diced chicken and veggies. "Come on."

I ruffled her hair. "Impatient, are we?"

She grinned up at me. "I'm a growing girl. I need my fajitas."

Mason patted his stomach. "Me, too. Hit it."

I poured the contents into a large skillet I'd found in one of Mason's cabinets. It was going to take time to get used to the space.

And he had a gadget for just about everything I could imagine. And plenty of things that I had no idea how to use.

I let Lyla help me stir but warned her to watch the sizzle and pop of the olive oil. "Justin, can you grate the cheese?"

"You got it."

Mason grabbed a cheese grater from a cabinet and handed it to him. "Extra for me."

Justin took the kitchen tool. "Do I look like an idiot?"

"No?" Mason answered but said it as more of a question.

Justin laughed. "I always do extra cheese. A mountain of it."

"Not the whole block," I warned.

"Do the whole block," Mason whispered.

I rolled my eyes and moved to put the fajita fixings onto a clean platter. Pulling open the oven I'd set to warm, I slid the food inside. "Where are your serving bowls?" I asked Mason.

He opened a drawer and pulled one out. "What needs to go in here?"

"Those chips." I pointed to the counter.

As he moved to grab the bag, a beep sounded from his pocket. Mason tapped a few times on his screen and then put the phone to his ear. "Come on down, Walker."

I stiffened at the police chief's name. He was a friend, but with everything going on, his presence set my teeth on edge. "Was he supposed to stop by?"

Mason shook his head. "Come on, let's see what he wants."

My gaze traveled around the kitchen. Justin watched me and Mason like a hawk, his alarm bells likely going off at Walker's name, as well. But Lyla was blissfully unaware as she put a stack of tortillas in a warmer. "Jus, can you finish up my guacamole? All of the ingredients are prepped. You just need to smash everything together."

We'd had plenty of Mexican feasts together, and he knew what he was doing. He pushed off the counter. "I want to hear what Walker—"

Mason cut him off with a head shake. "Let us talk to him first. We'll fill you in afterwards."

Justin looked as if he wanted to argue. I moved in and bumped his shoulder with mine. "Only the truth, right? I'll tell you whatever you need to know, okay?"

"Okay," he mumbled and turned to the counter where I'd set the ingredients for the guac.

Mason and I headed for the front door. My fingers couldn't stay still. I braided them together and then undid the action, only to start all over again. Mason reached out a hand, covering mine and squeezing. "Everything's going to be okay."

"You don't know that." I'd had too many experiences where things ended up the farthest thing from okay.

His gaze locked with mine as we stopped just shy of the front door. "I won't stop until we make sure it is. I promise you."

I had the sudden desire to lean into him. To bury my face in Mason's chest and have him wrap his arms around me. I closed my eyes for a moment, trying to fight the pull. "Thank you."

He released his hold on my hands, and I felt the loss immediately. It was as if the world was suddenly ten degrees colder. "I've got your back, Anna."

I didn't agree or disagree. I simply made a humming noise in the back of my throat. Mason didn't push. He only smiled at me and pulled open the front door. Walker was already heading up the front steps. He held up a tin. "These are from Taylor. She wanted you guys to have some treats your first night here."

I took the container he extended to me. "That was so thoughtful of her. She didn't need to go to the trouble of baking anything."

Walker chuckled. "Oh, she didn't bake. She got an assortment of things from the Kettle. If she'd made these, the box would probably still be smoking."

I pressed my lips together to attempt to hold in my laughter. "Well, thank her for sending them over."

"I will." His expression sobered, and I instantly knew the

goodies weren't the only reason he was here. "The social worker is going to do a visit tomorrow. Can you guys be ready for that?"

I had known it was coming. Appreciated that the system wanted to make sure Justin and Lyla had a safe place to call home. But I couldn't help the twisting my stomach seemed to do in response. I looked at Mason. "I think we're ready."

I hadn't had time to unpack fully, but I'd gotten the kids settled. Chelsea had stored the majority of their belongings in a storage unit in town. At some point, I'd have to go through everything. But for now, I'd taken out the majority of the boxes that had been marked for Justin or Lyla.

"We're ready," Mason assured me. "Keisha sent us a list of what to expect."

I nodded slowly. One of the dozens of emails my lawyer had already sent, outlining what we needed to be aware of. She hadn't blinked an eye when we told her that we were getting married. She'd only smiled and said, "That helps."

I had a feeling she knew this union was a bunch of bull, but she didn't ask probing questions. She had sent us a point-by-point breakdown of what a CPS home visit would look like. I'd gone over her list at least ten times. But I'd need to do it again now that we were here.

"Try not to worry too much. I asked around to find out who your caseworker was. It's Sadie Jacobson. She's one of the best I've worked with. Fair. Caring. Works damn hard."

That was good news. It should've eased the knot in my stomach, but it only intensified it. Mason seemed to sense my nerves and wrapped an arm around my shoulders. "What time should we be ready?"

"Two work?"

"We'll be here," Mason answered. "Do you want to come in for some dinner? Anna made a fajita feast, and Justin is mashing up what looked like some incredible guacamole."

"I'll have to take a rain check. I'm supposed to pick up takeout at the Saloon and bring it home. Taylor might murder me if I delay her dinner. And Cooper wouldn't be too pleased, either."

"I don't want Taylor mad at me because I came between her and her burger," I said.

Walker shot me a grin. "Smart woman. You guys give me a call if you run into any issues tomorrow. I'll help as much as I can."

"I really appreciate that." The words were a challenge to get out, my throat getting tight.

"Anytime." He waved and headed back to his truck.

Mason pulled me against him, his arms going around me, the embrace I'd wanted since the moment Mason had said Walker's name engulfing me. "It's going to be okay."

I let myself soak up the feel of the comfort, of not being alone, for a count of ten, and then I forced myself to straighten and pull out of Mason's hold. "We should go eat. I don't want Justin and Lyla to worry."

Mason studied me, his gaze calling bullshit on my subject change. But again, he didn't push. "Okay, let's go eat."

I wandered out of Mason's massive walk-in closet, my gaze firmly focused on the paper I'd highlighted half to death. My and Lyla's sleepover had been abandoned for me making sure that everything was ready for tomorrow. "Crap, we need a fire extinguisher. I can go to the hardware store tomorrow—"

"There's one in the pantry, one in the garage, and one in the barbeque area off the patio."

I looked up from Keisha's list of things a social worker might inquire about. "There is?"

Mason set his book down as he reclined against the pillows on his massive bed. True to his promise, he'd already erected a pillow wall of sorts in the middle of it. "Yeah. And there are fire ladders for the windows in Justin's and Lyla's rooms."

A burn lit in the back of my throat, spreading to behind my eyes. "Did you always have that?"

"No, but Keisha sent me the same list. I wanted to be prepared."

He was more prepared than I'd been, and they were my niece and nephew. The burn only intensified, and I blinked in an attempt to clear it. Mason swung his legs over the side of the bed and strode towards me, moving in close but not touching me. Since I'd pulled away on the front porch, he'd been careful not to. "Hey, what's wrong?"

I took in a shuddering breath. "I just—I feel like I'm failing already."

"Bullshit."

My eyes widened. I wasn't sure I'd ever heard Mason curse. "Excuse me?"

"You have done everything imaginable to help those kids. But there's been a lot to tackle in the past couple of weeks."

He wasn't wrong. There'd been meetings with Keisha, packing up the cottage, going through the storage unit. I'd been trying to pin down the detective in Vegas, but I felt like she was giving me the runaround. Oh, and I'd gotten married. I could feel a hysterical laugh bubbling up, but I tamped it down.

Mason reached out as if he were going to rest his hands on my shoulders and then stopped himself. Disappointment flickered, but I shoved that down, too. "We're as prepared as we can be," he assured. "What you need to do now is sleep. It's after midnight."

I'd been running around like a crazy person since we'd finished dinner. I'd gone over every detail of Justin's and Lyla's bedrooms, checked the garage for toxic chemicals, battery tested every smoke detector. As soon as Mason suggested sleep, I realized that I was bone-tired. I hadn't had a good night's rest since the horrible phone call that'd changed my world. "Sleep."

The corner of his mouth pulled up. "Yeah, you know, that thing we all need to survive?"

"Oh, that."

"Come on. Everything else can wait until tomorrow."

"All right." I suddenly felt a little awkward. I was already in sweats and a t-shirt that I could sleep in. "I'm just going to brush my teeth."

"Take your time." He headed back to the bed, but I couldn't seem to stop watching him go. The way he moved and the way his broad shoulders pulled his shirt taut.

I gave myself a mental shake and moved to the bathroom, shutting the door behind me. I leaned against it. "Get it together." My brain was short-circuiting or something. My hormones going haywire, and my mind playing tricks on me. Instead of thinking of the man in the bed feet away, I focused on my teeth. I flossed meticulously, brushed for the full three minutes. I washed my face and moisturized so thoroughly, I might as well have given myself a facial. And then there was nothing else for me to do.

Mason looked up as I pulled open the door. "Get every tooth?"

My face flamed. "Don't want any cavities."

"Good dental health is important," he said with a smirk.

I rolled my eyes. "Oh, shut up."

He laughed, and something about the sound eased the worst of my nerves. He pulled back the comforter on my side of the bed. "Think of it like a sleepover. We can whisper our secrets over the pillow wall."

I crossed to the bed and slid under the covers, pulling them up to my chin as he turned out the light. "I never went to one of those sleepovers." The words were out before I could consider how wise they were to share.

"You didn't?"

I pulled the covers tighter under my chin. "Chelsea and I were never allowed. Our parents didn't like us going over to other kids' houses." The more we were out of their sight, the more there was a chance for something to slip, for someone to see a bruise and start asking questions.

The sheets rustled next to me. "Well, you're going to make up for it now."

"Will you braid my hair and paint my nails?"

"Only if you ask nicely."

I grinned into the dark. "I'll make sure to save the glitter polish for you."

"You're such a good friend."

Friend. Deep down, I knew that wasn't what I wanted from Mason. It was a hell of a lot safer, though. And maybe that would be enough. We'd get through this next year and then part ways with a deep friendship. But something about that left a sort of hollow feeling in my chest. I'd been here less than twenty-four hours, and I already knew I'd miss the sound of that deep breathing as I slipped off to sleep.

CHAPTER
Fourteen

Anna

"Maybe I should change," I mumbled into the mirror. I'd gone with a simple sundress, trying to look put together while not trying too hard. But the social worker might see right through that and think I was being manipulative.

"Don't. You look beautiful."

I jumped at Mason's voice. "Maybe jeans would be better."

He moved into the bedroom, slipping his hands into his pockets. "I think it's perfect. And honestly, I don't think she cares what you're wearing as long as there aren't a bunch of curse words written all over it."

"That was the other outfit I was considering…"

"Me, too. It was hard to go for this instead."

My mouth curved. Mason looked effortlessly perfect. When I looked at my reflection in the mirror, you could tell I was *trying*, that this wasn't my natural state. But Mason in his dark jeans and button-down shirt looked simply at ease. I forced my gaze up to his face. "Where are Justin and Lyla?"

"I left them in the middle of a heated game of *Sorry* in the family room."

Games were good, they would keep them distracted until the social worker got here. Unless things got too heated, and one of them ended up throwing the dice at the other.

Mason's brows pulled together. "What's wrong?"

"Oh, I'm just imagining some sort of eye injury if one of them gets angry about losing."

"Neither of them strikes me as the kind of kid to get violent over losing a board game."

He was right, but I couldn't seem to rid myself of the panic. "There's a first time for everything." I started towards the stairs. "We should get down there, just in case."

Mason's hand caught my elbow, stopping me in place. But he dropped it just as quickly. "Take a deep breath. If you're nervous, they will be, too."

I closed my eyes and inhaled. The windows were open, letting in the early summer breeze. I focused on the scent of pine in the air, how clean and fresh it was. I imagined that air cleansing me, too, washing away all of the worries and anxiety. When I opened my eyes again, Mason was staring at me. I fought the urge to squirm. "I think I've got it together now."

"Good. And when we're done, we can all go out for pizza or burgers."

"Sounds good to me."

As we headed down the two flights of stairs, I heard Justin moan. "Aw, man."

Lyla let out a loud giggle. "Sorry!"

When we rounded the corner, Justin looked up. "She's kicking my butt," Justin complained.

"That's what little sisters are for," Mason said.

I sat down next to Lyla on the couch, tickling her sides. "Take pity on your brother."

"Never!" she shrieked.

Justin met my gaze. "Is she here yet?"

We'd explained the visit to them over dinner last night, telling them what we could expect, and that the social worker might want to talk to them alone. "Not yet. Just remember, all you have to do is tell the truth."

He nodded, looking down at the dice in his hands.

Lyla burrowed deeper into my side. "She's not going to take us, right?"

"No, sweetie. She just wants to make sure you're safe here."

"We are. The safest. She'll see all of Mase's cameras and his gate and then she'll know, right?" Lyla asked hopefully.

I brushed her hair back from her face. "I think she'll know."

Mason's phone beeped, and he tapped the screen. Putting it to his ear, he answered it. "Hello?" There was silence for a moment, and then, "Just follow the drive down and park anywhere."

He tapped another icon on his screen and then slid the device into his pocket. "All right, team. We're gonna get through this. And when we're done, pizza and ice cream."

Lyla shot her fist into the air. "Yes!"

Justin wasn't as easily put at ease, but he nodded, his expression stoic.

I pushed to my feet and took Lyla's hand. We made our way to the front door. I stayed back with Justin and Lyla while Mason opened it. A woman climbed out of a small SUV and headed up the front steps. She was younger than I'd expected, likely in her mid-twenties and beautiful. The smile she gave us was meant to put everyone at ease, but I couldn't relax.

Mason reached out a hand. "Hello, Ms. Jacobson. I'm Mason Decker. Welcome."

She shook his hand, the smile still on her face. "Please, call me Sadie. Thank you for having me in your home."

She said it as if it were optional or as if we'd invited her over for a barbeque. I did my best to keep my expression warm, but I knew it was fake. This woman had the power to potentially take

Justin and Lyla away, to place them with their grandparents. "It's nice to meet you, Sadie. I'm Anna, and this is Justin and Lyla."

"Hi, guys. I know you probably have a lot more fun stuff to do on such a pretty day, so I'll be as quick as I can."

"We're getting pizza and ice cream after," Lyla chimed in.

Sadie widened her eyes. "Lucky. That's my favorite."

"You can come with us if you want. Right, Anna?"

I couldn't help but pull my niece a little closer. "Of course, she can."

"That's so kind of you to offer, but I actually have another appointment after this one. Maybe another time."

Mason moved into our little circle. "Open invitation."

"Thanks." Sadie adjusted her tote bag on her shoulder. "How about this? Anna and Mason can show me around, and then I can have some one-on-one time with Lyla and Justin."

I hated the idea of Lyla or Justin being out of my sight right now, but I nodded. "Why don't you guys finish your game while we give Sadie the tour?"

"Sure." Justin wrapped an arm around Lyla's shoulders.

"Sadie, you saw the cameras and the gate, right?" Lyla asked.

Sadie looked a little confused. "I did."

"We explained to the kids that you were here to make sure they were safe and happy. Lyla wanted to make sure you saw all of Mason's security," I explained.

Sadie's expression gentled. "Looks like he's got lots of good things in place."

"He does," she assured.

We made our way through the family room and left Justin and Lyla on the couches. Sadie slid a clipboard and pen out of her purse. "Do you mind if I wander? I'll ask any questions as they come up."

"Go right ahead," Mason said. "We'll follow behind."

Most of the perusal of the downstairs was silent. And the quieter things were, the more my anxiety kicked up. Sadie kept marking things on a sheet. When we reached the bottom of the stairs, she looked up from her checklist. "Everything looks great down here. Where are Justin's and Lyla's rooms?"

"They're on the second floor. And we're on the third," Mason told her.

"Is that okay?" I asked. "That we're not on the same floor? Because we can move—"

"It's fine." She gave me another one of those reassuring smiles that did nothing to calm my nerves. "Try to take a deep breath. You're doing great."

Mason pulled me into his side. I hadn't realized how much I needed it. How much I'd missed his touch, simply not having it for twenty-four hours. I soaked up the feel of his warmth and strength. He pressed a kiss to the top of my head and then looked at Sadie. "This has been a nerve-wracking process, as I'm sure you understand."

"Of course. It's never easy to have a stranger assessing your home and talking to the children you love. But I promise I'll do everything in my power to make sure Justin and Lyla are in the best place."

"That's here," I said, my voice sounding almost rusty. "The best place for them is here. They wouldn't be safe with my parents."

Sadie's gaze sharpened. "What makes you think that?"

I swallowed against my suddenly dry throat. "My father was physically abusive to me growing up, and my mother covered for him. He hit Justin once right before they came to Sutter Lake."

Sadie scribbled on her paper. "Has there been any documentation?"

"No. Justin didn't tell his mom when it happened. He only told me after he knew there was a chance they might have to go live with their grandparents."

She looked up from her clipboard, a heat in her eyes that hadn't been there before. "I'm very sorry that happened to both of you.

Were there ever any hospital or doctors' visits that might help corroborate this?"

"I had to go to the hospital once for some broken ribs, but my mother told them I'd fallen while jumping on my bed. Most of the time, he was careful. He knew where to hit that would hurt but not leave outward signs." There were times I'd had blood in my urine from kidney punches, but he'd only broken a bone once. I'd never understood how he had the restraint to hold back in that way but not be able to stop hitting us altogether.

"If you can get me the hospital name, I'll request those records."

"I can email it to you after I look it up."

"That would be great."

Mason had gone stiff by my side, and when I looked up at him, I saw barely contained rage. I couldn't help but place a hand on his stomach, the muscles taut. "Are you okay?"

"No, I'm not. I want to kill your father," he whispered.

I forced some levity into my voice. "Somehow, I don't think you going to jail for murder will help our custody case."

I hoped for a chuckle or at least a corner of his mouth to rise. I didn't get either. He simply stared down at me. "He's not going to hurt any of you ever again."

"Okay." I wasn't sure what else to say. I wasn't going to tell Mason how good my father was at flipping the script and getting people on his side. I didn't explain how he'd turned my sister against me for so many years. None of that would help right now.

His hand slipped under my hair, squeezing the back of my neck. "I mean it."

"I know." There was a certainty in Mason's voice that brooked no argument. And for the millionth time, I wondered why. "*I know what it's like to have no power.*" His words echoed in my brain. I wanted to know who had taken that power away and why. Instead, I simply headed upstairs behind Sadie.

I leaned back in one of the lounges by the pool, tugging my hoodie a little tighter. I stared up at the stars as if they might have the answers I was looking for. If they did, they weren't speaking tonight.

A throat cleared, and I looked in the direction it had come from. Mason extended a mug. "Thought you might be able to use some hot chocolate."

I took the mug. "If it's that epic mix you used last time, the answer is yes."

"I don't mess around when it comes to hot chocolate."

"Good to know."

He wrapped his hands around his mug. "Can I join you?"

"Of course." It was his house. His pool. His land. He could go wherever he wanted.

Mason eased down onto the other side of the lounge. "How do you feel?"

"Exhausted." I was tired down to my bones. Lyla and Justin had been shaken after their time with Sadie. Not because she hadn't tried her best to go gently, but some hard questions had to be asked, and I knew Justin had needed to lay a weight at her feet. Instead of going out for pizza afterwards, Mason had gone to get us all takeout. We'd eaten in front of a movie in the family room.

"I think she's on our side."

I shifted so I faced Mason, my legs tucked under me. "What makes you say that?"

He took a sip of his hot chocolate and then set it on a side table. "Just a gut feeling."

"I hope your gut is right." We needed Sadie on our team. To report to the court that we were the best caregivers for Justin and Lyla. Without her vote of confidence, our custody case would be even more of an uphill battle than it already was.

We were quiet for a minute, soaking in the quiet night. There was a serene beauty to Mason's home. Everything felt calmer here. If it were mine, I'd never want to leave. I blew on my drink before taking a sip. "Does your sister visit much?" I'd seen photos around the house from various phases of life. The two of them seemed close, but he rarely talked about her.

Mason grimaced. "She's pretty busy with law school right now."

"What's with the frown? You don't want her to be a lawyer?"

"I'm not frowning."

I tried to copy his expression. "That's what your face looked like. Not exactly a happy reaction."

Amusement lit his eyes. "That is pretty bad. No, I want her to do whatever makes her happy."

"So, why the face?"

He sighed, turning so he faced me more fully. "Juliette is overprotective…"

He let the sentence hang, and I filled in the rest. "She's not happy you married me."

"She's always skeptical and thinks it's her job to look out for me, when it's really the other way around."

I traced the rim of my mug with a finger. "It's both of your jobs. You should look out for each other." Chelsea and I had built that kind of bond growing up. An early warning system to avoid Dad when he was in a mood. Friendship when we were so cut off from most of the world. But when I started seeing Derek, it had faltered. For the first time, I'd wanted to reach for more, and Chelsea was too scared. Our relationship fracture had left room for Dad's manipulations to take hold.

"You're right. But she takes it a little too far. And she wasn't exactly happy to learn I'd married someone she hadn't met."

I set my mug next to the lounge. "Mason, tell her the truth. That this is a favor. I don't want this to come between you."

He shook his head. "It's not a good idea. I think it would make it worse."

My stomach gave a healthy twist. The last thing I wanted was to create issues for Mason when he was giving me everything. I stiffened as something clicked into place. "She thinks I'm using you. After your money or something?"

Mason rubbed at the back of his neck. "She thinks everyone who comes into my life might have ulterior motives."

And why wouldn't she suspect me? We hadn't signed a prenup or anything like that. No paperwork other than the marriage license had been signed at all. "Mason, why don't I sign one of those…what do you call them? A prenup but after marriage?"

"A postnup. We don't need one."

"Why? I could try to take half of everything from you. Hell, maybe I like this house so much I could fight for it when we get divorced."

His mouth curved. "I'm glad you like my place."

"This isn't funny."

"It kind of is. Anna, I've seen you live your life for the past two years. How generous you are with your time and every resource at your fingertips. You don't think I know you paid for that computer programming class Kristin's daughter wanted to take but couldn't afford? Or the hockey gear Greg needed to play safely? I see you. And I don't think there's a person I'd trust more."

I suddenly felt raw and exposed. Every person who came through Hope House had a story. And the parents who were there in an attempt to make a better life for their children always got to me the most. I wished my mother had been strong enough to do that. And if there was ever a need that wasn't covered by the center, sometimes I stepped in. But I had no idea that Mason had seen so much of it.

"I…" I wasn't sure how to finish that sentence, how to even start it.

"Don't worry, I won't share your secret with the world. But I also won't have you signing some ugly paperwork that demeans the friendship we have. I trust you, and I'm not going to let my sister's doubts create issues here."

There was that *friendship* word again. One I both loved and hated. I pushed it from my mind and focused on Mason. "You never mention your parents. Are they not in your lives?"

The movement was slight, but I still saw it. A subtle stiffening of his shoulders, the twitch of his fingers as they tightened around his knee. "They're dead."

Mason's voice was flat as he said it. Not tinged with grief the way it might have been if he'd lost them to disease or a tragic accident. This was something else. I stayed quiet. There was an implied request for more in my silence, but I wouldn't push. I wouldn't make him tell me anything, even though he knew more about me than I'd shared with anyone since my time in juvie.

His gaze shifted to the trees beyond the pool, to the lake that peeked out from between them. "My father drove our car into a lake. He almost killed my sister and me. And he *did* kill my mother and himself."

CHAPTER
Fifteen

Mason

ANNA SUCKED IN AN AUDIBLE BREATH, BUT I COULDN'T make myself turn back to face her. This wasn't something I shared. Not with anyone. Cain knew, but not because I'd told him but because it would've come up in his extensive background check before offering me the job to head his company. Juliette and I never spoke of it because she didn't remember—too young and traumatized when it happened to have it stick in her brain.

But it had stuck in mine. Cemented itself into my bones, resurfacing every so often to taunt me. The screaming and crying. My mother's panicked wailing. Her begging me to get Juliette out when her seat belt stuck. The way my father didn't seem to hear any of it.

Fingers curled around my forearm. "I'm so sorry. Those words aren't nearly enough, but I don't have better ones."

Heat from that hand seeped into me. It was the first time Anna had reached out. The first time she'd made the initial contact. And damn it felt good. My gaze met hers. "We have more in common than you think. A club that neither of us ever wanted to be in."

Her eyes lit with understanding. "I hate that for you."

She didn't move her hand, and I laid mine over hers as if the heat from her touch could somehow replace the cold of the memories battering at my brain. "My dad was sick. I don't know what it was, but he had the highest highs and the lowest lows. Either could turn violent. And there was a paranoia in him. He'd accuse my mom of cheating or me of stealing things from him when he misplaced something."

"But your mom never left."

"No. She had this unquenchable hope in her. No matter what he did, she thought he would change."

"They never do."

"No, they don't." If someone was going to heal from that, it would take years of intensive therapy. Medication. And even then, I wasn't sure. But it didn't matter because he'd never once tried for help. Even when my mom would suggest seeing a doctor or counselor. On a good day, he'd blow her off, on a bad one, he'd backhand her and send her flying.

"How old were you?"

"Fourteen. Juliette was only two."

I could hear my father's words as the car picked up speed. "*You're not going to leave me.*" Maybe she had been planning to run. Maybe her daughter walking and talking had been a wake-up call. She hadn't protected me, but maybe something about Juliette had made her want to fight.

"God, Mason. I can't imagine."

I didn't want her to. I didn't want anyone to live with the images that haunted me. The feelings. The burn in my lungs as I broke the surface. Juliette's cries as she coughed up water. I'd wanted to dive back down and try to get to my mom, but I couldn't leave Jules alone on the bank of the lake. I didn't know how long I'd waited, hoping she'd surface. But she never had.

"We made it." It was the only thing I had to hold onto. Jules and I had survived. And now, we were thriving.

"Who did you live with after?"

My jaw clenched reflexively. "My aunt and uncle. They were absent at best. Overwhelmed with their own three kids. So, I pretty much raised Jules. Went to college near their house so I could stay close, and she came to live with me full time when I was in law school."

"You never got a chance to be a kid."

"Neither did you."

A soft smile curved her mouth. "It's one of the reasons I always loved when Justin and Lyla came to visit. I got to do all the things with them that I always wanted to do growing up. Chelsea was good about that. Giving them what we never had."

I traced circles on the back of her hand with my thumb. "We'll keep giving them that. I promise."

"That's why you did this. Why you're helping."

"I won't lie. It's part of it. I don't want anyone to go through what you and I have. But I care about those kids. I care about *you*."

There was the slightest hitch in her breathing. So small, I would've missed it if I hadn't been staring so intently. I lifted my hand that had been resting on hers, curving it around the side of her face where her jaw met her neck.

Anna's skin was so damn smooth but filled with heat and a buzz of energy. I'd never felt anything like it. Just this small contact lit everything inside me.

Her eyes locked with mine. Some invisible tether, one made of shared pain and understanding, of hope and fear, pulled us closer. Our lips were a breath away when her palm landed on my chest. "Wait." She closed her eyes. "This is dumb. Monumentally dumb."

"Or incredibly smart." I didn't move, not closer or to pull away. I simply waited.

"We can't. This is so much bigger than us."

An image of the two kids asleep in the house filled my mind. I knew she thought we didn't need the complication of feelings for each other, but that ship had sailed for me a long time ago.

Maybe the first time I'd ever met her. I brushed my thumb back and forth across her jaw. "We can. But I'm not in a rush, either."

She blinked a few times, her lips twitching. "Cocky, much?"

I shrugged. "I know there's something here. But I also know it scares you." I was putting together the pieces as Anna shared more of her history. The boy she'd loved had betrayed her, and I doubted she'd truly let someone past those walls of hers since— not in a romantic sense, anyway.

She scooted back, bending to pick up her hot chocolate. "You're allowed to think whatever you want, but I'm going to bed."

Shit. I watched her stride towards the house and pushed down every urge I felt to chase her. This would be a marathon, not a sprint. And I'd just stumbled out of the starting gate.

"What the hell happened to you? You look awful."

I looked up from my computer at Cain's voice. "Gee, thanks."

He lowered himself into the chair opposite me at my desk. "Married life not treating you well? Or is it treating you *too* well?"

I scowled at him. I wished I looked like death warmed over because my wife had kept me up all night. Well, I guessed she had, in a way. I'd been tossing and turning because my mind had been on her. But not Anna. By the time I'd gotten up to our bedroom, she'd been fast asleep, the wall of pillows firmly in place. "I didn't sleep great last night."

The humor in Cain's expression dropped away. "Did the social worker visit not go well?"

"No, I think it went as well as it could have. I've got a gut feeling she'll be on our side."

"But?"

"There's a lot going on." More than I'd talk about right now. "And the visit was tough on Lyla and Justin."

"I hate this for them."

"Me, too." I wished I could snap my fingers and make it all go away, but I didn't have that magical skill.

My cell phone buzzed on the desk, and I swiped it up.

Juliette: *Your wife went to jail. Did you know that? You need to get an annulment now. Call James.*

I muttered a curse.

"What now?" Cain asked.

"My sister getting the wrong idea about things." I typed out a quick text.

Me: *What the hell are you doing? Can you just quit it and be happy for me?*

This was getting ridiculous. Protective, I understood. But running a background check was going too far.

Juliette: *Here's a link to the full report. She didn't have a permanent address for almost eight years, Mase. She's a grifter and a con. You need to protect yourself. And if you won't, I will.*

Hell. I knew why there was no address on file. Because Anna had lived at the shelter for all of that time, going from resident to employee before finally being put in charge of the whole place. But Jules hadn't earned that information, not when she was already so set against Anna.

Me: *Quit it. I know Anna's past. But you don't have a right to go searching through it. That's her private business, and I don't appreciate you digging it up for ammunition. I mean it, Jules. Stop.*

There was nothing for a minute as I stared at my phone.

Juliette: *I'm just trying to look out for you.*

Me: *I know. But in this case, I don't need you to, okay?*

Juliette: *Just be careful.*

I groaned, leaning my head back and pinching the bridge of my nose where a headache was forming.

"She's not thrilled you got hitched without telling her?"

I forced my head down so I could see Cain. "Not the happiest. You know how she is."

"Vicious when she thinks someone is taking advantage of you."

Vicious wasn't a word I'd ever used to describe Juliette, but he wasn't wrong. "I'm hoping when she finally meets Anna, some of that will fade."

Cain made a noise that wasn't agreement or disagreement. "That going to happen anytime soon?"

"I doubt it. She's focused on summer classes right now." But, apparently, they hadn't taken enough of her focus because she'd had time to look into Anna.

"It's been the two of you for a long time. I know what that's like. You become this team forged in the worst of times. She might not want that to change."

Cain understood better than probably anyone. He'd had a sister he'd looked out for in much rougher situations than what I'd dealt with living with a neglectful aunt and uncle. But Cain had lost her, and it had marked him for a long time. Kennedy had brought him out of that dark place.

"I really do think that once Jules meets Anna, she'll understand. She'll see that Anna isn't anything Jules thinks she is."

"I hope you're right. But you might need to give her a sterner warning."

That wasn't exactly my strong suit. Juliette had wrapped me around her little finger from the moment she was born. I knew I spoiled her. Especially after I'd sold my first video game. But she'd never been a bad kid. She'd gotten good grades, hadn't been in any serious trouble. I'd rarely told her no, though. That might be coming back to bite me.

My phone buzzed again. But this time, it wasn't Juliette.

Anna: *Keisha got official word. My parents are filing for custody of Justin and Lyla. Their paperwork calls me unfit.*

Some part of me had hoped the Foleys would simply slink off into the night, too scared of what their daughter might bring up in court to stay and fight. But, of course, we couldn't be that lucky. And if they were going to fight, I knew it would be dirty.

CHAPTER
Sixteen

Anna

I DRUMMED MY FINGERS ON MY THIGH AND FOUGHT THE URGE to tear at my clothes. This suit had been Kennedy's suggestion. One to wear if fancy donors came to Hope House or if we needed to have meetings with outside people. If it was just our board, jeans were more than acceptable. But as much as the fabric made my skin itch, I was grateful I'd had it.

Today, it would be my armor. A coat of impenetrable material that my parents' scorn and hatred wouldn't be able to sink beneath. "Tell me again why we're doing this."

Mason kept his gaze on the road ahead. "Because there's a chance Keisha can get them to fold before we end up in court."

I didn't completely comprehend the dance going on between the lawyers right now, but a part of me understood it was a game of chicken. We were heading for a collision, both hoping the other would bail before impact. "They won't."

Once my father sank his teeth into something, he didn't let go. Not even if it meant his destruction.

"You might be surprised. Keisha can be pretty convincing."

I didn't doubt it. Mason's friend was a powerhouse. But my

father had a cruel streak that seemed to sustain him through anything. Instead of arguing, I stayed quiet, watching the fields and forests whiz by. "Thanks for coming with me."

"I wouldn't let you face this alone."

Of course, he wouldn't. Because Mason was a good man. The best. And that knowledge made my chest ache.

"I appreciate it."

His hands tightened on the wheel. "Stop acting like I'm a stranger. We're friends. Hell, even though this isn't the way people usually go about this kind of thing, we're married."

The hint of anger in his voice surprised me. I'd never heard it before. And as I took that in, I realized what I was doing. Pushing him away, back into the box of cordial colleagues. Back into what was *safe*. "Sorry," I mumbled.

"You don't have to be sorry, just quit it."

I opted for silence instead. Maybe if I kept my mouth closed, I'd stop messing everything up. Getting too close, pushing too far away. Nothing felt right.

I let myself zone out, trying to think of anything but what was to come or the man sitting next to me. Until those fields and forests changed to neighborhoods and then a town. Aspen Valley was larger than Sutter Lake, some big-box stores on the outskirts, and a vibrant central area. We passed a courthouse I hoped we'd never have to set foot in. Restaurants and shops. A movie theater.

Mason's GPS directed him to a brick building a few blocks off the main drag. It was picturesque, the kind of place that spoke of history. He pulled into a parking spot and shut off his SUV, turning to me. He held out a hand. "We're a team, right?"

I looked at his hand as if it had claws that could puncture and wound. But laid mine on top of his. "A team."

He wrapped his fingers around mine, squeezing. "We'll get through this."

I swallowed, trying to clear my throat. "Thank you." I held up my free hand before he could argue. "Just let me say it. It makes me feel better."

The corner of his mouth kicked up. "If it makes you feel better, say it to your heart's content."

"I'm gonna say it just to get on your nerves."

"You wouldn't."

I arched a brow. "Try me."

He chuckled. "You're vicious when you want to be."

"And don't you forget it."

"Never." He gave my hand another squeeze. "You ready?"

"Ready." I wasn't. Nowhere near it. But I could fake it until I made it.

"Liar."

"It's not nice to call someone a liar, you know."

He lifted my hand and pressed his lips to the back of it. "It is when it means I know you."

My heart hammered against my ribs. Not because I was about to face my parents and their ugliness, but because that easy brush of his mouth against my skin had sent a shock through me. As if all my nerve endings were standing at attention.

"You don't know everything." It was a tease and a warning all at once.

"I don't have to. I know what's important."

Each word killed. A pain that brought with it the deepest pleasure. A sensation I couldn't let myself lean into. I didn't jerk away, but I squeezed his hand and then slipped out of his hold. "We should go."

"We should."

Mason and I climbed out of the Range Rover, and he beeped the locks. When we met at the head of the vehicle, he twined his fingers with mine. I should've pulled away, but I didn't. I needed to know that I wasn't going into this meeting alone. That someone had my back.

We made our way inside, Mason giving our names to the

receptionist. She immediately led us back to a conference room. It was light, the large windows letting sunshine fill the space. Coffee, juice, and assorted pastries sat on the table. It gave me the sudden urge to laugh. This polite falsity before two groups tore into each other, fighting with everything they had.

Keisha breezed through a door the receptionist had left open. She was the picture of professionalism in a smart skirt suit, her wavy, black hair woven into a half-updo I never would've been able to perfect. "Anna, Mason, welcome. Do you want coffee or breakfast?" She gave me a quick hug and Mason a kiss on the cheek.

I instinctively placed a hand over my belly. "I don't think my stomach can take food right now."

She gave me a sympathetic smile. "I know this won't be fun, but it's necessary. Even if we don't have a shot at getting them to back down, it will help us see what they have up their sleeves."

A chess master. That was what Keisha was. Always thinking, not just one step ahead but ten. Arranging pieces on the board so she could make her move.

"I'm glad you're our lawyer and not my parents'."

She chuckled. "I'm going to take that as a compliment."

"It is," I assured her.

Mason pulled out a chair for me and then took the one next to mine. "Any idea what we should expect?"

"None. They've kept things pretty close to the vest so far. I'm hoping that changes today."

"Do you know their lawyer?" I asked.

Keisha nodded. "He's good. Old school. But he's not as good as me."

The receptionist appeared again. "The Foleys and Mr. Paisley are here. Do you want me to show them in or have them wait?"

Keisha looked at Mason and me. "You ready?"

Mason threaded his fingers through mine again. "We are."

I concentrated on blanking my expression. The best way to

keep my parents from winning was not to allow them to see how much they'd hurt me. How much they still were.

I didn't pull away from the fingers woven with mine. In that moment, I simply let myself pull strength from the contact. It would've been so much harder if I were in this room alone. If my parents saw me as vulnerable. But they wouldn't. They would know that, unlike twelve years ago, people had my back.

A portly man with glasses and a briefcase appeared first, shaking hands with Keisha. But I only had eyes for the two people behind him. My father strode in, his head held high. "Anna. It's good to see you."

I gripped Mason's hand harder but didn't say a word.

He kept right on going. "I'm sorry it's under these circumstances, but I'm so glad you're safe. We worried after you took off."

The false niceties and concern were the same picture he'd painted for teachers and neighbors. And it'd worked—every single time.

My mother moved to his side, but as she eased into a chair, I caught her wince. Dad had lost the targets for his rage, left only with Mom as the focus of his anger and frustration. The flare of concern and worry took me by surprise. Fear for the woman who had abandoned me to this man's mercies time and again, yet I couldn't help but want more for her.

Keisha took a seat at the head of the conference table. "Thank you so much for coming today. I'm hopeful that we'll be able to settle this matter outside of a courtroom and save us all some time, heartache, and money."

My father clasped his hands and rested them on the table. "I'm hopeful, too, Ms. Williams. I think Anna knows deep down that she's not equipped to care for two impressionable children. They would do much better in my wife's and my care."

Keisha's expression remained perfectly pleasant and polite. "Well, Mr. Foley, your daughter Chelsea entrusted her children into Anna's care on more than one occasion, and from the interviews we've done with Justin and Lyla, I know that they have never once been left with you."

Heat flared in my dad's eyes, his breathing growing a touch more labored. "Chelsea didn't have the full picture. Didn't know everything that Anna had done."

"I'm afraid she did," Keisha argued.

"She didn't know this." Dad grabbed two folders from his lawyer and slid them down the table. One landed in front of Keisha, and the other in front of Mason.

"What Mr. Foley is trying to express is his concern for someone with Ms. Foley's record having custody of his grandchildren. I suspect the court will be concerned, as well," Mr. Paisley explained.

I flipped open the folder, and the name at the top of the paper made everything around me freeze and my vision tunnel. The only thing I could see was Derek's name. As blood pounded in my ears, I forced myself to read the words. It was some sort of affidavit, talking about my alleged behavior in my teen years.

Lie after lie jumped off the page. That I had pulled him into dealing, bribed him with sex. He said I had connections to major cartels, and what the police arrested me for was only the tip of the iceberg. He said I used and took him to sex parties where I wanted to have multiple partners in a single night.

I wasn't sure why the betrayal cut as deeply as it did. Derek had already proven that his loyalty was fleeting. But why now? Why, when he had nothing to gain by spreading lies? I looked up and met my father's gaze, saw the satisfied smirk on his face.

He was why. My father. He'd probably offered Derek money or maybe just a chance to stick it to me one more time. I was sure Dad had told Derek the types of things he wanted him to say.

Nausea swept through me at the thought that it might work. That Mason might believe these words. The lies about my sexual history were clearly an attempt to change his opinion of me.

I forced myself to look at my husband, the man whose opinion of me had come to mean far too much in such a short period of time. I braced for disdain. Instead, I saw rage. But it wasn't directed at me—it was zeroed in on my father.

I squeezed Mason's hand, bringing his attention to me. "Don't let him see that it affects you."

"You're right." He pressed a kiss to my forehead and then took a deep breath. "Even though I want to deck him right now."

"Get in line."

He sat back in his chair, schooling his features. Keisha cleared her throat. "As vivid of a picture as this paints…I don't think the court will put too much stock in a felon's stories from over a decade ago. This man has been in and out of jail since he was seventeen. Anna has never had another issue with the law. In fact, we have people right now, looking to overturn her conviction. The case had major holes in it and wasn't prosecuted correctly."

I straightened in my chair, whispering to Mason. "What?"

He took my hand again, his thumb brushing back and forth across my knuckles. "They're looking into it. I didn't think Keisha should get your hopes up before we knew more."

Annoyance and gratitude battled within me. "I want to know everything. Even if something's a longshot. Remember what you said. This only works if we're honest."

"No fair throwing my perfectly sensible words back at me."

Mr. Paisley straightened in his chair. "Ms. Foley may have only been convicted once, but when a judge has a choice between a couple with a sterling record and a woman who's been to juvenile detention and lived in a homeless shelter for most of her life, who do you think he's going to choose?"

My stomach hollowed at the mention of my home. Whose fault was it that a homeless shelter had been my only option? And what did they know about the beautiful life I'd built at Hope House? Nothing. They only had their judgement and anger.

Things only devolved from there. The ping-pong match between Keisha and Mr. Paisley only succeeded in giving me a headache. No agreement was reached, and my parents and their lawyer left in a huff. Keisha assured us that everything was good. We had a much clearer picture of what we were up against, and she was ready to fight.

I could barely take her words in, my head hurt so badly. The pulse of my heart seemed to have taken root there, thrumming an angry beat. Mason kept a hand on my lower back as he led me out of the building and helped me into his SUV. "You okay?"

"My head's killing me."

"Do you want some Tylenol? I think I have some in the first-aid kit in the glove box."

Of course, he did. Mason was prepared for everything. He was basically a grown-up version of a Boy Scout.

"I don't think my stomach would handle it too well." It was already churning. I needed a soda and some food before anything.

"All right. Why don't I just get you home?"

I nodded, closing my eyes as he shut the door. I kept them closed as he drove. But the words from Derek's statement taunted me. The ugly images they invoked. The way my parents and their lawyer had sliced me to bits without a second thought.

But it was Derek that hurt the most. The pictures that filled my brain now were worse. Us cuddled on the couch in his new apartment, making plans for what our future would hold. Tossing names back and forth for what we'd call our children someday. The tender way he'd frame my face in his hands and tell me that he'd love me forever. That he'd always protect me.

"Pull over!" I jerked up in my seat.

Mason cursed but brought his Range Rover to a stop at the side of the road. My seat belt was already off, and I leapt out of the car. My knees buckled as I landed in the dirt. And then I was heaving. Emptying whatever meager contents remained in my stomach.

Mason was by my side in a matter of seconds, pulling my hair away from my face and rubbing my back. He didn't stop as I continued heaving until there was nothing left to empty, but my stomach continued to revolt. I didn't know how long it took for me to will my body under control, but I was gasping for breath when I did.

"Nice and easy," Mason said as he kept rubbing my back. "You want some water?"

"Yes," I croaked.

He released his hold on my hair and stepped away. I felt the loss instantly. And I wanted his touch back so badly it terrified me. I leaned back on my heels, trying my best to get my breathing back to normal.

Mason reappeared, handing me a bottle of water and some napkins. "I've got a travel mouthwash, too. When you're ready."

"Boy Scout," I muttered and then washed out my mouth. Wetting one of the napkins, I patted down my face, as well.

He handed me the mouthwash. "Boy Scout?"

"You're always prepared." The minty flavor was everything I needed, and I rinsed out my mouth twice.

Mason helped me to my feet, his hands remaining on my elbows to make sure I was steady. "Are you okay?"

Something about the earnestness in his gaze broke me. The tears came fast and hard. "No. I'm not okay."

CHAPTER
Seventeen

Mason

THE TEARS MIGHT AS WELL HAVE BEEN DAGGERS TO THE heart. I'd never seen Anna cry. Not once. I'd seen her fight back tears. But not even when she'd gotten the call about her sister had Anna let those tears fall.

But today had been too much. Everyone had a breaking point. And this was Anna's. I pulled her into my arms. She might break for a moment, but I refused to let her fall. "We're going to get through this."

"I don't know if we are." Her body shook against mine as her tears came harder. "It—it's too much. I can't—"

"You can, and you will. These assholes don't get to win."

Anna couldn't seem to get out another word. And she didn't need to. All she needed was to let some of this out. All of the pain and grief she'd been bottling up for way too long.

"Let it out. Keeping it all in was what made you sick in the first place."

I could feel her trying to rein it in, even now. But the dam had broken, and there was no getting it back now. As much as I hated that she was hurting, I was glad it wasn't eating her alive anymore.

I held her as she sobbed. For her sister. The innocent love that had turned so wrong. For the parents that were supposed to care for her but never did.

I didn't know how long we stood on the side of that highway, vehicles whizzing past every few minutes. I didn't care how long it took for Anna to let everything free. I'd stay with her until she unlocked it all.

Slowly, her breathing evened out, and the tears lessened. I framed her face with my hands, wiping away what tears I could. Her cheeks were red, and her eyes were bloodshot.

"I'm sorry, I—"

"No." The single word came out more harshly than I'd intended, and I did my best to soften my tone. "You don't have a damn thing to apologize for. You needed this. And it's my honor to stand with you while you let some of that toxic stuff out. If you don't, it'll kill you."

"I'm scared that if I start, it'll never end. There's too much hurt. And if I really sit and think about it, I'll drown."

I stared into those red-rimmed eyes that still somehow managed to be beautiful. "You're too strong to drown. Especially if you take the hand that someone's holding out." It wasn't an outright request, but Anna knew what I was asking. For her to let me in. To let me support her.

Her hands fisted in my shirt. "I've leaned on you more in the past two weeks than I have any other person in the last ten years."

The statement rocked me. Made me see our shared history through another lens. Anna was warm and friendly with most people. She was always ready to reach out a hand to help. But she rarely took that help in return. If something was wrong, she figured it out on her own.

I brushed her hair away from her face. "That doesn't make you weak. You know that, right?"

"I know. But it does make me vulnerable."

There was such pain in her statement—a bone-deep hurt at

leaving herself open to the kind of betrayal she'd experienced before.

"I'm not Derek."

Anna's gaze shifted to her feet. "I know you're not him. In my head, anyway. But people hurt each other every day. They might not mean to, but it happens."

"They do. But the good ones do everything in their power to repair that hurt. To make it right and not do it again."

"Sometimes, it's too late."

God, I knew that was true. Sometimes, the wound was deadly. And even if you recovered, it meant that you'd always be looking out for someone or something to hurt you in the same way. "Think you can let me try?"

Anna looked up into my eyes. "That's what I'm doing."

She was, I realized. By taking the help I had offered. By sharing her life with me, even if it was under false circumstances. By letting me stand by her side. And it wasn't often, but every now and then, she leaned, let me lend her a little of my strength. "Okay."

We were quiet for a moment as we stood on the side of the road. Frozen in time, in this bubble of hurt and hope, fear and the desire to fight. I wanted to dip down and close those few inches between us. To lose myself in her and forget about the storm swirling around us.

A truck honked as it drove by, breaking the moment. Anna stepped out of my hold. "We should go."

"Probably a good idea." I helped her back into my SUV and then rounded the hood.

"I should stop by Hope House and make sure they don't need anything."

"No way."

"Excuse me?"

I pulled back onto the road. "You've been through hell today. The only thing you're doing is going home, getting some food, and resting. Someone at the shelter will call if they run into any issues."

"I might shove that food in your face if you keep ordering me around like that."

I stole a quick glance at Anna, who looked more than a little annoyed. "Let me rephrase. Please, give yourself a day off. A slug day."

"A slug day?"

"That's what Juliette and I used to call them. If either of us had an especially rough week, we'd pick a day and do nothing but watch movies and eat way too much junk food. It always helped."

Anna shifted in her seat. "I guess a slug day wouldn't be all that bad. *If* you ask nicely."

"Please, Queen Anna, will you be a slug for a day? I promise to only feed you things with zero nutritional value and watch movies that make you laugh."

"I could suffer through it…"

I shook my head and kept driving. I kept the conversation light, focusing on Anna's favorite movies and candy. It made the trip pass in a flash. I hadn't realized that we'd never had any normal get-to-know-you conversations. But they would happen more and more now that we were living together.

I made a quick stop at a burger place on the edge of town, telling Anna to wait in the car. I ordered enough burgers, fries, onion rings, and milkshakes to feed an army. Her eyes widened as I opened the back door and slid in the box of food.

"Are you secretly the Hulk and didn't tell me?"

"Better too much than too little."

She let out an adorable little snort. "That's enough food to get us through the apocalypse."

I climbed in and turned over the engine, pulling away from the curb. "Or an epic movie marathon."

The drive through town was quick, and I hit the remote on my visor to open the gates. By the time we reached the house, Kennedy, Cain, Lyla, and Justin appeared on the front porch. I didn't bother pulling into the garage, simply parked out front. I looked over at Anna. "You okay?"

"Nothing a cheeseburger or ten won't fix."

"That's my girl." The words spilled out without me giving much thought to them. They weren't the truth, but I wanted them to be.

Lyla knocked on Anna's window. "Why are you taking so long?"

Anna chuckled and pushed open her door. "I'm trying to figure out how Mason's going to get all of that food in the house."

Lyla peeked into the back and sniffed. "Burgers?"

"You know it," I answered.

"Milkshakes?" Justin asked as he appeared behind his sister.

"Do I look like an idiot to you?"

He grinned. "You definitely do not."

"I want strawberry," Lyla called as she ran up the front steps.

I motioned for Anna to follow her. "I've got the food. You set up the couch and pick out a movie."

"Slug day," she mumbled and followed her niece and nephew.

I grabbed the food and met Cain on the steps. "Want to stay for food and a movie, or do you need to get back to the office?"

He patted his stomach. "It's technically lunchtime, and I do own the company."

"Perks."

"Damn straight." His expression sobered. "How'd it go?"

Anna's tear-streaked face flashed in my mind. "They're fighting dirty." I suspected they would but seeing it firsthand was another thing altogether. "Can you do me a favor?"

"Name it."

"Ask Dante to look into the ex, Derek. He's pulling shit, even now. That says he holds a grudge. Not sure why since he's the one who screwed Anna over, but something isn't sitting right. Might be as simple as the parents paying him for his testimony, but we need to know."

Cain immediately pulled out his phone and began texting his private investigator. "The little I know Dante's turned up about this guy isn't good. He's mixed up with some bad people. It doesn't make sense that he'd want to involve himself in a legal case. Any attention would be bad attention in his book."

"I doubt he's going to be involved. He gave a sworn statement that will be submitted into evidence. But we need all the ammunition we can get against him. That statement needs to be thrown out on day one."

Cain clapped me on the shoulder. "If there's something to find, he'll find it."

I wanted Cain's assurances to put me at ease, but there was no such luck. I wasn't sure I'd be able to take a full breath until that judge's gavel landed, and the Foleys were gone.

CHAPTER
Eighteen

Anna

"**B**ANANA OR STRAWBERRIES ON YOUR CEREAL?" I ASKED Justin and Lyla as they slid onto stools at the island.

Justin wrinkled his nose. "Neither?"

"It's the tradeoff for eighty-two burgers, a dozen fries, and at least five milkshakes."

He grinned. "Slug day is the best."

Lyla nodded, taking a sip of her juice. "I want to have slug day every day."

I opted for banana, slicing it and dividing it between the two bowls of Cheerios. "Pretty sure you'd get sick if that happened."

"Nuh-uh," she argued. "I've got a steel stomach, Mom says."

Lyla froze at her slip of *Mom*. I kept right on completing my task. I'd been worried that neither Lyla nor Justin had talked about Chelsea much, and I wasn't sure if I should push or let them go at their own pace. I pulled milk from the fridge. "Did you know your mom always used to get sick on rollercoasters?"

Every year, our elementary school's upper grades took an end-of-year trip to a local amusement park. And every year, Chelsea thought she could handle the big coaster with its massive drop and upside-down loop. She always tossed her cookies right after, and then we'd spend the rest of the day sipping Sprite and walking around. Everything in me hurt at the memory. But it was a good kind of hurt, the kind that reminded a person of just how many memories they had to pull from.

"She would never go on any of the rides at the fair. I always wondered why," Justin mumbled.

"Barfing one too many times scarred her for life," I told him.

He smiled, but it was a little sad. "Do you have more stories like that?"

"Only a million. I'll tell you one anytime you want."

"I miss her," Lyla whispered.

I rounded the island and pulled her into a hug. "I know, sweetie. It's because she was such a good mom."

"The best," Justin agreed.

"Is she gonna have a funeral?" Lyla asked.

I wished I had an answer for that. I'd left a number of messages for the detective in Las Vegas, but I was getting the runaround. I wasn't sure if that was because the case was still active or what, but it was starting to piss me off. "Do you want to have one?"

"I dunno," Lyla answered, looking towards her big brother.

He swallowed. "We should do something."

"I agree. Something special to remember her. And it can be whatever you want. Just the three of us or a big party."

"You mean the four of us," Justin said.

"Of course."

As if he were beckoned by me leaving him out, Mason appeared from around the corner. "Hey, guys." Reading the room, he asked, "Is everything okay?"

"We're talking about what we might want to do for Chelsea," I explained.

Mason nodded and leaned a hip against the counter. He was wearing another pair of those expertly tailored dress pants. I'd come to realize that he preferred to be casual most of the time, jeans and a button-down. But on days when he had meetings with clients, he dressed up. "Whatever you want to do, count me in."

Justin smiled. "Told ya."

I ruffled his hair. "Too smart for your own good."

Mason grabbed a water bottle from the cabinet and filled it. "I've got meetings this morning, but I can pick Justin and Lyla up from camp if you need to work past three."

I desperately needed to. And while we had aftercare for the parents who worked late, it was a long day for the kids when they were just getting back into the swing of things. "Sure. Thanks for doing that."

He gave me a wink. "No problem. Just call or text if you need anything. And my secretary knows to patch you through if anything's urgent, even if I'm in a meeting."

My stomach gave a healthy flip at that. Such a silly thing to react to. But it was because he'd made me a priority. Even in this weird pseudo-friendship, fake marriage that we had going, he made sure I knew I was important. "Thanks," I whispered.

"See you guys at three." He gave a high-five to Justin and Lyla as if he'd been doing it all his life and headed for the front door.

Justin swallowed his bite of cereal. "Bananas are kinda good on cereal."

"Told ya."

My landline rang, and I pushed my laptop back. I was going to kiss whoever was calling because approving kitchen supply spreadsheets was never at the top of my list of favorite things. "Hello, this is Anna."

"Hi, Anna. It's Keisha."

"Hey." It was the only word I could get out, my throat suddenly dry.

"I've got some updates for you if you have a minute."

"Of course." I wanted every piece of information I could get my hands on. Somehow, it made me feel more in control. If I could emotionally prepare for everything that might be headed my way, I could stand strong. Not have another meltdown like the one I'd had on the side of the road yesterday.

"I've got good news and bad news."

"Give me the bad first."

"I received the first list of people Mr. Paisley is calling to give testimony."

My grip on the receiver tightened. "And?"

"They've listed Justin and Lyla's birth father, Jeff Angler."

Jeff had left my sister high and dry, wanting nothing to do with her or the kids after realizing that he wasn't cut out for a family, after all. He'd been only too happy to sign over his parental rights if it meant not having to pay child support. Lyla had no memory of him, and Justin's memories were minimal at best.

"Why would they call him? He has no legal rights."

Papers shuffled over the line. "I've got our P.I., Dante, looking into him. I can only guess why they'd put him on the stand. Perhaps to say where he'd like Justin and Lyla to go as their closest living relative."

"Wait. If he's taking the stand, does that mean he'll be in town?"

"I'd guess he's already there. My good news is that our first court date is at the end of this week. We're going to get this underway and wrapped up as soon as possible."

My stomach cramped. Jeff was here. Would he try to see Justin and Lyla? That would only confuse them. Especially after just losing their mother. "Do you have a recent photo of him?"

"Dante just sent me one. I'll text it to you now."

"Will you send it to Mason, too? Explain who it is. I just want us to be on the lookout."

"Of course. Hold on just a moment."

The silence stretched, and each second ticking by felt like an ice pick jabbing behind my eyes—another of those brutal headaches coming on. I spun in my chair and grabbed a Diet Coke out of my mini fridge, hoping the caffeine would fight it off. As I popped the top, my phone dinged. There was a text from an unknown number with a message and a link. *Do they know who you really are?* I shouldn't have clicked the link, but I couldn't seem to help myself.

Instead of a photo of Jeff Angler, my mug shot looked back at me. There was only one word to describe the girl in the photo. *Terrified.* The article was from a smaller newspaper in the Portland area that had a reputation for being sensational in their news coverage. The headline read: *Teen Kingpin Arrested.* Bile crept up my throat.

"Anna, did you hear me?"

"Sorry, what?"

"Did you get my text?"

"Hold on." I exited out of the internet browser and returned to my messages. One from Keisha was at the top. I clicked on the photo. He looked incredibly normal. Unremarkable in every way. But I memorized the planes of his face, the jut of his chin. The color of his eyes and hair. Because this man had the potential to ruin everything.

CHAPTER
Nineteen

Mason

"**Y**OUR AUNT IS GOING TO KILL ME," I MUTTERED AS I walked down the street with Justin and Lyla in tow.

"But at least you'll go with ice cream in your stomach," Justin argued.

I chuckled. "Fair point."

Lyla looked up at me with those wide, innocent eyes. "What she doesn't know won't hurt her."

I blinked down at her. "Kid, I think you might have a future as a lawyer."

She shook her head. "Naw. I think I want to be a doctor that helps kids."

I wrapped an arm around her to guide her into the ice cream shop. "That would be a great job."

"I think so, too. I bet it's hard, but I could make everyone feel better, and that would be awesome."

I looked at Justin. "What about you?"

"I dunno. I like soccer a lot, but that's probably not a job."

"You could always be a coach. Or a teacher and coach on the side."

He looked thoughtful for a minute. "That might be fun. I like my history classes a lot. Maybe I could teach that."

"History was my favorite subject when I was growing up. We learn a lot from what happened before us."

Justin grinned. "I like the battle stories."

"Those don't suck."

A girl who looked to be in her later teens appeared behind the counter. "Hi, guys. What can I get for you?"

Justin ordered cookies and cream, while Lyla opted for strawberry. I settled on a mint Oreo milkshake.

Justin took his cone from the girl. "Next time, I'm trying what you got, Mase."

"It's always a winner." I paid the girl, leaving a healthy tip in her jar. "Want to walk down to the park?"

"Yeah! I want to do the monkey bars after I finish my ice cream."

As we walked, they told me about their days. Lyla had worked on an arts and crafts project that had gotten more than a little messy, and one girl had gotten paint stuck in her hair. Everything about the moment was so normal. Ordinary—and everything I'd been missing for so long.

Once they finished their ice cream, Justin helped Lyla tackle the monkey bars, and then they created some sort of obstacle course race that I couldn't understand no matter how hard I tried. Justin even let his sister win once or twice.

I checked my watch and then waved them over. "We should head home. Anna should be getting off soon, and we'll have dinner." I eyed them both. "You better not say you're too full for vegetables, or I'm gonna be grounded from picking you up."

Lyla looked thoughtful. "We should get a dog."

"Where did that come from?" I asked.

She shrugged. "If we had a dog, I could sneak him my vegetables under the table."

Justin held out his hand for a high-five. "I like the way you think."

"Justin, Lyla," a voice called.

I stiffened as I turned to see Mr. and Mrs. Foley approaching with another younger man. While Anna had custody of Justin and Lyla, there was no restraining order in place that said their grandparents couldn't approach them in public.

Lyla burrowed into my side, and Justin moved in close, but his shoulders were squared, and he stood straight as if ready for battle. The posture alone was enough to make me want to cause serious harm to Mr. Foley.

Mrs. Foley smiled. "Well, come on, give your gran a hug."

Neither child moved. I cleared my throat. "We were just leaving. We need to get home for dinner."

"They should at least be able to say hello to their father. They haven't seen him in years," Mr. Foley said. His voice was pleasant but his eyes had a glint that told me he enjoyed inflicting this kind of pain on his grandchildren.

I pulled Lyla in closer, feeling her tremble against me.

The man who looked to be in his forties shuffled his feet. "Hey, Justin. Lyla."

"Stay away from us," Justin growled. "All of you. I'm going to tell the judge who I want to go with, just like I told Sadie."

"You don't have the first clue what's best for you and your sister," Mr. Foley said. He was struggling to keep his anger contained, the façade cracking around the edges.

"Let's go." I didn't wait. I picked up Lyla, who clung to me instantly and kept a hand on Justin's shoulder, guiding him away.

"Wait!" Mrs. Foley called. "You can't just take them away."

I can, and I would. But I hated that there wouldn't be any more spontaneous trips to the ice cream parlor or park, not when I knew they could potentially end this way.

"Is he going to try to take us?" Lyla asked in a shaky voice.

Anna pulled her niece in close on the couch. "He can't, Lyla Bean. He signed a paper that says he isn't allowed to."

"Because he's a jerk and a loser," Justin muttered, arms crossed.

"I normally don't like that language, but in this case, I think *jerk* is the perfect word. As is a loser because he lost the most precious gifts he could've ever been given—you two."

I sat back, watching Anna weave her magic with the kids. Repairing wounds and bringing comfort.

Lyla sniffed. "He didn't want us."

Anna brushed the hair away from her face. "Which is his loss." She looked up at her aunt. "D-do you want us?"

"Oh, sweetie. More than anything in the whole wide world."

Tears slipped from Lyla's eyes, tracking down her cheeks. "Good."

Anna pulled her into a tight hug and met Justin's gaze. "I will do anything I can to make sure you guys stay with me, okay?"

He nodded jerkily. "Can I go play video games for a little while?"

"Sure," she answered. "But only one hour, okay?"

"Yeah, okay." He took off for the stairs.

I understood. He needed time alone to process. Maybe he didn't want to let the tears fall in front of us. I'd give him that space, but I'd be checking on him in an hour. Because if there was one thing I wanted Justin to be sure of, it was that he wasn't alone.

"What about you, Lyla Bean? What do you want to do?" Anna asked.

"Can I watch a movie?"

"Sure. Where do you want to do it?"

"In my room. I can set it up."

Anna studied Lyla's face. "You sure you don't want me to help?"

Lyla shook her head. "No, thank you."

"Love you big time," she whispered.

"Love you, too," Lyla mumbled and pushed off the couch to head upstairs.

When she disappeared, Anna leaned back on the cushions

of the couch and pinched the bridge of her nose. I couldn't stop myself from going to her. I sat down next to Anna and pulled her against me. She went willingly, letting her head fall to my chest. "What are we going to do?"

I slipped my hand under her hair, massaging her neck and scalp. "I think we need to call Walker and Keisha and see what our options are. I'd like to get a restraining order, but I don't think we have enough justifiable reason."

Anna straightened. "He hit Justin. That should be more than enough."

My hands fell away. "It should be. But there was no documented proof. All we have is Justin's testimony. Do you want to put him through that?"

Her shoulders slumped. "No. I don't. I just feel like there are no good options."

"We keep fighting. I think there's enough stacked on our side that we'll win this. It's just going to take time."

Anna pressed the bridge of her nose again. "I don't know how long I can keep this up."

I gently pulled her hand away from her face. "Another headache?"

"Yeah. I've been getting them like crazy."

"Come here." I grabbed one of the throw pillows and put it on my lap. "Lay down."

Anna hesitated for a moment and then obliged. That was how I knew it was bad—that she went so willingly. I massaged her temples and forehead, the top of her scalp.

"Give me your hand."

Her eyes flew open. "Why?"

"Trust me, okay?"

She paused again but slowly lifted her hand to me. I took it, pressing hard on a spot in the juncture between her thumb and pointer finger.

"Ow," she groused.

"Just stay with me for a few more seconds." I held it for a count of sixty and then released. "How do you feel now?"

She opened her mouth and then shut it, eyes widening. "So much better. How did you learn that?"

I sifted my fingers through her hair. "I used to get bad headaches in law school. That should've been my first clue that it wasn't the career path for me. My doctor recommended doing acupuncture, and the practitioner showed me this trigger point. It's been my secret weapon ever since. But I think it works better when someone else does it to you instead of you doing it to yourself."

Anna's eyes locked with mine, her mouth curving. "I guess I'm going to have to keep you around."

"I guess so." I couldn't look away from those lips. Pillowy soft and rosy-pink. "Anna?"

"Mm-hmm."

"I'm going to kiss you."

"Okay."

My head dipped at the same time she rose to meet me. This was bigger than the last kiss that had haunted me ever since. There was more between us now, shared pain and hope, and a fight we were waging together. All of that poured into the kiss.

It deepened in a flash, my tongue stroking hers. Anna's taste exploded in my mouth. I wanted everything she would give, even if that meant she had to hold back for now. I would take any crumb. She let out a little moan, pushing closer.

"Anna! I can't get the DVD to work."

Lyla's voice was a bucket of ice water on our overheated bodies. Anna shot up. "Shit. That—"

"Don't say that shouldn't have happened. Just say, 'Now isn't the time.'" I couldn't take another moment of her retreating and pushing me away.

She let out a shuddering breath. "Now isn't the time."

But as I watched her disappear up the stairs, I knew that it would be the time someday. I just had to hold on until then.

CHAPTER
Twenty

Anna

I STEPPED OUT ONTO THE BACK PATIO, MASON'S AND THE KIDS'
voices muting as I shut the door. Only the occasional loud
giggle from Lyla or shout from Justin cut through the glass.
They'd rebounded quickly from their run-in with their birth father.
The only hint of unease that remained was the fact that they hadn't
asked to go for ice cream the last two days.

The knowledge that my parents and Jeff had ruined that for
them had hot anger rolling through me. But I took a long breath,
letting the fresh pine air soothe away the worst of it. The kids
were safe, and Mason was currently teaching them how to make
homemade pasta. He had some sort of fancy machine that could
form the noodles.

I moved farther away from the house until my bare feet met
cool grass. Tapping on the screen of my phone, I pulled up a contact and hit the number. Someone answered on the fourth ring.

"Detective Johnson."

"Hi, this is Anna Foley." What I wanted to ask was why her
department had been giving me the runaround for the past few

weeks. Every time I had called to ask for an update or see when my sister's body might be released, I could never get a direct answer.

"Hello, what can I do for you?"

"I've been calling the number you gave me to see when you might release Chelsea's body, and I can never get a direct answer. Do you know what's going on?"

There was silence for a beat before Detective Johnson answered. "Her body was released to your parents over a week ago."

My footsteps faltered, stopping just shy of the paved area near the pool. "What?"

"They said they were going to let you know."

But they hadn't. And why would they? Not when they wanted to cut every connection I had to my family. "I have to go." I hung up without even saying goodbye and tapped another contact. Keisha answered on the second ring.

"Hi, Anna."

"Can you do me a favor? Or ask the P.I. maybe?"

Her voice lost the warm casualness it had held just a moment ago. "What's going on?"

The only thing that made me realize that I was shaking was the fact that my phone kept bumping the side of my face. "The Las Vegas police said they released Chelsea's body over a week ago. Can you find out what my parents did with her?"

"Of course. I'll move as quickly as possible, but it might take a little while."

"Okay."

"Hang in there, Anna. We'll figure this out."

"Thanks, Keisha."

I hung up and moved towards the lounge by the pool. My legs trembled as I sat. I pulled them up, wrapping my arms around them so that I was sitting in a tight ball. The sun hung low in the sky, but I was suddenly freezing.

I didn't want to imagine that my parents could be so heartless that they would bury their daughter without her children present.

But, deep down, I knew they were capable of anything. I wished I knew if my mother had always been that way. Always contained that chip that made her callous, able to turn away in the face of cruelty. Or if my father had turned her into that. Maybe she'd been a completely different woman before meeting him. I'd never know.

But I couldn't imagine my father being anything but what he was—cold and vicious. As if he lacked even an inkling of empathy. And the rage that flared to life when anything impinged on his control…I'd never seen anything like it.

I'd heard similar stories, though. In the voices of women at Hope House who had fled abusive husbands. I knew that sort of flip wasn't unique. But that didn't make it any less terrifying.

My phone buzzed in my hand, making me jump. I hit *accept* as Keisha's name flashed across the screen. "Hey, that was fast."

"I stayed on the phone with Dante while he researched."

"And?"

"I'm so sorry. They buried her a week ago."

It shouldn't have hurt as much as it did. Not when I knew the truth about my father's need for revenge. I'd seen him exert his dominance in every way imaginable for the smallest infraction. A neighbor had once asked him not to mow the lawn so early on the weekend. My father had started a campaign against him in the neighborhood, slowly but surely sowing doubt with everyone in the area. The man had been single and lived alone. My father insinuated that he might be a pedophile and that he looked at us girls funny. The man was finally forced to move.

There were countless stories like that. So, it shouldn't have shocked me that he would steal my chance to say goodbye to my sister. Yet, it did. And, God, it hurt. So much so, I had trouble taking a full breath.

"Anna?" Keisha asked.

"I'm here," I wheezed.

"Where's Mason?"

"Inside making pasta with Justin and Lyla."

"Do you want me to call him?"

I shook my head and then realized she couldn't see me. "No. I just need a minute to get it together."

"Want me to stay on the phone with you?"

It was so kind of her to offer. Especially when her normal billable-hours rate was something that made me wince. "No, that's okay. Thank you for finding out."

"Of course. Let me know if you need anything else."

"I will. Bye."

"Bye."

It took me three tries to hit the right button on my phone to disconnect from the call. The shaking had intensified until a sob finally tore free. The tears came in torrents, and I pressed my face to the pillow on the back of the lounge. I screamed and wailed into it, letting all of the pain and rage and fear free.

Memory after memory slammed into me. A kaleidoscope of the ugliest images of my childhood. Huddling with Chelsea, trying to hide from my father. Watching him punch my mom in the stomach. The blood in the toilet after an especially brutal beating.

It was too much. Where was the justice? Where was God? Where was anyone?

Arms came around me, making me jolt, but Mason's familiar scent quieted my panic. He lifted me, settling me in his lap and holding me close. "What is it?"

I didn't have it in me to pull away, even if that might have been smarter. Instead, I leaned into Mason, soaked in his strength and the fact that he cared. "I-I—" The words barely came to my lips. "My parents…they buried Chelsea. She's gone."

He went as still as stone beneath me. "What?" I nodded against his chest. Mason let a slew of curses fly, the likes of which I'd never heard from his mouth before. And then he pulled me tighter against him. "I'm so sorry."

"What am I going to tell Justin and Lyla?"

"The truth. We'll find our own way to remember her. And it

will mean more because there won't be any ugly energy from your parents to contend with."

God, I loved him for that. I stilled at the realization. It wasn't simply a common phrase passing through my mind. I loved this man. For what he'd done for me and Justin and Lyla, for who he was. And that terrified me more than anything. Because what would happen when I lost him?

CHAPTER
Twenty-One

Mason

"SHE WOULD'VE LOVED THIS SPOT," JUSTIN SAID, A HITCH in his voice.

I wrapped an arm around his shoulders. "I think it's a good place to remember her."

After a talk with Justin and Lyla about how they wanted to honor their mom, I'd made a call to my interior designer to see if she knew anyone who made custom benches. She'd, of course, come through. Two days later, we were standing at the edge of the lake on my property, where we'd placed the bench.

It was the perfect spot to take Justin and Lyla if they felt sad or wanted a connection point to their mom. A small plaque on the back of the bench read: *Chelsea Foley, beloved mother and sister. Her light will shine on us always.*

"Are you guys ready?" Anna asked as she held Lyla's hand.

Lyla nodded, holding tight to the special paper Anna had purchased. It was biodegradable and contained seeds for all sorts of different flowers. Each of the kids had written a letter to Chelsea, and now we were going to bury them not far from the water's edge, near the bench.

I let my arm slip from Justin's shoulders and reached for my shovel. "Put them in there, and I'll cover them up. Then we can water them."

Lyla came forward first, kissing her paper and placing it in a hole to the left of the bench. She gently patted it down. "Okay."

I heaped a pile of dirt on top and then looked at Justin, giving him an encouraging nod. He stepped forward to the hole to the right of the bench and crouched down. As he stared at his paper, his shoulders began to shake. I let the shovel fall and moved to him in a flash, pulling him into my arms and holding on tight.

His small body shook with the force of a much larger one. "I-I miss her so much."

"I know."

Anna moved in with Lyla, and we ended up in a huddle, surrounding Justin as he cried.

"It-it'll never be the same. She won't see me play soccer or make my favorite cookies. We used to make these forts and camp out in the living room. We'll never get to do that again."

Justin's broken voice shredded whatever was left in my chest. I would've given anything to take away his pain. "It won't be the same, you're right. And you're always going to miss her." I locked eyes with Anna over his head. "But maybe you can share some of those things with us, and we can do them together."

Lyla let out a little sniffle. "Mase and Anna are really good cooks. I bet they can get Mom's chocolate chip cookie recipe and make them."

Anna squeezed Justin's shoulder. "I know there's a box of cookbooks and recipes in the storage unit. We can go get it tomorrow."

"O-okay," Justin agreed. His voice was still shaky, but he straightened.

"You ready for this, or do you want to wait? There's no rush," I told him.

"I want to do it now."

"Okay."

He stared at the paper again, but this time when he crouched low, he didn't break down. He pressed the letter into the hole and patted it down. "Love you, Mom."

A tear of my own slipped free as I shoveled dirt into the hole. Anna appeared with the watering can we'd brought, and Lyla helped her wet the ground over each letter. I tossed the shovel into the back of the ATV we'd taken out here. "Do you guys want to stay out here for a bit or go back?"

Lyla gave me a sheepish smile. "I'm hungry."

"I could eat," Justin said.

Anna ruffled his hair. "You can always eat."

"How about breakfast for dinner? I always used to make that for my little sister. It was one of our favorites."

"Waffles?" Lyla asked hopefully.

I gave her a high-five. "Sounds good to me."

"Only if there's whipped cream on top," Anna said.

I wrapped an arm around her shoulders, pulling her close. "Do I look stupid to you?"

She rolled her eyes and then looked at Justin. "Do you see what you started?"

He shrugged. "I can't help it if my jokes are good."

We piled into the ATV and took the small dirt road back to the house, Lyla squealing with glee when I went fast. I slowed as I rounded the bend to the front of the house. A sedan was parked in front that I didn't recognize.

Anna leaned forward in her seat. "Who's that?"

"I don't know, but they shouldn't have been able to get in." I'd left my phone at the house, not wanting to be interrupted. I would've gotten a security alert, even if someone had the code. I brought the ATV to a stop as my sister climbed out of the car. I grinned, turning off the vehicle. "It's Juliette."

I climbed out and crossed to my sister, enveloping her in a tight hug. "Why didn't you tell me you were coming? I would've picked you up at the airport."

"I wanted it to be a surprise." She straightened from my hold, sending a scowl towards the ATV. "And I wasn't sure if my presence here would be appreciated. Your circumstances have changed."

"Jules…don't be like that. You know you're always welcome here. But I also expect you to be kind to Anna and her niece and nephew."

Her lips thinned. "I have nothing against those kids."

I fought the urge to pinch my brow. "Please. Don't make this hard on me."

"Fine," she huffed. "Introduce me."

Lyla was already bounding over, Justin on her heels. "This is your sister?"

"Yup. Lyla and Justin, this is Juliette. Jules, this is Lyla and Justin."

My sister smiled at them, and there was nothing false about it. "It's great to meet you both. Did Mase drive you fast?"

Lyla nodded enthusiastically. "So fast."

"That's the best."

"It's pretty fun," Justin agreed.

I patted his shoulder. "You want to go get out the waffle mix with Lyla? And then when I get inside, I'll start cooking."

"And the whipped cream," Lyla added.

I grinned. "That, too."

The kids ran for the house, and as soon as they disappeared, all warmth fled from Juliette's face. I turned to find the cause and came face-to-face with Anna. I wrapped an arm around her shoulders. "Jules, this is Anna. Anna, this is Juliette."

Anna started to reach out a hand to shake, but before she'd fully extended her arm, Juliette was speaking. "You mean the con artist?"

Anna stiffened in my hold, dropping her hand to her side.

"Jules," I warned, my voice low.

"What? It's the truth. She barely exists on paper."

And if I told my sister why, she would only see it as more evidence that Anna wasn't to be trusted. "Don't do this."

Anna placed a hand on my chest. "No, it's okay. Why don't you and your sister go out to dinner so you can have some one-on-one time? I'll make dinner for Justin and Lyla."

My back teeth ground together. I didn't want to leave, but I also didn't want to force Anna to put up with whatever snit Juliette was in. "We'll be quick."

"Take your time," she urged.

I brushed my lips against hers, and Jules coughed. I didn't spare my sister a glance. "Save me a waffle?"

"I'll do my best."

When Anna disappeared, I turned to my sister. "Seriously, Jules?"

CHAPTER
Twenty-Two

Anna

Busy. That was the key. If I kept moving, then I wouldn't think about Juliette calling me a con artist. I emptied the contents of Mason's junk drawer onto the island counter. I grouped items. Scissors, glue, and tape. Band-Aids, alcohol swabs, and Neosporin. A Sharpie, pencil, and pen. A pile of keys to who knew what. A lighter and flashlight. I threw away stray paper clips and half-melted birthday candles.

Moving to the cabinet under the sink, I grabbed a container of multi-surface wipes. I went to town making sure I got every speck of dirt in that drawer. But Juliette's voice still echoed in my mind. "*You mean the con artist?*"

Wasn't that exactly what I was? Conning the courts into giving me custody of Justin and Lyla. Conning the world into believing Mason could really be mine.

Music. I needed sound to keep that ugly voice at bay. And all of the other voices that followed. My father's calling me useless and a slut. Guards at juvie telling me I'd ruined my life and would never have a chance for a fresh start. Derek telling me he'd protect me forever.

I pulled out my phone and grabbed earbuds from my purse in the mudroom. Happy. I needed music that had a beat, and catchy lyrics you could sing along to. I settled on a nineties and early 2000s pop mix with boy bands galore. Then I turned it loud enough to drown out any lingering critics in my head.

I moved from drawer to drawer, pulling everything out, cleaning, and organizing. I wasn't sure how long I worked. I lost myself in the simple purpose of it all. Anytime my thoughts began to waver from my task, I doubled down on what the best organizational structure might be for the drawer or cabinet in question.

I reached to the very back of a shelf, stretching so I could clean the farthest nooks and crannies. Someone pulled one of my earbuds free, and I let out a scream. It cut short as Mason filled my vision. "God, don't do that!"

The corner of his mouth kicked up. "Maybe don't listen to your music at a decibel that will burst your eardrums."

My chest heaved as the adrenaline slowly left my system. "Just enjoying a little escapism."

Mason surveyed the kitchen. "You know I have a housekeeper, right?"

"I know."

His expression sobered. "You okay?"

I nodded. It was a total and complete lie, but I'd get there eventually. "Where's Juliette?"

"She's staying at the resort."

There was a five-star resort on the edge of town that would make the pickiest traveler happy. I tore at the wipe in my hands. "Because of me?"

Mason tugged at the material between my fingers and tossed it into the trash can I'd pulled out for my project. "Because of her."

"Just tell her what this really is. A favor you're doing for a… friend." I struggled to get the word *friend* out of my mouth. That too felt like a lie.

Mason leaned against the counter. "Is that what you still think this is? A favor?"

His tone was deceptively calm, but I could see the anger heating in his eyes. "I don't know." The lingering touches and soft kisses were enough to make a smart woman lose some of her brain cells. I knew there would be a line at some point. We would either cross it, or we wouldn't. Smart Anna would stay firmly on this side of the line. Reckless Anna would hurl herself over it for a chance to lose herself in Mason.

He moved in closer so I could feel the heat pouring off him. Mason lifted a hand, tucking a strand of hair behind my ear. His fingers trailed down my neck and slipped beneath my hair. "This isn't a favor, Anna. It's so much more. I think you know that, but you're scared to let yourself recognize it."

I swallowed, my throat catching with the action. "You terrify me." The words were out before I could stop them. The brutal truth.

Mason froze, his fingers still at the back of my neck. "Why?"

I had nothing to lose by telling him the truth. Maybe it would scare him away, and I would have my solution. But the thought of Mason walking away was almost too much to bear. "You already mean too much to me. That gives you the power to destroy me. I've been ruined before, Mason. I don't want to go there again. I don't want to give someone everything, only to have them break me apart and spit on the pieces. I never want to feel that alone again. If I keep my heart to myself, that will never happen."

Mason didn't look away as I spilled everything in my head. He listened. And then he was quiet. "I don't know how to ask you for a shot when you've been through so much. But that doesn't change that I want it. So, I guess I just have to ask. Take that first step. Just one. We can go as slow as you want, and I'll meet you wherever you're at. Just one step."

I felt a tugging somewhere deep inside. As if my soul wanted that step so badly, it was already on its way. My heart hammered against my ribs, almost seeming to rattle them with its force. The two halves inside me warred for supremacy. But it was the reckless side that won.

I took a single step forward so my body was flush with Mason's. His eyes flared, the green in them almost seeming to shift to gold. He moved in a flash, taking my mouth in a hungry kiss. I lost myself for a moment, nothing existing but the press of Mason's body, the feel of his tongue tangling with mine, the way my nerve endings woke with the promise of more.

My phone buzzed in my front pocket, making us both jump. I let out some sort of ridiculous giggle, my fingers flying to my mouth. My lips tingled. "Sorry, I should check it in case it's Keisha."

The hearings had started, but Keisha had warned us that staying away until we were required to testify might be the best thing. She was smart and could already tell that my father was using these legal maneuverings to hurt me. She didn't want him to have that opportunity. She'd told me and Mason that she thought it would increase my dad's frustration, and that those cracks in his veneer would eventually show in court. Keisha was clearly a master at the legal game, and I was thankful for it.

I slid my phone out of my pocket, unlocking the screen. A text from an unknown number popped up. A photo filled the screen, but even on that small space, it still had the ability to turn my blood to ice. It was of me, walking down the street, Lyla holding my hand and Justin grinning up at me. The text read: *Do you really think you're fit for the role of mother? Wait until your little town knows all of the skeletons in your closet.*

"What the hell?" Mason tugged the phone from my hand and unplugged my headphones. He trailed up the text chain, seeing the article I'd been sent earlier. Clicking on it, his jaw went hard. "Why didn't you tell me someone had been texting you this shit?"

My spine stiffened. "Not that I owe you a report of who has texted me, but I forgot. I was on a call with Keisha when the text came through, and we were dealing with more important things."

Mason straightened to his full height, and I was suddenly aware of just how much taller he was than me. "I want to know if someone's messing with you."

"It's probably my dad." Though something about that didn't sit right. He was far from techy, and I didn't think he'd be able to find my unlisted phone number. But he could've hired a private investigator. If he'd tracked Derek and Jeff down, someone must be helping him.

"I don't care who you think it is. This is the kind of shit you share with me."

I took a slow breath, not wanting to let my temper get the best of me. "Make that request nicely, please."

Mason closed his eyes and pinched the bridge of his nose. "Please, for the love of God, tell me when someone texts you something like this."

"That's better. Your tone could use a little work, though."

Mason pulled me into his arms, resting his chin on the top of my head. "I need you safe."

"I am safe. Someone's just trying to mess with my head."

"They were close enough to take this photo, and you didn't even notice they were there."

A chill skittered down my spine. I pulled back to look at the phone. "This was yesterday. When we went to pick up the bench. You were just out of frame."

Mason studied the photo. "You're right. Hold on." He pulled out his phone and tapped a few things on the screen. "Hey, Dante, it's Mason." There was a brief pause. "Anna has been getting some weird texts. Can I forward them to you and see if you can trace them?" Another pause. "Thanks, man."

He did something with my phone, and I heard the whoosh of texts being sent. Then Mason handed the device back to me. "He's going to try to trace the number."

"I hope it's my dad."

Mason pulled me in close again as if he couldn't bear even that little bit of separation between us. "Why do you say that?"

"If it's him, then we'll have even more evidence for the court." I'd take any harassment if it meant I got Justin and Lyla.

He pressed his lips to the top of my head. "We're going to get custody. We won't stop until we do."

God, I hoped he was right. But something told me that my dad wouldn't stop. And I knew how vicious he could be.

CHAPTER
Twenty-Three

Mason

JUSTIN TOOK A RUNNING LEAP AND CANNONBALLED INTO THE pool. Anna laughed as the water splashed her. Justin's head broke the surface. "What do I get?"

Anna pressed a single finger to her perfect lips in an exaggerated thinking gesture. "Eight and a half."

"Aw, man," he muttered, swimming over to the side of the pool. He looked up at Juliette and me. "What about you guys?"

I grinned. "The belly flop was better. I say seven."

Justin flicked water in my direction. "You lie. You're just jealous you can't beat me in a cannonball competition."

"I think it's at least a nine. Justin's right, big brother, you're just jealous," Juliette said, peeking out from under the wide brim of her sun hat. She'd been on better behavior today, and I had to hope that Jules had heard what I'd said at dinner last night and was getting her act together. But Anna was still giving her a wide berth, and I didn't blame her.

"We'll just have to see about that." I stood, pulling off my t-shirt.

Lyla cheered from the shallow end. "Then will you throw me?"

"You know it." Just as I was about to head for the pool, my

phone rang on the side table. I stole a quick glance and swiped it up. "Hey, Dante."

"That number came back."

No time for pleasantries with Dante, he was always straight to business.

"And?"

"It's a Google Voice number. I tried to get some information on it, but it's all smoke and mirrors. I've got nothing."

I grabbed the back of my neck and squeezed, trying to keep my expression blank. "I appreciate you doing what you could."

"Forward me any other texts that appear. I want to keep a record for my profile."

"Will do."

Dante hung up without another word. When he was done, he was gone.

Anna climbed to her feet, moving towards me. "What did he say?"

I pulled her in closer, needing to feel her body flush with mine. She hadn't put the pillow barrier in place last night. Anna had curved herself against me and let me hold her all night long. I hadn't pressed for anything more than that. What she'd given was already such a gift. "It's a Google Voice number, and there's no data on it." I knew from my time in law school that we wouldn't be able to get any additional information from the company since the texts hadn't been overtly threatening.

Anna's shoulders slumped. "I was really hoping there would be something."

I pressed my lips to the top of her head. "Me, too."

"What's going on?" Juliette asked.

I hadn't even heard her get up from her chaise lounge. I looked around to see if the kids were within earshot, but they'd become engrossed in a splash fight. "Anna's been getting some less-than-kind texts."

Juliette's lips pressed into a thin line. "And you had a P.I. trace them?"

"Yeah. It comes back to a Google Voice number."

Her shoulders straightened as she faced off against Anna and me. "Wake up, Mase. She probably sent them herself. Those things are ridiculously easy to set up and hide your identity."

Anna had gone stiff as a board in my hold. I pulled her tighter against me, trying to keep my anger in check so I wouldn't say something I regretted. "Jules, that's enough."

"What? I can't even have an opinion anymore?"

I looked down at Anna. Beneath the carefully blank mask was hurt. I felt the beginnings of a pull that had started the moment I'd told Jules that I'd gotten married. The tug between my sister and the woman who was beginning to mean everything to me. "I think it's best if you leave." The words burned as I let them loose.

Her mouth fell open. "Are you serious? She has completely blinded you. I've asked around about her in town, and people know almost nothing about her, even though you said she's lived here for ten years. Where? Scamming off some other idiot?"

"I lived at the homeless shelter," Anna said. Her voice was soft, but it was in no way timid. "I lived there for six years before I started working there full time and took an employee apartment in the building. I lived there because when my boyfriend framed me for selling his drugs, my parents decided I wasn't worth their time and cut off all contact with me. I had no one. But Hope House gave me a safe place to rebuild. That's where I've been."

There was shock on Juliette's face for a moment. It gave me hope that maybe she would finally hear the truth. That hope fled as anger filled Juliette's expression. "If you think some sob story you've invented to snare my brother will convince me, you're crazier than I thought."

"Jules," I barked.

The kids had stopped playing and were watching the exchange

with worried expressions. That only made me more furious. "Leave."

"You'd pick her, someone you barely know, over me? Your sister? The person who has been with you through everything?"

"You're the one making that choice," I said quietly. "By being so hateful to my wife, in front of two kids who have been through hell. And now you're scaring them."

Juliette glanced over to the pool quickly, a hint of regret passing over her features. "I don't want to scare them, but I'm terrified for *you*. Get that through your thick skull."

"No, you're not scared, you're angry. And you need to figure out why me being happy makes you that way. When you've done that, we can talk. But for now, you need to leave."

Tears filled Juliette's eyes, and they twisted something deep inside my chest. But I didn't let them break my resolve. She turned her furious gaze on Anna. "I hope you're happy." She grabbed her bag and stormed off to the side of the house where her rental car was parked.

"Mason, I don't want—"

"No," I cut Anna off. "She doesn't get to come in here and spew that shit, ruining our day. It's been a good one, and I'm not going to let her change that." We needed all of the good days we could get right now. Yet it seemed as if we kept getting knocked down.

"How about we talk later?" she asked in a quiet voice.

"I'll take that deal." I pressed a gentle kiss to her lips, slowly deepening it. "You're important to me. Don't ever forget that."

A hint of fear cascaded through her eyes. "You're important to me, too."

"I hope I still am after I do this…"

"What—?"

Her question cut off as I swept Anna up and threw her into the pool. She made a massive splash and spluttered as she kicked to the surface. "I was still wearing my cover-up you—you—you caveman."

I chuckled and catapulted into the water after her, splashing Anna, Justin, and Lyla.

Lyla clapped as I surfaced. "When you threw Anna? That was so totally a ten."

I grinned at Anna. "See? I've got style and form."

"What you've got is a target on your back, Decker. I'm coming for you."

"I can't wait."

CHAPTER
Twenty-Four

Anna

"I'M STAAAAAARVING," JUSTIN MOANED.

I looked up at Mason from where I was curled into his side on the lounge on the back patio and smiled. "I'm so shocked he's hungry only an hour after he had a snack."

"It's probably a world record for how long he's gone without food," Mason said.

Justin rolled his eyes. "I'm growing, you guys."

I pushed off Mason's chest, even though it was the last thing I wanted to do. "How about veggies and hummus, and cheese and crackers?"

Justin scrunched up his nose. "How about pizza?"

"Yeah!" Lyla said, bounding up the patio steps. "I want pizza."

I glanced back at Mason. "I blame you for this. Your pizza addiction has stretched far and wide."

He shrugged. "There are worse things."

"How about pizza *and* salad?"

Justin gave me a very serious look. "I will suffer through whatever salad you bring home if it means I can get some Hawaiian goodness."

I couldn't hold in my laughter. "Fair enough. I'll go pick it up, so we don't have to wait forever." The only downside of Mason living so far from town was that those deliveries were rarely hot when they arrived.

"I can go," Mason offered.

"No, I'll do it." I didn't want to chance Mason running into his sister when she was still pissed off. "If I call it in now, it'll be ready by the time I get there."

He leaned forward and gave me a long, slow kiss. "Drive carefully."

I couldn't answer. Mason's kisses stole my breath and made me stupid. He wasn't shying away from physical affection. The lingering touches and toe-curling brushes of his mouth were driving me crazy. Every night he held me as we fell asleep, but not once had he pushed for more. I was both grateful and about ready to rip his clothes off.

Justin made a gagging noise. "Enough with the lovey-dovey stuff. I need pizza."

Mason chuckled. "Just wait until you meet someone you like one day."

"No way. Never gonna happen."

I pressed my lips into a firm line to keep from grinning. It would be fun watching Justin get his first crush, go on his first date, maybe get married. A blow of grief hit me, so intense it nearly brought me to my knees. Chelsea would never get to see any of that. Those special moments in her son's life.

Mason squeezed my arm. "You okay?"

I forced a smile. "Of course. I'll be back in a few."

I pushed to my feet and hurried inside. The last thing I wanted was to lose it in front of the kids. They didn't need the weight of my grief on top of theirs. I made it to my car, calling the pizza place on the way and ordering three pies and a salad. I didn't let the tears flow until I hit the dirt road past the gate to Mason's property.

They weren't heaving sobs, simply a quiet stream of tears. It was a silent cry for my sister, the one I had just started to get back. I'd tried to write her letters while I was in juvie, but they'd been returned to sender. I wasn't sure if that was her or our father. I'd finally gotten through on her cell phone not long before I was released, but Chelsea had told me that she didn't want me in her life and had hung up.

That blow had nearly been my breaking point. That night, I'd lain facing the cinderblock wall on my bunk and cried as quietly as possible. You never cried in public. It made you look weak. And the weak were always used as punching bags. But I'd had fifteen years of hiding my emotions as training. I was a master of the blank mask. And it had been my greatest tool.

I called on it now, wiping the tears away from my face as I pulled into town. The Old West façades of the buildings and the baskets of flowers hanging from lampposts welcomed me. This tiny community had been more of a respite than it would ever know.

I guided my hatchback into an empty spot a few doors down from the pizza parlor. It was still on the early side, so things didn't look too crowded. But the streets of Sutter Lake were still plenty busy. Lots of unfamiliar tourist faces peeking in windows or buying souvenirs.

I climbed out of my car and closed the door with a hip, beeping the locks. My phone dinged.

Mason: *Justin and Lyla asked if you could pick up some brownies, too.*

I grinned down at my phone and typed out a reply.

Me: *Are you sure it's Justin and Lyla and not you?*

Justin might have the never-ending appetite, but it was Mason who had the insatiable sweet tooth.

Mason: *I wouldn't hate it…*

Me: *You owe me.*

Mason: *I always repay my debts.*

A pleasant shiver trailed down my spine, and I picked up my pace, slipping my phone back into my purse. Before I could straighten, I bumped into someone, their hands going to my shoulders.

"Anna. Damn, you grew up good."

A new shiver enveloped me, but this time, there was nothing pleasant about it. I stumbled back, out of the man's grasp. "What are you doing here?"

Derek grinned as his eyes raked up and down my body. "Gotta give a little testimony in front of the judge."

I tried to take in the man in front of me, to see any of the boy he used to be. But there was nothing. The hardness in Derek's eyes said there was no longer room for the tenderness I used to soak up from him. It was that gentleness and warmth that had pulled me in. I'd had so little of it growing up that when I'd gotten it from Derek, I'd been a goner.

I couldn't help but wonder if it had all been a lie. An intricate web of deception designed to ensnare me. "You mean so you can lie to a judge?"

Derek made a tsking sound. "Now, Angel. That's not very nice. I tried to make it right when you got out, but you wouldn't let me." He gave an exaggerated pout, but his eyes hardened even further. "That hurt my feelings."

Everything in me was strung tight, twisting into a spiral that might snap at any moment. "There isn't one thing that you could do to make up for what you put me through."

His jaw worked back and forth. "You were fifteen. You got cush juvie. I was seventeen. I would've been tried as an adult."

"Because you *were* an adult. One who made stupid decisions and wasn't man enough to take responsibility when you got busted."

"Watch your fuckin' mouth." He moved in a flash, backing me against the building. "You should show a little respect. I provided for you. Got you a phone, gave you a place to stay. You *owed* me."

The rough wood of the building bit into the backs of my bare legs. My eyes darted around the street, but it was suddenly so much emptier, no curious tourists. Nothing at all. "Back up."

I did my best to keep any tremble from my voice, but it must not have worked because Derek's mouth curved into an ugly grin. He leaned in closer. "Haven't you realized it yet? I don't play by your rules."

A hand clamped down on Derek's shoulder and yanked him back. He jerked out of Walker's grip. "What the hell, man? I was having a word with *my* woman."

A muscle in Walker's cheek ticked. "Since that woman is married to a friend of mine, I don't think she's yours."

Derek's gaze zeroed in on my hand, where my wedding band flashed in the light. The planes of his face hardened to granite. "And what's it to you?"

Walker pulled his badge out of his back pocket and flashed it at Derek. "I don't appreciate anyone hassling the residents of my town."

"Fuckin' pigs," Derek muttered. "I don't need this." He turned to me and gave me a wink. "I'll be seeing you, Angel."

The use of the nickname I used to love had my stomach roiling as he disappeared. "I think I'm going to be sick."

Walker took my arm. "Come on, let's get you out of here."

But it didn't matter where we went because Derek knew where I was now. He knew that I was happy. Without him. And he wouldn't stand for that.

CHAPTER
Twenty-five

Mason

I JOGGED UP THE FRONT STEPS TO THE POLICE DEPARTMENT, pulling open the door. It slammed against the wall, making the officer behind the counter jump. He eyed me warily. "Can I help you?"

"Walker's office?"

"Name?" he asked.

"Mason Decker. He called me."

The young officer checked his notepad. I was about ready to jump behind the desk and throttle him, he was moving so slow.

"Can I see some identification please?"

"For fuck's sake." I pulled out my wallet and slid out my driver's license. "Here." I slapped it down on the counter.

The officer took his time examining it before handing it back to me. "Down the hall, third door on the left."

I grabbed my I.D. and hurried down the hall. I felt as if I hadn't taken a full breath since Walker's call twenty minutes ago. I would've been here in ten, but I had to wait for Kennedy and Cain to get to the house to watch Justin and Lyla. I counted the doors as I walked, not bothering to knock on the one that read *Chief Cole*. I pushed it open.

"Mason," Walker greeted.

I didn't bother looking at him. I moved straight to Anna, framing her face in my hands. "Are you okay?"

"I'm fine. He just surprised me, is all."

But I felt the slight tremor in her hands as they wrapped around my wrists. It was more than that, and that knowledge had my gut tightening. I pressed a kiss to Anna's head and breathed in the scent that was only hers, a mixture of her shampoo and whatever flowed from her skin.

When I'd done my best to assure myself as much, I straightened, easing into the seat next to her and taking her hand in mine. I wove our fingers together, needing that point of contact. I would've pulled her into my lap if I could've. "Tell me what the hell is going on."

Walker leaned back in his chair, his gaze settling on our interlocked hands. "Derek Raymond is apparently in town to testify."

I glanced at Anna. "Keisha didn't say anything about that."

"She didn't know. Paisley hasn't listed him as a witness yet."

"What did he say to you?"

Anna's gaze shifted away. "Just talked about some stuff from the past."

Walker rested his hands on his desk. "You need to fill Mason in. On everything."

Her head snapped in his direction. "How do you know?"

"I'm a cop. As soon as this whole thing began, I did my research. I didn't want to push if I didn't have to. The situation has changed. Raymond's here. The people in your circle need to know everything so they can be prepared."

"Will someone tell me what the hell is going on?" I growled.

Anna tugged her hand out of mine. She toyed with a string on her denim shorts. "Derek tried to get back together with me after I got out of juvie. He wanted me to move in with him. Kept showing up at the coffee shop I worked at, would wait across the street from the shelter where I was living in Portland."

"What did you tell him?" I hated the idea that she might've considered it. He'd been her first love. All she ever knew.

"I told him I wanted nothing to do with him. But he didn't give up." She took one string and wove it with another. "He did everything to isolate me. Made calls to the coffee shop to say I was stealing. A report that I had been rude to a customer. Even though the manager believed me, the owner didn't want to deal with the hassle, so they fired me."

"Asshole," I muttered underneath my breath.

"He made several calls to the shelter where I was staying, saying that I was bringing drugs into the facility. They kept searching my room. They didn't find anything, so they didn't kick me out, but I knew it was only a matter of time."

"What did you do?" I couldn't imagine how terrified Anna must have been. She had only been eighteen years old and completely alone in the world. Which was what Derek had been counting on. That, eventually, she'd be forced to come back to him.

"I spilled my guts to Detective Markum. He was the one who questioned me when I was arrested. He did his best to get the district attorney to charge Derek and not me, but he didn't have any luck. I was pissed at him for a long time, but he kept coming to visit me in juvie."

A tear rolled down Anna's cheek, and she quickly brushed it away. "He was the one to pick me up the day I was released. Found me a good shelter to stay at. Helped me get that job. I told him everything, and he knew I had to get out of Portland. Another detective friend of his had sent a woman to Hope House. She was hiding out while she brought charges against her abusive husband. That was how he knew about Sutter Lake.

"He drove me all the way out here, three hours. Bought me the basics I needed. Hid all traces of where I would be. And it worked. Derek never popped up once." She let out a bitter laugh.

"He never was one to put in an effort when things got challenging. I figured he'd moved on."

"But now you're not so sure." My fingers curled around the arm of my chair, knuckles bleaching white.

"He wasn't happy that she was married," Walker offered.

"It's not that simple," Anna cut in. "It's ego more than anything. He was always the only safe place I had—or that's what I thought, anyway."

"He won't like that you made a safe place on your own," I surmised.

She nodded. "Hope House was everything I needed to get my sea legs again. And I wasn't worried about running into Derek or my family. I started to breathe. I would go on these long walks in the woods behind the center. For hours. And for the first time, I didn't hear all of the voices saying ugly things about me. I started hearing my voice again. I started believing that I might have a purpose in this life, after all."

I moved my chair closer, my hand slipping under Anna's hair at the back of her neck. "You do have a purpose. I've seen it time and again. In the way you reach any resident from the grumpiest hardened men, to women scarred by trauma, to terrified kids. I've never seen anything like it."

She swallowed audibly. "I don't want to lose any of that. I don't want to lose Justin and Lyla. And Derek might try to make trouble just to spite me."

"He might try, but he won't succeed," I vowed.

"Mase is right," Walker agreed. "Raymond has too long a record for any judge to take his word. Especially when you haven't had a single brush with the law since they released you from juvie. I've got a call in to Detective Markum. I think it might be worth talking to your lawyer about having him as a character witness. He can speak to what he saw of your parents, as well."

Anna untwisted the two little strings she had a death grip on. "I don't want to get him involved in this."

Walker looked her straight in the eyes. "Trust me. He'll be happy to help."

"How do you know that?"

He shrugged. "Markum sounds like a really good cop. It burns when we know justice hasn't been served, and there's nothing we can do about it. This might let him right a few wrongs."

Anna released her hold on the strings. "I'll text Keisha."

"Good. Now, why don't you get out of here and relax for the rest of the night?" Walker said. "I'll send a copy of Raymond's mug shot to all of my officers so they can keep an eye out."

"Thank you." I rose and reached out a hand to clasp Walker's in a half-shake, half-grasp.

"Anytime."

Anna barely said anything as we walked out of the station. Then her steps faltered. "I forgot about the pizza."

"I'll have them make us fresh ones. We can wait."

"Okay." She started towards the pizza parlor, but I stopped her. Anna looked up at me, her gaze turning wary.

"Is that everything?" I did my best to keep my voice even.

"What do you mean?"

"You can't keep hiding huge things like this."

She stiffened, her spine going ramrod straight. "I wasn't *hiding* it."

"Feels like something pretty big to conveniently forget about."

"Just because we've started something doesn't mean I owe you every detail of my life."

Her words cut. Because I wanted every detail. I wanted to know every single joy and sorrow of her twenty-eight years. But Anna didn't want to share them with me. She was content to have her walls sky-high. "You know all of my stuff."

I thought we'd shared everything in those late nights talking in the dark. Me sharing what it was like to practically raise Jules. Her telling me what it had been like living in Hope House for so long. But shadows and secrets were everywhere.

"I'm sure I don't know everything."

"Maybe not, but I'm not consciously hiding things from you."

"I'm not either," she argued.

I raised a brow. "You don't think this was something you might have shared when Derek's statement first came up? That doesn't feel a little wrong to you?"

Some of the fire went out of Anna with that question. "I don't like thinking about it. It was the hardest time in my life. Even worse than juvie. Because at least juvie was predictable. Once I knew the spoken and unspoken rules, I knew how to survive. When I got out, anything could happen. That was scarier, somehow."

I pulled Anna into my arms, and she went willingly. I held her close, resting my chin on the top of her head. "I just don't want you to lock me out."

"I'm not trying to. It's habit."

"Okay." I rubbed a hand up and down her back. "It's a habit you can try to break."

"I'll do my best."

For now, that would have to be enough.

CHAPTER
Twenty Six

JUSTIN LEANED BACK IN HIS CHAIR, GLANCING AT MASON. "Ready for me to kick your butt in Mario Kart?"

Mason arched a brow. "You really think you can take me?"

"Mase, I lapped you yesterday. I was thinking about giving you a thirty-second head start just to make things interesting."

I covered my laugh with a cough.

Mason shot me a dirty look. "You're supposed to be on my side."

I held up both hands. "I'm not taking sides, but I think we should have a movie night instead of video games. I'll pop popcorn…"

"Kettle corn?" Lyla asked hopefully.

"I think there's some in the pantry." I stood, gathering up my plate and bowl. "Help me clean up, and then we can all pick a movie."

Lyla toyed with her fork, not moving.

"What is it, Lyla Bean?" I thought we'd assuaged the kids' worries when Mason and I had returned home from the police station, but maybe Lyla had been more concerned than I'd thought.

"Could we make a fort? And watch the movie from there?"

The hesitancy of her voice cracked something in me. A little more grief pouring out. But I kept my voice light. "I think that's a great idea. You and Justin can show us all of the tricks."

Justin stood, picking up his plate and glass. "Mom was really good at making sure everything balanced."

Lyla let out a little giggle. "Except that one time. Remember? Everything collapsed on us."

Justin grinned. "When we were watching *Hocus Pocus*. You thought a witch did it."

"It could've been," Lyla argued.

Justin shook his head and brought his dishes to the sink. "You should've heard her. Lyla was shrieking so loud, I thought I was gonna go deaf."

Lyla climbed out of her chair. "You were scared, too."

"Only for a second. Then Mom started laughing and couldn't stop. I thought she was going to pee her pants."

The battle going on in my chest was fierce. Sorrow for the amazing mother these kids had lost. Joy that they were remembering the happy times and talking about her. I hadn't wanted to push, but I'd been starting to worry if that was the right move. We were bringing Chelsea out into the light.

Mason wrapped an arm around my shoulders. "You okay?"

I hadn't even seen him move, too lost in my thoughts. "I think we should put some photos of Chelsea and the kids up around the house. Would that be okay?"

"Of course. Move anything of mine you want."

I knew there were photos in the boxes in storage. It might be good to go through them with Justin and Lyla, pick which ones they wanted to display. And we could add some to their bedrooms, as well. "I should've thought of that before."

"Cut yourself a little slack. We've had a lot going on lately. And we're learning as we go."

I looked up and brushed a kiss against his lips, sinking into Mason's warmth. It was the first time I'd sought that kind of comfort from him. But it felt right. "Thank you."

He grinned against my mouth. "If this is what comes with a thank you, you can thank me anytime you want."

I rolled my eyes and turned back to the sink to rinse the dishes.

"There's one rule about the fort," Justin said.

I looked up. "What's that?"

"No kissing."

Mason barked out a laugh. "I thought we were friends, man. That is cruel."

Justin stuck out his tongue and made a fake heaving sound. "I won't be able to eat my popcorn if you're doing all of that mushy stuff."

"I like it," Lyla argued. "They're like a real-life Cinderella and the prince."

My cheeks heated at Lyla's words. I needed to remember that kids at this age were little sponges. They soaked up everything. "Why don't we focus on picking a movie?"

Mason moved in behind me, his lips skimming the side of my neck. "Don't get embarrassed."

"Mason," I hissed. "They are impressionable."

He chuckled against my skin, sending a delicious shiver down my spine. "I don't think kissing is going to scar them for life."

"It will, too. I'm going blind," Justin moaned.

I covered my face with my hands. "You have to stop touching me."

"He can't," Lyla said. "He likes doing it too much."

Mason held out his hand to her for a high-five. "I always knew you were the smartest one around here."

Her little chest puffed out. "That's why I'm going to be a kid doctor."

"And you'll be a great one," Mason told her. "Do you know what they call a doctor for kids?"

She shook her head.

"A pediatrician. Or if they are a special kind of kid doctor, they're called a pediatric and then their specialty."

"What special kinds are there?" Lyla asked.

"A ton. If you want to treat the heart, you'd be called a pediatric cardiologist. If you want to treat the brain, you'd be called a pediatric neurologist."

"The heart. That's what I want to do. Be a pedi-pedi—"

Mason sounded it out for her. "A pe-di-a-tric car-di-ol-o-gist."

"A pe-di-a-tric car-di-ol-o-gist." She extended the *oh* sound adorably.

My rib cage tightened at how good Mason was with Lyla. With both of them. He would be an amazing father someday. The thought made it suddenly hard to breathe. Because I couldn't imagine letting down my guard enough that I would get to share children with this man. But the thought of him having them with someone else was too much to bear.

Justin shut the dishwasher with a bang. "That's all of the dishes. Fort time?"

I forced a smile. "Fort time."

Mason got a pile of sheets, blankets, and pillows from his linen closet. After a few false starts, we found our rhythm, creating a tent over the family room's massive sectional. We layered comforters on the floor to have cushioned beds to lay on.

"Noah told me this movie was super good," Justin said as Mason hit play on *The Karate Kid*.

"It was one of my favorites when I was your age," Mason said.

I burrowed into Mason's side, needing the closeness. I felt as if he were slipping away, even though he was right here. All because I wasn't ready to make that next step. I knew he was waiting for a sign from me. That was just the kind of man he was. Yet, I was terrified to move forward.

He pressed his lips to the top of my head. "I could live in this fort forever, I think."

Something about his words made my chest ache even more. Because Mason was destined for this life. Husband. Father. I just wasn't sure it would be with me.

CHAPTER
Twenty-Seven

Mason

CAIN SET HIS COKE DOWN ON THE RESTAURANT TABLE. "I think adding that fourth tier will open us up to an additional market."

"I agree." Attempting to find demographics that Halo wasn't serving was a key to our success. Right now, we were discussing adding another option for home security above our most budget-conscious line but before our middle tier. "And I don't think it will take much of the tech team's time to create the hardware."

Cain flipped the page of his legal pad over and began sketching something. "I'm thinking about this for window censors." He moved quickly, incorporating a few elements from our higher-end lines with our budget system's basic alarm components.

"I'll have to run the numbers, but I think it'll work."

He set down his pen. "See, sometimes getting out of the office is all it takes."

Cain had a point. I'd been distracted at the office lately. My mind on Anna, Justin, and Lyla, a million and one worries hounding me. "And it doesn't hurt that the Saloon has the best burgers in town."

"It definitely doesn't."

My phone buzzed, and I flipped it over to read the text.

Juliette: *Mase, we need to talk.*

Guilt pricked at me. I'd been a shitty brother the past couple of weeks. As mad as I'd been at Jules, I never should've left things unsettled for this long.

Me: *Lunch tomorrow? Meet me at my office, and then we can figure out where we want to go.*

Juliette: *See you then. Love you.*

Me: *Love you, too. Always.*

Maybe now that she'd had time to cool down, Jules would see how wrong she'd been about Anna. But until I was sure, I wasn't putting Anna in range of Juliette's biting words.

"What's with the scowl?" Cain asked.

"Just trying to execute a peace treaty between Juliette and Anna."

He raised a brow. "It didn't go well?"

"Understatement of the century. Jules just can't see Anna for who she really is."

"That could make things rocky for you."

I scrubbed a hand over my jaw. "I'm hoping Jules has had enough time to cool down to see reason."

"You might have to be a little firmer with her, and I know that's hard for you."

"Not when it comes to Anna. I mean, don't get me wrong, I never want to hurt Juliette, but I won't let her around Anna if she's going to be cruel."

Cain met my gaze dead-on. "What are you going to do about holidays?"

A lead weight settled in my gut. Jules and I always spent from Christmas through New Year's together. We usually took a trip, going on some adventure that we'd remember forever. But that would be different this year. I was sure Anna and I would want to celebrate Christmas Day at home with Justin and Lyla opening tons of presents. And if we took a trip, it would have to be with everyone.

"See? Harder than you thought," Cain said. "All of our relationships have threads. And it's going to take some adjusting now that your priorities have changed."

"Why do you have to be so damn wise all the time?" I muttered.

Cain chuckled. "It's my burden to carry."

A familiar figure caught my gaze. Jeff—Justin and Lyla's father. He was in the corner with a guy I knew was a lowlife and bookie, at least according to Walker. Cash passed between their hands.

"Why do you look like you want to murder someone right now?"

I did my best to mask my fury and focused on my mostly empty plate. "Take a quick look over your right shoulder."

Cain did as I instructed, and when he turned back around, his anger was showing. "Dante said that asshole was a piece of work. Same M.O. with every woman he dates. Gets them hooked, mooches off them until they're fed up, and then moves on."

I straightened in my seat. "He didn't fill me in on that."

"I don't think he thought it was overly pertinent. It's in the written report he emailed."

I'd only had time to hit the bullet points of that document, and I'd focused more on Derek. But there hadn't been much on him other than his criminal record and known associates.

Cain took another quick glance at Jeff. "It's interesting that he's placing bets when Dante said he was tapped out."

"And if he's in Sutter Lake for weeks on end, he sure as hell isn't working a job in Portland."

Cain pulled out his phone. "I'm texting Dante. He needs to do a deeper dive into Jeff's financials. Maybe there's some proof that the Foleys are paying him."

I couldn't see how. They seemed too smart for that. If they had bribed Jeff and Derek, I was sure they hadn't written them a check. "It seems insane that people can get away with stuff like this."

"But it happens all the time. They just think the rules don't apply to them."

"We're going to make sure they do."

"We're sure as hell going to try—" The beeping of my phone cut off Cain's words.

I scanned the screen, my fingers tightening around the device.

Dante: *Anonymous source tells me Mr. Foley withdrew fifty grand from his retirement account two days after being notified of Anna's petition for custody.*

I turned the phone around so Cain could read the screen. "Who the hell is this anonymous source?" I asked. "We need them to go on record. Testify."

Cain shook his head, keeping his voice low. "Anonymous source means he hacked into their bank accounts to get the lay of the land."

I let out a string of curses. "Any way we can get a warrant?"

"I'll have to talk to Walker, but I doubt it. Not on an anonymous tip alone."

I gripped my phone tighter, the edges of the device biting into my palm. "I need to tell Anna. She'll kill me if I know this and don't share." It was the last thing I wanted to do. The last few days had been good. No run-ins with Derek, Justin and Lyla happy, finding our routine.

"Come on. I'll drive us over to the center. Kennedy's working there today, and I can always use an excuse to see my wife."

Typically, I would've made a crack about him dragging her off to some dark corner, but the only thing I could think about right now was that I was about to ruin Anna's day. But I had no choice. I was working on earning her trust, and that meant being honest with every piece of information I found. "Let's go."

We tossed some cash onto the table and headed for Cain's SUV. The drive was silent as I imagined various ways to send Anna's parents to prison. Anywhere they couldn't hurt her anymore. Cain pulled into a spot near the front of the community center, and we hopped out, moving towards the Hope House buildings.

Jefferson, the daytime security guard, opened the door from the inside as we approached. "Afternoon, guys."

Cain gave him a friendly clap on the back. "Holding down the fort?"

"You know it."

I gave him a lift of my chin in greeting but didn't say anything. I didn't have pleasantries in me at the moment. I peeled off from Cain, who headed for Kennedy where she played with two little girls. I moved towards Anna's office and rapped twice on the door.

"Come in," she called.

I pushed it open.

Anna looked up from her computer, expression brightening. "Hey. What are you doing here?" That brightness dimmed as she took in my face. "What happened?"

I moved to her, leaning on the desk and bending to kiss her. As if I could somehow pour all of my reassurance into her with that one action. "Your dad took fifty grand out of his retirement account two days after he found out you'd filed for custody."

She sucked in a sharp breath. "That's good, isn't it? We have proof they may have bribed someone."

"The information was uncovered through less-than-legal means."

"Shit," she whispered, her gaze drifting out the window to a group of kids playing on the playground. Justin and Lyla ran among them. "I know my dad is cruel. I've known for as long as I can remember. I just wish I knew why he hated me so much."

"He doesn't hate you."

Anna's head swiveled in my direction. "No? I'm pretty sure he does."

"No. He hates that he can't control you. That you won't bend to his will. So, he does everything in his power to break you. But you never give in, you're too damn strong." I wished my mother had contained an ounce of Anna's strength. The ability to stand up to my father. To get us out of there. But she hadn't. And we'd all paid the price for it.

"I'm not that strong," she whispered. "I'm terrified all the time."

"Strength doesn't mean you aren't scared. It means you do what you have to, regardless of your fear."

"I still haven't taken that next step with you."

I framed her face with my hands. God, I wanted her to take that next step. So badly, I could practically taste it. But I would never rush her. "When you're ready, you will."

She searched my face. "You're so sure."

"I am." Because I had some bone-deep knowledge that Anna was made to be mine, and I was made to be hers.

CHAPTER
Twenty-Eight

Anna

"STOP FIDGETING."

My hands stilled, and I looked over at Kennedy in the chair next to me. "I'm not fidgeting."

She snorted. "You haven't been able to sit still since the moment you got here."

Lyla let out a shriek as she jumped off the giant trampoline in the middle of Cain and Kennedy's lake, Justin on her heels.

"I'm sitting."

Kennedy raised an eyebrow. "You know, it's good to take an afternoon off now and again."

I felt as if all I'd been doing was taking time off. Only it wasn't for rest and relaxation. It was for meetings with social workers and lawyers. "I feel like I haven't been pulling my weight lately."

Kennedy sat up in her chair and turned to face me fully. "You aren't a robot. If some other employees and volunteers need to take on a little more responsibility at Hope House right now, so be it. You know you've done the same for them when they've had things going on in their lives."

I toyed with a thread on my shorts. I knew I'd pitched in on things when staff had lost a loved one, had a child, or were overwhelmed, but somehow having them do the same for me made me feel vulnerable and exposed.

Kennedy reached over and squeezed my hand. "It's okay to need help sometimes. It doesn't make you weak."

"I know that. In theory."

"But reality is a whole different ball game."

"Exactly."

She released my hand. "You're not used to it, so you're just going to have to practice."

"What do you mean?"

"Let people help you in small ways. When someone offers to take something off your plate, let them."

I tugged the string loose. "I can try."

Kennedy burst out laughing. "Oh, God, you should see your face. You look like I told you to jump off the Empire State Building without a parachute."

I scowled at my best friend. "You're not funny. You know that, right?"

She made a pssh sound. "I'm hilarious."

"Anna! Watch me!" Lyla yelled from the trampoline.

"I'm watching, Lyla Bean."

She took a running start and catapulted herself into the water. My hand flew to my chest as I braced to jump in after her. Lyla popped up. "How awesome was that?"

"Super awesome," I called back—and enough to take ten years off my life.

"Now me," Justin said. Instead of taking a running jump, he bounced at the edge of the trampoline, getting more height with each pass until he finally launched himself into the air and flipped, landing with a splash.

"They are going to make my hair turn gray," I told Kennedy as I clapped for Justin.

"I think that's part of their job."

"I'm figuring that out."

She looked over at me. "How are they doing?"

I leaned back in my chair as Justin and Lyla raced from the trampoline to the dock and back again. "I think pretty well, all things considered. We've had our rocky moments, but we're finding our way."

"I think the only thing that truly helps in these circumstances is love and time. You've got the love piece handled. Now, you just have to let the time part unfold."

I knew she was right, but I wanted every reassurance I could get that I was doing all I could for Justin and Lyla. "I second-guess just about every choice I make for them."

"I think that's natural, too. But especially when they unexpectedly came into your care."

"What about you and Cain? Any word from the foster-to-adopt program?" I couldn't imagine two people who would make better parents to a child who needed a home. But they'd had the rug ripped out from under them more than once now.

Kennedy sighed, looking out at the water. "I really thought our last placement was it, but—" She wiped at her eyes.

"Oh, Kenz." I leaned over and took her hand, squeezing. "You are going to find the babies that were meant for you. I have no doubt. You just have to keep pushing until you do."

"It's so much harder than I thought it would be. And every time I have to give them back because someone changed their mind or circumstances changed, it takes a piece of me."

"I don't think it could be any other way. Because you love so freely." I envied Kennedy for her ability to do that. She didn't hold back even one piece of herself. But I knew that gift came with pain and hardship.

She took a shaky breath. "The right pairing will come. It's just going to take time. I hate it for Cain, though. You know him. He wants to shield me from all forms of pain, and this is one area he has no control over."

Cain was another level of overprotective when it came to Kennedy, and I was honestly surprised he'd handled this process as well as he had. But being with Kenz had changed him, helped him let go a bit. "You've made him loosen his hold on the reins a bit."

Kennedy snorted. "A little, but he still wishes he could plan for every possible outcome."

"That's not so bad."

"No. And it can be pretty adorable at times."

The soft smile that overtook her face made my heart clench. It was wistfulness of missing her man but also knowing he was wholly hers. I wanted that. It was as if I had Mason at my fingertips, but he wasn't mine. I had to make that leap but doing so felt like I was launching myself at an unknown so terrifying it froze me to the spot. I'd promised myself a long time ago that I'd never put myself in the position to lay my heart in someone's hands again.

"Anna?"

"Sorry, what?"

Kennedy's brows pinched together. "Are you okay?"

"Fine. Just lost in thought." More like a downward spiral of what-ifs. No matter what direction I moved, there would be pain.

"Mason?"

My gaze jumped to hers. "What makes you say that?"

"You have this look on your face…"

I wasn't stupid. I knew I was falling in love with Mason. If I were really honest with myself, I was already there. I just wished I could take that final step and let go. "He makes it so damn hard not to fall in love with him."

A laugh tore out of Kennedy. "Oh, God, Anna. You sound so pissed about that."

"I am. He just had to be kind and gentle. Yet fierce and protective, too. Sometimes it feels like he was made for me. He understands my wounds like maybe no one else would."

Her laugh slipped away. "Would it really be so bad? To let yourself love him?"

"Yes." The last time I thought I loved someone, they destroyed my entire life. I knew in my head that Mason wasn't Derek—he couldn't be further from him—but translating that to the rest of me was another story.

"At some point, you're just going to have to throw yourself off that cliff. Either that or walk away. You can't be half in and half out forever."

"I know," I whispered. An ache spread through my chest, so strong and fierce I had to run my hand along my sternum to try to relieve it. But nothing I did helped.

My phone dinged from the arm of my chair. I snatched it up, grateful for the distraction. The photo that flashed across the screen made my stomach drop. It was grainy, from an old camera phone. I was straddling Derek's lap, a beer in one hand, and my head tipped back in laughter. It had seemed like such innocent fun at the time—getting a little tipsy at one of the parties Derek had taken me to.

That was before he'd started using. At least, from what I could tell looking back. But there was an ashtray on the table with a couple of joints inside. The message below the photo read: *Mother of the year.*

"Anna, what is it? What's wrong?"

My hand shook as I handed her my phone.

Kennedy's expression went hard. "Seriously? You had a boyfriend and drank beer at a high school party. If that disqualified someone from parenthood, we'd go extinct as a species."

"Look at the ashtray. I know people smoked at those things, but I never did. But that won't matter if this photo gets turned in as evidence."

"What I want to know is how this asshole has your phone number."

There were a million ways. Being married to someone who specialized in security, Kennedy knew that; she was just pissed at the moment and not thinking straight.

She handed me back the phone. "You need to call Mason."

I opened my mouth to say no, that I didn't need to worry him, that I could handle it myself. But I stopped the words from tumbling out of my mouth. I needed to take the baby steps Kennedy had talked about. Let him in, let us be more of a team.

I tapped a few icons on my screen and then put the phone to my ear. It rang and rang before Mason's voicemail picked up. I'd never heard it before because he always answered when I called. "Hey, Mason. It's Anna. I got another picture text. I just wanted you to know. I'll forward it to Dante and let Keisha know."

"Try his office line."

"I don't think I need to." I was already feeling all sorts of exposed.

Kennedy leveled me with a stare. "Call."

I sighed and tapped the other number I had programmed in my phone for Mason. His secretary picked up on the second ring. "Mason Decker's office."

"Hi. It's, um, Anna. I was wondering if Mason was in?"

"Hello, Anna. He's in a meeting right now and asked not to be disturbed. Can I have him call you back, or is it an emergency?"

"No. No emergency. I left a message on his cell, so you don't even need to tell him I called. Thank you." I hung up before she could say anything else. It was silly. Logically, I knew that, but I still felt so incredibly alone in that moment. I'd reached out, and he wasn't there. Just another reminder of why letting myself fall was the stupidest choice of all.

And I had promised myself I'd never be that dumb again.

CHAPTER
Twenty-Nine

Mason

"EARTH TO JULIETTE."

She looked up from her phone, blushing. "Sorry. Grades posted for an exam from my summer classes."

"How'd it go?"

She looked down at the screen again and shoved it into her bag. "Fine."

"Which means not as well as you wanted it to."

Juliette gave me a sheepish grin. "You know me. If I'm not at the top of my class, I'm not happy."

Understatement of the century. Jules brought perfectionism to a whole new level. I'd never forget her fourth-grade hysterics over getting a B on a spelling quiz. "Maybe it's time to cut yourself a little slack."

My cell phone rang, and I moved to answer, but Juliette cut me off. "Can't we just have some time? You and me, without distractions?"

Anna's name flashed on my screen, and I itched to answer it, just to make sure everything was okay. But I knew she was safe. Locked behind the Fort Knox of Cain's security system. If it were truly urgent, she'd call back. "Okay. Where do you want to go to lunch?"

She grinned. "How about that cute little café we went to the last time we were here?"

"Sounds good to me. But before we go, we should talk." I didn't want to get into a public space and have Jules create a scene when I brought up Anna.

She made a face. "Conversations that start like that never go well."

"I'm hoping this one will."

Juliette sat up straighter in her chair. "Oh, God. She's not pregnant, is she? Please tell me you're at least wrapping it up."

I stared at my sister, trying to figure out where this hatred and ugliness had come from. I'd seen her get vicious before when someone had truly wronged one of us. I'd seen it directed at the aunt and uncle who were supposed to care for us. At the first boy who had broken her heart. At the father Juliette had never known. But at the time, all of that anger had seemed justified.

Now, I wondered if I'd missed bigger signs. Her view of the world had always been black and white. People were either for us or against us. And if they weren't on our side, she wrote them off. But I'd never seen this kind of anger directed at someone who hadn't done anything to Jules.

"She is, isn't she?" Juliette stood and began to pace. "Hell. You're going to have to pay a ridiculous amount of child support and alimony now. But I know a P.I. we can put on it. I'm sure he'll be able to find plenty of dirt on her. You'll be able to get sole custody—"

"Juliette." I kept my voice calm, even though it was the last thing I felt. "Anna isn't pregnant, and I'm not divorcing her." I hoped we'd never have to bring up the subject of ending our marriage. I wasn't sure I could walk away anymore. Because as much as I'd been transfixed by Anna from afar—her strength and beauty and compassion—seeing it all up close, experiencing it firsthand...I was a goner.

Juliette's cheeks reddened. "Has she hypnotized you or something? How can you not see everything about her is an act?" She pulled her bag off of her shoulder, setting it on my desk and riffling through it.

"You haven't given her a chance, Jules. And I think you need to look closely at why that's the case. I know that I've always made you the number-one priority in my life. But at some point, I was going to meet someone, get married, have a family. There's room in my life for all of you."

Her eyes filled. "You would put her before me? I've always had your back. '*You and me against the world.*' That's what you always said. So, what? Now that's just done?"

I *had* said that. Time and again, when struggling to keep my head above water, running on only a couple of hours of sleep, and trying to make sure Jules had everything she needed. "I always want us to be on the same team. But my team has Anna, Justin, and Lyla on it now, too."

Juliette's jaw clenched, and she worked it back and forth. She pulled a folder out of her bag and threw it onto my desk. "I was looking out for you. I can't believe you'd want those children to be with a woman like this, instead of two loving grandparents who would have all of the time and energy in the world to devote to them. She must have some sort of golden vagina to make you forget what we went through."

Before I could say a word, correct the stream of bullshit that had just fallen from Juliette's mouth, she turned on her heel and stormed out of my office. I could only stare after her. How had we come to this?

I gritted my teeth and tapped out a text.

Me: *You have a world of misinformation. If you could listen to me for five minutes before throwing a tantrum, you'd see that.*

It only took a few seconds for a reply.

Juliette: *Look at that folder and tell me I'm wrong.*

Me: *I don't need to. I can already tell you that you are.*

But the folder was already flipped open. There was an array of photos and newspaper clippings. Some of the articles I'd seen, some I hadn't. All wove a picture of a young girl who'd used her innocent looks to get away with pumping drugs into her high school.

The photos made me nauseous. Anna with glassy eyes, Derek's hands all over her. They looked like pictures friends had taken at a party. I knew it was all normal, the typical kind of high school rebellion, yet a lead weight settled in my stomach. I hadn't had that kind of rebellion. I'd been too busy taking care of Juliette. And if the courts got ahold of this, it might be enough to skew things in Anna's parents' direction.

I tapped out another text—this time to Dante. I paused before hitting send, knowing it was a violation. But I couldn't wait for Anna to tell me what we needed to know. There was too much riding on this custody battle. We had to cover all of our bases if we were to keep Justin and Lyla safe. I could take Anna's anger, and I knew she'd eventually understand why it needed to be done.

Me: *I need you to dig into Anna's background. See what the other side could dig up that could hurt us.*

Dante: *On it.*

I should've felt relieved. Knowledge was power, and if my sister could find this much, what could a motivated legal team get their hands on?

CHAPTER
Thirty

Anna

I RIFLED THROUGH CABINETS, BANGING POTS AND PANS AS I went. It wasn't fair to the dishes, but I had to take my frustration out somewhere. And going for an hours-long walk in the woods the way I had when I'd first come to Sutter Lake wasn't an option.

My gaze caught on Justin and Lyla as I straightened. They laughed as they kicked the soccer ball back and forth. I should be happy. Relieved. I had what I wanted most—Justin and Lyla safe. And with any luck, the judge would rule in our favor soon.

The social worker had recommended that the kids stay where they were. Justin and Lyla had braved speaking with the judge and had told him that they wanted to live with Mason and me. Derek hadn't testified yet, but Keisha had assured me that the judge wouldn't put much stock in whatever he had to say.

Instead of resting in the building hope of my niece and nephew being happy, I was angry. With Mason, but more with myself. It had been six hours, and he'd never returned my call.

I was angry because it hurt. Because I let myself reach a hand out for support, and he was nowhere to be found. The mix of pain and anger bubbling inside me was why I hadn't wanted to do this with Mason in the first place. When you opened yourself up, when you counted on someone besides yourself, you could get dropped—and the crash could leave you broken.

The oven beeped, and I pulled the chicken I'd been marinating all day out of the fridge. When I'd thrown everything together this morning, I'd done it with Mason in mind. Knowing he'd like the salty-sweet combination of the honey mustard glaze. Now, the fact that I'd made the dish simply pissed me off.

I shoved it into the oven with a little more force than necessary. Maybe Mason wouldn't even come home tonight and wouldn't get my damn chicken. I took the pot off the counter, filling it with rice and water and setting it on the stove.

Just as it came to a boil, I heard the garage door open. I stiffened but forced myself to keep moving, turning the heat down and covering the rice to steam. I moved to the island where I had an array of veggies to chop for a salad.

The door opened, but I remained focused on my task. Mason's shoes sounded on the hardwood floor. "Hey," he greeted.

"Hey." I didn't look up.

"Oh, shit. I completely forgot to call you back."

"No problem." I diced a carrot into tiny pieces and dumped it onto the bed of mixed greens.

"If it's no problem, then why aren't you looking at me?"

I raised my head, forcing myself to meet his gaze. Mason was too handsome for his own good. Too charming and sweet, and it made women like me stupid. It made me think that something could work between the two of us when it was actually impossible. "I didn't want to chop off a finger."

His lips twitched, and my eyes followed every flicker of movement. "Safety is important. Still, I'm sorry."

"Okay."

He studied my face, trying to read between the lines. "What did you need?"

He hadn't even listened to my voicemail. If that wasn't all the evidence I needed, I didn't know what would be. "Nothing important."

Mason opened his mouth to say something, but Justin and Lyla barreling through the back door cut him off. Justin held up a hand for a high-five. "Mase! We went to Cain and Kennedy's, and I taught myself to flip off the trampoline into the lake. It was so sick."

Mason grinned. "We'll have to go back this weekend so you can show me."

"I did the biggest cannonball. I have to show you!" Lyla cut in.

"Maybe after dinner, you can show me in the pool."

"Totally," she agreed.

I lost myself in preparing the meal, in the din of the chatter. I should've been happy. Justin and Lyla were flourishing, even amid the trauma of these past months. But inside, a piece of me was dying. Because I knew I'd never have what I wanted most—for all of us to be a real family.

I paused and listened as I reached the second floor. There wasn't a peep of sound coming from Justin's or Lyla's rooms. I still couldn't resist peeking inside. Justin slept like a starfish, arms and legs thrown wide. Lyla was the opposite, curling herself into a ball so tight, I didn't know how it was comfortable.

I envied them both in that moment. I wanted the sweet oblivion of deep sleep. But I knew I'd be lucky if I got a few fitful hours. I'd thought briefly about pretending to fall asleep on the couch downstairs where I'd been working on my laptop. But it only meant delaying the inevitable. Tomorrow night, I'd have to sleep in that bed, feel Mason's body next to mine but know we were worlds away.

I climbed that final stretch of stairs to the third floor, sending up a silent prayer that he was already asleep. The deep timbre of

Mason's voice told me that I was out of luck. I paused on the landing, trying to brace myself to walk inside.

"Were you able to find any more photos?"

Silence.

"Were there drugs in any of them?"

My body tensed, and I took a step forward. I could see Mason through the sliver the open door provided. He sat up in bed, the glasses he wore to read perched lopsidedly on his nose.

"I just want to see what we're dealing with, Dante. Know if more skeletons are going to jump out and surprise us."

I'd thought I was hurting before. The knowledge that I wasn't as important to Mason as I thought I was had cut. But that was nothing compared to this. Going behind my back, trying to get information on me… Ironically, information I'd been trying to give him if he would've simply called me back.

I stepped into the room, my gaze hot. Mason's eyes flew to me. "I need to go. I'll call you tomorrow." He hung up, swinging his legs over the bed and standing. "Anna—"

"Don't." I held out a hand to keep him from coming any closer.

"It's not what it sounded like."

"So it wasn't you asking a private investigator to look into me without asking me if that was okay?"

He ran a hand through his hair, giving the ends a firm tug. "I was going to tell you tonight. Juliette had some internet results about you, and I wanted to make sure more wouldn't surface that could hurt the legal case."

My jaw worked back and forth. I wanted to destroy every single internet search engine. "Did you ever once consider asking me if that was okay?"

"I only wanted to protect you."

"Bullshit. You wanted to know things that I wasn't ready to share yet. You wanted to open every dark closet I have without my permission. And you want to know what's hilarious? I called you today to tell you that someone sent me a photo. That we might need to prepare for more coming to light. I treated you like we were on the same team. But you? You're treating me like the enemy."

"Anna."

Mason's voice was pained, but I forced down the flash of sympathy that flared to life. I met his gaze dead-on. "I trusted you. The thing that is hardest for me to do, and you shat all over that."

"I didn't mean—"

"No." I held up a hand. "I don't want any excuses. I can't deal with this right now." I started for the door.

"Where are you going?"

"I'm going to sleep in a guest room for a while. Unless you'd rather I get the kids and leave altogether. It's clear you don't trust me."

"I do trust you."

I stared at the man who'd just crushed me, not believing a word from his mouth. "No, you don't."

CHAPTER
Thirty-One

Mason

"**W**HAT THE HELL HAPPENED TO YOU?"

I looked up from my computer, blinking a few times and trying to bring Cain's face into focus. My eyelids felt as if they were made of sandpaper. "I fucked up."

Cain stepped inside my office and shut the door. "Anna?"

I nodded and pressed my fingers into the corners of my eyes, trying to alleviate some of the pressure.

"What'd you do?"

I took a deep breath and leaned back in my chair. "I asked Dante to look into her. See if there was anything that could come out and bite us. She found out."

Cain let out a low whistle. "That was dumb."

I glared at my friend. "I can see that now." I'd thought she might be pissed when I told her. But I hadn't seen things through her eyes. I hadn't meant to break her trust, but that was precisely what I'd done.

Her words about me wanting to know things that she wasn't ready to share echoed in my mind. She might have been right there. I *did* want to know. Every secret and every single thing she hid away. The good and the bad. I wanted all of it because I wanted *her*.

I'd fallen in love with a woman who gave so much to others. Who never gave up, no matter the odds stacked against her. Anna's unique mix of tenderness and fire was unlike anything I'd ever experienced. And now, I might have lost her.

"How are you going to fix it?" Cain asked, breaking into my thoughts.

"If I knew that, I wouldn't be sitting here, would I? I can't even get her to listen to me."

Every time I'd tried to get her alone this morning, Anna had used the kids as shields. I'd asked if we could talk, and she'd insisted that she was late—she'd been thirty minutes early.

Cain eased into a chair across from my desk. "You're going to have to shock her into pausing long enough for you to throw yourself on her mercy and tell her you're an idiot."

"I think I've got the groveling part down." I'd been running through what I wanted to say in my head all night.

"You need a grand gesture." He drummed his fingers on the arm of the chair. "Let me and Kenz take Justin and Lyla for a sleepover tonight. Get an elaborate dinner for Anna, candles, the works. That should make her pause long enough for you to at least start talking."

"I'll make her dinner."

Cain raised a brow. "You a good cook?"

I grinned. "I'm damn good."

"That'll make it more meaningful." He paused.

"What?"

"You need to make peace with the fact that Anna may never be ready to open up to you the way you want her to. If you can't handle that, you need to walk away. It's not fair to either of you to expect her to be someone she's not."

I knew it would always be a struggle for her to let me in. But

I believed she would get there, bit by bit—as long as I didn't keep pulling bonehead moves like I had yesterday. "I love Anna for exactly who she is. I just want her to feel safe enough to let down her guard with me."

"Hell," Cain muttered. "You're done for. I can see it already. Just don't get your hopes up that things will change overnight."

"I won't." I looked at the clock icon on my computer. "Can I play hooky today?"

He chuckled and waved me off. "Go get your girl."

That was exactly my plan.

I heard the garage door go up, and my gut tightened. I hadn't been this nervous since I'd taken Cynthia Shepard out on my first date in the ninth grade. I glanced towards the dining table. I'd done my best, picking up some flowers from a local florist, and candles, too. It wasn't expertly put together, but I'd done my best.

Two filets were warming in the oven, along with some mashed potatoes. A Caesar salad chilled in the fridge. And a Chateauneuf-du-Pape from one of my favorite wineries sat on the table.

Anna's movements slowed as she crossed the space, taking in the low light and soft music. "What's going on?"

"We need to talk."

She sighed, letting her eyes fall closed for a moment. "I don't have it in me, Mason. It's been a long day, I'm exhausted—"

"Then let me feed you. Just give me five minutes to say what I need to. If you want me to shut up after that, I promise I will. Not a word for the rest of the night."

"Not one?"

I mimed zipping my lips and throwing away a key.

Her mouth twitched as if she wanted to smile but then tightened into a thin line. "Okay."

I gestured to the dining table. "Sit. I'll get everything."

Anna didn't argue, as if she were grateful for a little distance to breathe. I hurried to get everything ready. I brought out the salad and mashed potatoes. Then topped our plates with the steak, the peppercorn sauce already on the table.

Anna looked down at the plate I set in front of her. "You didn't have to go to all of this trouble just to talk to me for five minutes."

I eased into the chair at the head of the table so we were next to each other. "I should've been going to all of this trouble from the moment I kissed you. I should've made sure you knew how much you mean to me."

"Mason—"

"I messed up. I knew you'd be mad, but I didn't see how much it would hurt you." I didn't look away, praying she could see the honesty in my gaze, hear it in my words. "I was too wrapped up in preparing for every awful thing that could happen. And you were right, I wanted to know things you weren't ready to share. Because I want to know everything about you and because I want to keep you safe."

"You have to give me time. And I may never share every single detail of my past with you."

"I know. I shouldn't have gone behind your back." I wanted to take her hand so badly. To brush my mouth against hers. But I resisted. "I was wrong. But that mistake didn't come from wanting to hurt you. I care about you, Anna."

"*I love you,*" was on the tip of my tongue. "I'm going to mess up. But I will try not to make the same mistake twice. I'll try to learn and do better. To hear what you need."

Tears glistened in the corners of her eyes. "I don't know if I can do this."

Her words were a sledgehammer to my chest. "Why?"

"It's not just that it's hard for me to trust. I was irrationally angry simply because you didn't call me back. That's not fair. But my head reads it all as a rejection. Abandonment. Which is messed up, Mason. I'm messed up. My brain doesn't process things the way a normal person's would. Yes, I was furious when I found out that you called Dante behind my back, but I already had one foot out the door."

I took her hand then, tangling our fingers. It felt so good just to have that skin-to-skin contact with her again. "We just have to deal with it together. Neither of us is going to be perfect. We have our traumas and wounds. But the more we talk it out, the more we'll understand where the other is coming from."

Anna's hand gripped mine harder. "The accident."

"I'm always going to be someone who looks for danger. Who wants to mitigate it as much as possible. I might go overboard sometimes, but I'll always try to reel myself back in. I hate that I hurt you. I'm so damn sorry."

She stared at me, barely blinking. "You can't go behind my back again. Promise me. It hurts too much."

"I promise." God, I'd do anything if it meant I never had to see the look of betrayal in her eyes again.

She looked down at our joined hands. "I want to try. Really try. But I'm probably going to be awful at a real relationship. I'll drive you up the wall, and you'll want to get rid of me."

"I hate to break it to you, but we're already in a real relationship. This was just our first fight."

"What?"

I burst out laughing. "Anna, we're married. We share a bed. I know what it feels like to sleep with my body curved around yours. We're there."

Her eyes flared with a heat I'd only seen hints of before. "Then let's jump."

CHAPTER
Thirty-Two

Anna

"WHAT?"

I couldn't help the small laugh that bubbled out of me at Mason's shocked expression. "Let's jump." Something about realizing that we were both a bit of a mess, with wounds that influenced our choices, made it feel safer somehow. I didn't need to have it all together because Mason didn't, either. But maybe we could figure it out as a team, find a way to make it work.

The truth was, I was exhausted from fighting. And spending last night away from Mason, without his arms around me and the steady beat of his heart, had made me realize I never wanted to do it again. I was giving in to this thing between us. And I would do whatever I could to hold on for the ride.

His hazel eyes flared with heat. "What does jumping mean, exactly?"

My mouth curved. He was going to make me spell it out. It was such a Mason thing to do. Extra-careful to make sure he wasn't misreading anything. I didn't look away from him. "Take me to bed."

It was all he needed. Any lingering air of carefulness was gone in a flash. He was on his feet and lifting me out of my chair in a flash. My legs encircled Mason's waist instinctively as his lips met mine. Nothing about the kiss was polite. It was desperate and hungry. Born of all the holding back he'd had to do these past months.

I'd never felt more wanted than I did in that moment. It was both a balm to my soul and the spark of a fire low in my belly. As if my body were waking up after hibernating for years.

I let out a yelp as Mason strode towards the staircase. "Put me down. You can't carry me up two flights of stairs."

He kept right on moving but arched a brow as he looked down at me. "Watch me. I'm not letting you go for a second."

Mason had always done his best to make his hulking form unintimidating when he was at the shelter. But nothing about him was small. From his broad shoulders to his muscled arms. And now, I would see all of him.

A shiver trilled through me, making my nerves seem to dance under my skin. I couldn't resist trailing my lips up his neck and breathing him in.

"You keep doing that, and I could drop you."

I laughed against his skin. "You're the one who said you were up for a challenge."

"You would find it funny that you have the power to drive me crazy. Have from the moment I saw you."

I leaned back a bit so I could take in his face as he climbed the last of the stairs. "Really?"

I'd felt the buzz of chemistry the moment we met. I'd instinctively clenched and flexed my fingers after our hands had grasped in a shake. It had been a red light of warning for me. A sign to stay far away. But Mason had seemed wholly unaffected.

He came to a stop in the middle of the bedroom, slowly lowering me to my feet. "I was supposed to volunteer at a few different organizations around town. But as soon as I met you, I asked

Cain if I could dedicate my time to Hope House. I needed to know you. I can't explain it, but there was this…"

"Pull," I finished for him.

"Exactly."

"It's what made me stay far away."

Mason framed my face with his hands. "I'll do everything in my power not to hurt you. And if I do, I'll give everything I have to fix it." He pressed his lips to one side of my face, then the other, before finally settling on my lips.

Three little words were on the tip of my tongue. I bit them back, but all I wanted was to let them loose. "I trust you," I whispered. Those weren't the words I wanted to give him, but they were still a gift.

Mason's hands left my face to trail down my body and tug my sundress up and over my head. He sucked in a sharp breath. His fingers traced my nipple through the lace of my bra. "So damn beautiful."

My nipples puckered, drawing some invisible cord in me a little tighter. "Mason," I breathed.

"Hmm?"

I couldn't find words. All I knew was that I needed him. My hands went to the buttons on his shirt, fumbling in my haste.

The corner of his mouth kicked up. "In a hurry?"

I nodded, tugging his shirt off those broad shoulders. Skin lightly tanned from the sun stretched tautly over lean muscles. My fingers itched to explore all of it. Instead, they moved to the button on his jeans. Mason chuckled as I got frustrated with his zipper. He finally took pity on me and shucked the jeans himself. His boxer briefs, too.

And then…there he was. So gorgeous it almost hurt to look at him. And this man wanted to be mine.

Mason's fingers hooked in the sides of my lace thong, slowly tugging the panties down my legs. The drag of his knuckles against my skin pulled that cord within me impossibly tighter. As if it would only take one slight movement to have me breaking apart.

He knelt on the floor, looking up at me through hooded eyes. I felt so exposed, bare but for my bra, but at the same time, so incredibly safe. Mason trailed a finger down my center, and I let out a soft moan.

As he rose, his exploration continued. Teasing and taking all the time in the world. My head fell forward against his chest as my fingers wrapped around his shaft. My strokes were almost lazy when I felt anything but.

Mason hissed out a breath as I hit an especially sensitive spot. "Anna," he growled.

I raised my head, meeting his gaze but still stroking. "Yes?"

"You are going to kill me."

"But it'll be a damn good way to go."

He moved so fast, I barely had time to blink before I was in the air and landing on the bed with a whoosh. The movement startled a laugh out of me.

"You keep laughing that you're my undoing."

The look on his face, the intensity in his gaze, stole the laughter from my tongue. "You're mine, too."

He stalked towards me, then paused. "Shit. Condom."

"I'm on the pill. And I have a clean bill of health. It's been a long—"

Mason cut off my words with a kiss, leaning over me and letting me feel all of him against me. "I'm clean. And it's been a while for me, too. Are you sure?"

I nodded. I didn't want anything between us—nothing to steal even the slightest sensation.

Mason's tip bumped against my entrance, and then he was pushing inside. I inhaled sharply, trying to adjust to his size. He stilled, lowering one bra strap and then the other, his fingers circling my nipples, turning the bite of pain into heat. "You okay?"

"More, please." I rocked my hips against him to punctuate my request.

Together, we found our rhythm. The back and forth, give and take. The gentle movements became more desperate as if we both needed to burn ourselves into the other's bones. To leave no question that we had been there.

That hint of feral need broke the last tether I had to control. I gave in and let myself go for the first time in over a decade. I lost myself in Mason, his touch and the thing that would only ever be ours.

I arched against him as my nails dug into his back. Mason thrust impossibly deeper, and I fractured. Lights flickered across my vision, but I never lost sight of him as I came apart. And I vowed I never would.

CHAPTER
Thirty-three

Anna

MASON LINKED HIS FINGERS WITH MINE, STOPPING MY fidgeting. "You're going to do great."

I was glad he was confident, but I wasn't quite there. Between facing my parents and opening myself up to a cross-examination from their lawyer, my insides were tied into knots. "We're the final two people to testify. I want our case to finish strong." And I didn't want to be the reason it failed.

Keisha had done a good job of giving us an update each day, but she'd also said that she didn't have a read on the judge. As our social worker testified, he had been stoic. And, unfortunately, my father and mother had apparently been convincing on the stand. Keisha hadn't been able to trick my father into exploding. I just had to hope the judge would put the most weight on where Justin and Lyla wanted to be.

Mason swept his thumb back and forth across my hand. "You practiced with Keisha. You know what to expect from Paisley. You're ready."

I nodded, but as he pulled into a parking spot outside the courthouse, my stomach pitched. The building had an antique charm to it, but I couldn't appreciate it. Instead, it seemed to loom in the distance.

Mason leaned across the seat and brushed his lips against mine. "I'll be with you the whole time."

"I know." It should've scared me how much comfort I took in that. But, instead, I let myself sink into his reassurance.

Mason's phone dinged, and he grabbed it from the cupholder.

"Juliette?" I asked. I felt awful that I was the reason for the strife between the siblings. As much as Juliette was acting like a brat, I knew it came from a place of worry for her brother.

"No, it's Cain. Jules still isn't texting me back."

"Maybe after the judge rules, you should go see her in California."

Mason looked up from his phone. "I'm not sure it's time yet. She needs to calm down first. Have a chance to see that she's the one who screwed up."

I linked my fingers with his. "Or you could meet her in the middle because you love her."

He pulled me in close, kissing me again. "You've got a good heart in there."

"Just don't tell anyone," I whispered against his lips. "I want people to think I'm a badass."

He chuckled. "You can be both."

"Sounds good to me." I took a deep breath, straightening and then pushing open the passenger door. I couldn't put this off any longer.

Mason and I met at the front of the SUV, linking hands again. Keisha waved from the top of the steps. "Perfect timing. You guys ready?"

"I feel like I might throw up," I mumbled.

"If you do, just aim it at the opposing counsel."

Her retort startled a laugh out of me. "Think I'd go to jail for that."

"Naw," Mason said. "It's a natural reaction to B.S., don't you think?"

Keisha grinned. "I can make that argument for sure."

I looked at them both. "Between the two of you, they don't stand a chance."

"Damn straight," Keisha agreed. "Now, let's do this."

As we walked into the courthouse, I drew up short, almost walking straight into my parents. My father's chin jutted. "It's nice of you to finally make the time to make an appearance. But it's too little, too late. The judge has already seen that Justin and Lyla aren't important to you."

"Don't listen to him," Keisha urged, hurrying Mason and me forward. "The judge is aware of your full-time job and the fact that you're caring for Justin and Lyla."

I gripped the strap of my purse tighter. "Do you think it's possible the judge will see it as me not being involved?"

"No," Mason assured me.

Keisha nodded. "He's right. These types of cases come with intense emotional entanglements. Judges are well aware that it may not be in the participants' best interests to come to court every day."

I could only hope that she was right and that the judge would see my truth when I spoke. Everything became a blur as we sat. Commands from a bailiff. A foreign language of terms tossed back and forth between the lawyers and the judge. They called Mason's name first.

I tried to study the judge as Mason answered Keisha's questions and then Mr. Paisley's. I couldn't get any sort of read on him, either. There was no flicker of reaction on his face that I could find. Something about that was unsettling—too similar to the masks my father wore all too well.

My stomach cramped as Mason returned to our bench, and they called my name. Mason gripped my hand briefly, squeezing for reassurance. But it wasn't enough. Blood roared in my ears as my heels clicked against the linoleum floor. The stairs to the witness stand felt like Mount Everest.

The bailiff approached and made his speech, and I recited the words I had been instructed to say. But I barely heard them. Keisha gave me a small smile as she approached. Her questions started off easy, asking me to describe my relationship with Justin and Lyla, what our days were like, and my plans for their futures. Then they got a little tougher. She asked me about my relationship with Chelsea and why we didn't speak for years.

I tried to keep my voice even and my explanations as clear as possible. But I braced. For the question I knew was coming. Just as Keisha asked something, I caught sight of a figure in the back row.

I hadn't seen him come in, but he glared at me now, anger pouring off him in waves. Derek had testified two days ago. He'd spilled lie after lie, and I had no idea if the judge had believed him. But I couldn't figure out why he was still here. Whatever job my parents had likely paid him for was complete. The only reason he might be sticking around was in the hopes of seeing me suffer.

"Ms. Foley?"

I gave myself a little shake and met Keisha's concerned gaze. "I'm sorry. Can you please repeat the question?"

"Why are you concerned about your parents having custody of Justin and Lyla?"

I swallowed against the burn tracking up my throat. "Because my father was physically abusive to both my sister and me for as long as I can remember. And my mother covered for him."

"Can you please describe the physical abuse?"

My fingernails dug into my palms. "He was good at hiding it. Punches to my abdomen. Sometimes a knee. But he broke my ribs once that way."

Keisha turned to the judge. "We have x-rays of those broken ribs in evidence." The judge nodded, and Keisha continued with her questioning. I recounted incident after incident, and each retelling felt like living through the event all over again. By the time Mr. Paisley rose for my cross-examination, sweat trickled down my spine.

"Ms. Foley, is it true that you were a rebellious child?"

"I would need more clarification on what you mean by that."

He pushed his glasses up his nose. "Did you sneak out of the house to meet your boyfriend?"

"Yes."

"Did you attend parties with alcohol and drugs when you were only sixteen?"

"Yes." It killed me not to defend myself. Not to ask if he had only drunk a beer once he turned twenty-one. To tell the judge I'd never done a single drug in my life. But I stayed with the one-word answers that Keisha had urged me to use.

"Were you sexually active with your boyfriend at the age of fifteen?"

Keisha stood. "Objection. Relevance?"

"Goes to character," Paisley ordered.

"I'll allow it but tread carefully," the judge said.

"Yes."

"And you were arrested and convicted of the distribution of narcotics, correct?"

It went on like this. Question after question, each one so carefully asked, I knew my parents had helped their lawyer skirt the line of what I had no choice but to admit to. Tears burned the backs of my eyes, but I refused to let them fall. I wouldn't give my parents the satisfaction of knowing how much it all hurt. How much it killed.

And worse, how it made me doubt myself. Wonder whether I was good enough to raise Justin and Lyla. But when I lifted my gaze from my lap, I met Mason's. His was so full of rage, but I instantly knew that it wasn't directed at me but at my parents and their lawyer. His anger was a balm to my shredded soul. It was what I needed to press on.

"Ms. Foley," Paisley interrupted my connection with Mason. "You married Mr. Decker a week after your sister died?"

"Yes."

"Did you do that in an attempt to convince the court you were equipped to take custody of two minor children?"

I stiffened against the wooden chair. "I did it to give Justin and Lyla the best home possible. Because Mason is the most caring man I have ever known. And because we are all incredibly lucky to have him."

"Is it true that you and Mr. Decker didn't have a relationship prior to your marriage?"

"No." I kept my voice even, but inside, I was panicking. Where was this information coming from? No one but our closest friends knew that Mason and I had spent little time together before marrying. And none of them would throw us under the bus.

"Mr. Decker's sister informed us that she had never heard of you until a week after your marriage. What would you say to that?"

I froze. Juliette. She was the one who'd betrayed us. I knew she wasn't my biggest fan, but I couldn't imagine why she would hate me this much.

"Objection," Keisha said, rising.

"Withdrawn," Paisley retorted before the judge could rule.

But it didn't matter. The accusation was out there, and there was nothing we could do about it.

CHAPTER
Thirty-Four

Mason

I LOCKED EVERYTHING DOWN AS WE HEADED OUT OF THE courthouse. I'd barely heard Keisha's assurances that this wasn't a death blow to our case. That it made the opposition look desperate and as if they were grasping at straws. None of that calmed the raging storm inside me.

My sister. The one person I had thought would always have my back had been the one to stick a knife in it. I knew she'd been upset, unable to see Anna clearly, but I'd never thought she'd go this far.

"Mason." Anna's fingers curled around my forearm, bringing me to a stop. "Take a breath before you get behind the wheel."

She sounded so calm. As if my sister hadn't just almost ruined everything for us. I sucked in air through gritted teeth. "Did you not hear Paisley?"

"Of course, I did. But I don't want you to do something you'll regret right now or drive us when your mind is a million miles away."

I pulled Anna into my arms. I let the feel of her body pressed against mine, the scent of that which had somehow come to mean home, ease me a fraction. Enough that the pulsing heat behind my eyes abated. "I can't believe she did something like this."

Anna's hand slipped under my suit jacket and traced an infinity symbol on my lower back. "I'm so sorry."

"I'm the one who should be apologizing to you. This could've been so much worse. If she'd had any sort of information that would blow us sky-high, she would've used it."

Anna tipped her head back so she could meet my gaze. "Why? What's making her so angry? I get not liking me or thinking I'm using you, but this is extreme."

I brushed the hair away from her face. "After our parents died, we went to live with our aunt and uncle. But they had three kids of their own. Our aunt looked after Jules while I was at school, but she was my responsibility as soon as I got home. And once Juliette was old enough to be left to her own devices, we were completely on our own. She doesn't know the full story of your family.

"I think part of me didn't want to bring up bad memories for her. I'm so used to protecting Juliette, it's second nature at this point. I should've pushed, made sure she understood what was at stake. But we had so much going on, and every encounter with her ended in drama."

Anna's hand fisted in my shirt. "She thinks Justin and Lyla are better off with my parents."

"That's part of it." I let my hand slide beneath the fall of her hair. "Honestly, I think she's being triggered in a lot of ways. I've always been her person. And for the first time, I'm building a family beyond her."

"I'd never ask you to choose between us."

"I know that. But fear like this is subconscious." That didn't excuse her actions, though. Nothing would. I pulled out my phone. Jules and I had always left the tracking apps enabled, just in case. "She's still at the resort."

Anna's lips pressed into a firm line. "Are you sure you want to talk to her right now? Maybe you should cool off for a while first."

I leaned back, taking her shoulder in my hands. "Why are you defending her?"

Anna's eyes shifted to the side. "I don't want you to end up resenting me because I hurt your relationship with your sister. And I understand what it's like to feel like you have no one. I don't want that for her."

"Anna." I took her face in my hands. "None of this is on you. It's on Juliette. And maybe me for not making sure she understood what was at stake."

"There wouldn't be this hurt between you if it wasn't for me."

"And I'd be half the man I am right now if you left. I didn't realize just how lonely I was before you showed up. My house was just that: sterile and empty. You and Justin and Lyla brought life to its walls. You've made me feel understood in a way I never have. And, God, you guys have brought me so much fun. I wouldn't give that up for anything. Not one single thing."

Her fingers curled around my wrists. "I love the home we're building. I don't want to lose it."

"We're not going to. But I have to talk to my sister."

"Okay," she whispered.

The drive to the resort was mostly silent. Juliette was staying in one of the high-end cabins at the back of the property. My anger flared back to life when I realized that I was footing the bill for that cabin. She was spending *my* money and using it to stab me in the back.

I parked next to her rental car and climbed out of my SUV. Anna did the same but stayed by the vehicle. Juliette must have heard us drive up because she opened the front door as my door slammed shut. She glared at Anna. "She's not welcome here."

A muscle in my cheek ticked. "She's welcome wherever I am. And since I'm the one paying for your extended stay, I'd say she's welcome here."

"Mason," Anna said in a low tone, moving in behind me.

Juliette's mouth slackened. "Are you seriously throwing that in my face? I'm in school. You said you wanted me to focus on that and not go into debt."

"And that hasn't changed. What has is *you*. I never thought you'd betray me. After everything I've given you. I've never asked for a damn thing in return except for you to give Anna a chance. One thing. You couldn't even do that. Instead, you opted to be bitter and selfish. And in the process, you hurt the people I care about most in this world."

"Mason," Juliette whispered. "What are you talking about?" She took in our apparel and put two and two together. But instead of apologizing, she doubled down. "I did what I thought was right."

"What you did was potentially deliver two children into the hands of an abusive asshole."

Juliette blanched. "What are you talking about?"

"Foley beat Anna and her sister all of their lives. He hit Justin. And you couldn't pause your downward spiral of hate long enough to let me tell you that's what we were up against. You didn't even bother to ask if Justin and Lyla wanted to go live with their grandparents. They don't because they don't like getting smacked around."

Juliette's gaze darted from me to Anna and back again. "You're wrong. She's lying. I met with the Foleys and their lawyer. They're kind people."

"They're manipulative," Anna cut in. "My father would go to church Sunday morning and lock me in a closet Sunday afternoon."

Heat hit Juliette's cheeks. "I don't believe you."

Anna's gaze hardened. "Would you believe Justin if he told you that his grandfather punched him so hard it knocked the wind out of him just because he didn't want to play peewee football?"

"Y-you probably coached him to say that. It's a better sob story for my brother."

"Enough," I barked. "Jules, I love you, but I am done. I won't have a relationship with you unless you can learn to stop."

Her eyes filled with tears. "Mase. You can't mean that."

"I never thought I'd have to do this. It kills me that you can't see the truth. But I won't let you poison the life I'm building. And that's what you're doing. When you come to your senses, I'll be there."

Juliette's gaze snapped to Anna. "This is because of you."

"No," I cut in. "It's me. Anna told me to go easy on you, but I've been doing that for far too long. Now, we're done."

But I was afraid I was too late. Lessons Juliette should've learned a long time ago might be out of her reach now.

CHAPTER
Thirty-Five

Anna

I WAS QUIET ON THE RIDE BACK TO THE HOUSE. THE SCENE with Juliette replayed over and over in my mind. I knew what it was like to lose a sister. I'd lost Chelsea for years after my sentencing. And now, I'd lost her forever.

Heat flared in my chest, a burning pain. I didn't want that for Mason. Especially not because of me. He didn't see it now, but that kind of thing would destroy us. He would slowly come to blame me for it.

My phone dinged. It was a picture text from Jensen. She and Tuck had offered to take Justin and Lyla to see the wild horses with Noah and Drew. It was a photo of Lyla, sheer joy on her face as she took in the majestic creatures from a distance. At least, they were happy. Their days hadn't been a series of pain and disaster. And I'd do anything to keep it that way.

"Who is it?" Mason asked as he pulled into the garage.

"Jensen." I handed him my phone.

His mouth curved into a grin. The first one I'd seen in hours. "She looks like she's having the time of her life."

His happiness at that fact made the burn in my chest intensify, but for an entirely different reason. Mason loved the kids. He was so good for them. He was good for me. And I didn't want to lose that.

He handed me back my phone. "Lunch?"

"Sure." I wasn't hungry in the slightest, but I could force some food down.

We climbed out of the SUV and headed for the kitchen. I began pulling things out for turkey sandwiches. I didn't stop moving. If I stopped, the last five hours would hit me like a freight train. Instead, I washed lettuce, sliced tomato, cut thick slabs of my favorite sharp cheddar. I layered honey mustard on bread.

Hands landed on my shoulders. "Anna."

"I'm almost done. I just need the turkey."

"Stop."

"I'm almost—"

Mason spun me around, concern lacing his features. "Talk to me."

My hands balled at my sides as if keeping them locked tight would keep every emotion bottled up, too. "Hard day."

"I know." He pressed a kiss to my temple. "I'm sorry my sister made it so much worse."

"Mason, you can't cut her out of your life."

He blinked down at me. "I thought you'd be relieved."

"I'll never be relieved by something that hurts you."

Mason brushed the hair away from my face. "Don't worry about me."

"This is a two-way street. I don't think it's possible to care about someone and not worry about them."

His expression softened, and he brushed his lips against mine. "Always feeling for others."

My hands fisted in his shirt, and I tugged him closer to me. "I'm serious. She's your entire family. I don't want you to lose that."

"I won't. She will come around eventually, but I can't have Juliette acting the way she is now. I won't have her around you like that. Justin or Lyla, either."

"It's not like I want her over for family dinner, but you should still see her, talk to her. Maybe she'll soften over time."

He stared down at me. "Do you honestly think I could bear to be in the same room as someone who would say the ugly things she said about you?"

"Mason," I whispered.

"I can't. It's like I don't even know her anymore."

"You do. She's just…going through something." And she was spoiled. Mason had always let Juliette have her way. But it seemed as if that might be changing.

He stepped out of my grasp, pacing the kitchen. "That might be true, but it doesn't justify her behavior. I've never known Jules to be cruel for no reason. Especially to someone who's important to me."

"Have you introduced other people who were important to you to Juliette?" I didn't know much about Mason's dating history. I didn't want to know. The thought of him with someone else made me want to vomit.

He stopped mid-stride and turned. "I dated, but there was never anyone serious enough to introduce to her."

"She feels threatened and she's lashing out."

"Hell," he muttered. "There are better ways to deal with it."

"I know. But you need to give her time."

He moved into my space, boxing me in against the counter. "I'll give her time, but she doesn't get to take her anger out on you."

I pressed a kiss to the underside of his jaw. "Deal."

One of Mason's hands slipped from the counter. He trailed it up my leg to the apex of my thighs. The featherlight touch sent a jolt through me. "Need you, Anna."

"You have me." More than he would ever know. Bit by bit, he was claiming every piece of me, body and soul.

His fingers went to the buttons on my blouse, slowly and methodically undoing each one. He eased the shirt off my shoulders and let it fall to the floor. His thumbs brushed my nipples through the lace of my bra. "So damn pretty."

With a flick of the clasp, my bra joined my shirt on the floor, and I was bare from the waist up. Utterly exposed, the light from the large windows pouring in. Something about it sent a pleasant shiver up my spine as Mason's hands went to my pants. In a flash, they were also dropping to the floor.

"Step out," he instructed, his voice husky.

I kicked off my heels and stepped out of the slacks. The only thing I had left on was my thong. The see-through lace made it feel as if I had nothing on at all.

Mason moved, lifting me into the air and depositing me on the kitchen island. I let out a little shriek. "Warn a girl, would you?"

He sent me a devilish grin. "Now where would be the fun in that?"

He laid me back on the island, the marble surface making me shiver. His fingers went to the lace at my hips, tugging it free. And then there was nothing between me and his gaze, his touch.

Mason trailed his fingertips up my legs, teasing the flesh between my thighs but not giving me the touch I craved most. "Close your eyes."

I opened my mouth to argue, but the heated look he sent me had it snapping closed again, along with my eyes. I heard what sounded like the refrigerator door open and close.

"So much beauty. The most I've ever seen."

He was right next to me. I could feel the tease of his breath, the heat of his body.

"Keep your eyes closed."

His mouth took mine in a searing kiss. My back arched off the marble, yearning to get closer to him. One hand palmed my breast, his thumb circling my nipple, teasing it to a peak. And then, without warning, ice-cold flashed there.

I sucked in air, about to curse at the man with the magic hands, but then I realized how the feeling of it drove me higher. My back arched again.

"More?" he asked.

I nodded, keeping my eyes shut.

His lips latched onto my nipple, sucking deep. I couldn't contain my moan. The ice cube replaced his mouth.

"More," I begged. I didn't know what I wanted, but I knew I needed something to take me to the next level of this beautiful torture.

Mason grabbed my hand and sucked on two fingers, releasing them with a pop. "Touch yourself."

I fought the urge to open my eyes and squirmed on the island.

"It's just me," he urged, tweaking my nipple. "I want to see how you pleasure yourself. How you make yourself come."

The ice, his mouth, his fingers. It was enough to have me moving without further thought. I took a finger, spreading the wetness pooling between my thighs to my clit and circling. Mason let out a growl as he twisted my nipple.

"Mason…" It was a plea as I circled again.

The ice was back, and I arched into the sensation. The heat of my blood against the cold of the ice sent shockwaves through me.

"Need you," I begged.

His hands were gone, the ice rattling into the sink. I didn't open my eyes, but I kept circling that tight bundle of nerves. I didn't want to lose anything I was feeling.

I heard the sound of a zipper, and then he tugged me towards the edge of the island. He was inside me in one swift thrust. It was desperate and carnal and rough. It was pleasure and pain and everything I needed.

"Open your eyes, Anna."

They flew open, and the need I saw in his gaze was enough to break me. Another of my walls crumbled as I arched into him. I called out Mason's name as I came, clutching him with a desperation that should've terrified me. But I couldn't find it in me to care. I was his, and he was mine. And I wasn't letting go.

CHAPTER
Thirty Six

Mason

ANNA LET OUT A SLEEPY LITTLE MOAN AS SHE BURROWED deeper into my hold. "Too early, turn it off."

I hit the button on my alarm, silencing it, and pulled her so she lay on top of me. "How are you feeling?"

"Tired," she grumbled.

"Sore?"

Her cheeks pinked. "In a good way."

I pressed a kiss to the top of her head. "Long bath for you today."

"I wish I could play hooky."

"Maybe we both could…" I could think of a million ways to spend the day.

"I have a meeting I can't cancel, and the staff has already been pulling more of my weight than they should."

"It's okay to take their help, you know."

Anna scrunched up her face. "You sound like Kennedy."

"She's a smart woman so I'm going to take that as a compliment."

She rolled her eyes but then kissed the bottom of my chin. "You going to call Juliette today?"

I sighed and trailed a hand up and down her back. "I am."

"Good—"

"*But*—"

"But what?"

I tickled her side. "If you'd let me finish, I'd tell you."

Anna pinched my stomach. "Two can play this game."

I rolled her onto her back, holding her hands over her head and taking her mouth in a slow kiss. "That's better."

Anna nipped my bottom lip. "Finish what you were saying."

I released her and sat up against the pillows. "The way things are between Juliette and me isn't working."

"Okay…"

"I need to make some calls and change that. She won't be happy."

"Mason…"

I tucked a strand of hair behind her ear. "I thought a lot about what you said yesterday." I'd been up half the night thinking about it. "It's time for some better boundaries, but I'll make it clear that I'm her brother, and I'm not going anywhere."

Anna absentmindedly traced a pattern on my chest. "As long as you've thought it through."

"I have." I lifted her chin so our gazes met. "But none of what Juliette does or doesn't do is on you, okay?"

Anna took way too much of the weight of other people's actions onto her shoulders. Jules might pitch a fit, but that wasn't Anna's responsibility. "Okay," she whispered.

I slid my hand along her jaw to her neck and under those golden locks. "You have to tell me if she approaches you. Promise me." The last thing I wanted was Juliette doing something to get in Anna's head.

"Promise."

"Good. Now, what do you say to waffles this morning?"

Anna beamed. "That should get Justin out of bed at least ten times faster. Especially if there's whipped cream."

I slid my lips along her jaw. "I thought you were the one partial to whipped cream."

"I don't hate it," she said a little breathlessly.

"Why don't you tell me about that in the shower?"

"I like the way you think, Mr. Decker."

I had the sudden urge to call her Mrs. Decker. Anna hadn't changed her name, but I wanted her to. I wanted everything about this marriage to be real. The lines had blurred, and it was hard to tell what was pretend and what wasn't anymore. But as I carried her to the shower and lost myself in her body, I was reminded that what mattered most was the realest thing I'd ever had. This unnamed connection between us. And soon, I would give it a name, either mine or one we chose together that would be ours.

I leaned back in my chair, staring at my computer screen. I'd run the numbers a few different times. I'd looked at a series of options. And this was what I'd settled on.

Juliette had two years of law school left. She was right that I'd told her to concentrate on that effort and not to worry about a job. I'd had to juggle a job, school, and Jules, and it had nearly killed me. I didn't want that for her.

But there would be no more credit cards for extravagant shopping trips and vacations that miraculously got paid off each month. No more spending without a thought. I was setting up a transfer that would cover her basic expenses each month, plus tuition. If she wanted extras, she'd have to get a job.

I picked up my desk phone and dialed my financial advisor. Lucille answered on the third ring. "Morning, Mason. How are you?"

Lucille was in her fifties but sounded like she smoked a pack a day.

"I'm hanging in there. How about you?"

"Still kicking, so I can't complain."

"Glad to hear it. Listen, I need to change some things regarding Juliette."

"All right." There was a click of a pen. "What do you need?"

I walked her through what I was thinking. "I'm going to be calling Juliette next, so she'll be aware of the changes."

She let out a low whistle. "I'm glad you're not leaving that to me. She won't be happy."

I'd worked with Lucille since I'd gotten my first big check selling the video game I'd developed. She always shot straight and was a good steward of my money. More than that, she'd been a teacher, showing me what I needed to know about my growing fortune. And in the process, she'd gotten to know Juliette and me quite well.

"I know she won't. But some developments have made me realize that things need to change."

Lucille was quiet for a moment. "Love that girl. But she doesn't deal with change well."

"Life is full of change. She'll have to get used to it."

"That means you need to stop standing between her and every hardship that comes her way."

"I don't—"

"Mason," Lucille cut me off.

Heat crept up the back of my neck. "It's always been my job to protect her."

"And you've been excellent at it. But she has to learn to fall and get up on her own."

"I'm realizing that."

The squeak of Lucille's ancient office chair came across the line. "I'm glad to hear it. You know I'm here if you need to talk anything out."

"Thank you. I really appreciate that."

"All right. I'll make these changes. Come visit soon, would you?"

"I'll plan on it and bring Anna and the kids."

A smile sounded in Lucille's voice as she spoke. "I can't wait to meet them."

"Talk soon."

"Bye, Mase."

I pressed down on the receiver button and took a deep breath. I needed to get it over with. Delaying would only make things harder. I dialed a number almost as familiar as my own.

"I thought you weren't talking to me." Juliette's voice was a cross between haughty and hurt.

"I was wrong to say that."

Juliette sniffed. "It really hurt, Mase."

"I'm sorry. I shouldn't have said it, but things need to change."

"Why? Because you married a gold digger, and she hates me?"

I pressed my fingers to the space between my eyes. "She doesn't hate you. She actually defended you."

"Sure," Juliette scoffed.

"She did. But I'm talking about how you and I operate. I want you in my life, but Anna is also a part of it now, so you're going to have to learn to deal with that."

Juliette was silent.

I pressed on. "I'm cancelling your credit cards. You'll get a transfer into your checking account each month to cover tuition and living expenses. I've been generous, but you'll have to budget."

"*Anna* doesn't want me to have access to your money, does she?"

"*Anna* doesn't give a damn what I do with my money. She hasn't taken a dime from me."

"Bullshit."

"Enough," I barked. "We're not going down this track. My decision is final, unless you don't want anything from me."

Jules was quiet for a moment. "I never thought someone would be able to turn you against me."

"I'm not against you. I never will be. But I want you to stand on your own two feet. I want you to realize that I can care about you *and* her. And I'm sorry, but you don't get to dictate who I'm in a relationship with."

"I'm trying to protect you," she said through gritted teeth. "But if you want to throw away half your money, maybe half your time with a kid if she gets pregnant, fine. I'll be here to help you pick up the pieces when it's over."

"Or maybe you'll be surprised and none of that will happen."

"Time will tell, I guess."

"That it will." I waited a beat. "Love you, Jules. Always."

"I love you, too." Her voice broke as she spoke, and then she quickly ended the call.

I felt sick. The last thing I wanted was to cause my sister pain. But I reminded myself that sometimes broken bones needed to be set right if you were to walk again. I just hoped that things would heal right for Juliette and me.

CHAPTER
Thirty-seven

Anna

WE WERE ALL QUIET AROUND THE DINING TABLE AS our breakfasts sat in front of us. I wished the silence came simply from exhaustion, the fact that we'd had an epic weekend of fun. Taylor and Walker had invited everyone over to their place for a barbeque on Saturday. The kids had all played, and the adults had laughed and caught up. Sunday, we'd spent the day at the lake, wanting to feel close to Chelsea.

But that wasn't the reason for the lack of voices and joking this morning. We'd been as honest as we could be with Justin and Lyla. And they knew that the judge would be ruling on who would get custody of them today. If he ruled against us, Sadie would have to come and get the kids and take them to my parents.

The thought almost sent me running for the bathroom with the urge to throw up my orange juice. I inhaled slowly through my nose, trying to still my roiling stomach.

"Hey," Mason started. "Why don't we do pizza in a fort while we watch a movie tonight?"

Justin looked up from where he was pushing his breakfast around on his plate. "If they don't take us away."

Lyla started to cry, and I pulled her into my lap. Holding her close, I pressed a kiss to the top of her head. "We have to keep the faith. No matter what the judge says, we'll figure it out."

I eyed Mason from across the table. He knew what my look said. If the judge didn't rule in our favor, I'd run. There was no other choice. I wouldn't let these kids go with their grandparents.

Mason cleared his throat. "I think the judge heard the truth."

"I hope so," Justin whispered.

"Can we go with you?" Lyla asked, wiping her tears.

"No, sweetie. Court isn't for kids."

"We talked to the judge," she argued.

"That was different. An exception to the rule. But we'll hurry home as quickly as we can, okay?"

She nodded into my shoulder, and my heart clenched. I hadn't been there when she or Justin were born, but that didn't change the depth of our bond. They were a part of me, and I would do anything to protect them.

An alert sounded on Mason's phone, and he picked up. "It's Cain and Kennedy."

I stood, Lyla wrapping her legs around me. "Want to come with me and let them in?"

"Yeah."

I walked with her in my arms like a little spider monkey and pulled open the front door just as Cain and Kennedy climbed out of their SUV. "Don't you have to work today?" I asked him.

He shrugged. "I can work from here. That's the good thing about the internet."

I heard what he didn't say. That if there was an unfavorable verdict, he wanted to be here to help us plan. "Thank you," I said, my voice thick.

He squeezed my shoulder. "Anything you need. *Anything*. We've got your back."

I nodded, unable to say more. Kennedy gave Lyla a bright smile. "How's my bestie?"

"Okay," she mumbled.

Kennedy pulled open a bag. "I brought nail stuff. I thought we could do mani-pedis."

Lyla lifted her head, brightening a fraction. "Sparkles?"

"Duh."

Lyla reached out her arms to Kennedy, and Kenz took her. Cain took the bag of nail polish and supplies. I forced a grin in his direction. "You gonna go for sparkles, too?" I asked as we headed inside.

"I think I'll pass. Justin and I can kick around the soccer ball."

"I'm sure he'll love that."

Justin and Mason appeared, and Mason checked his watch. "We should go. We don't want to be late."

My stomach dropped. "Okay."

Kennedy squeezed my shoulder. "Text if you can."

"I will." I looked around at everyone. "Love you guys."

The words were echoed back, and Mason slipped his hand into mine, tugging me towards the garage. I felt like a robot, climbing into the SUV, watching as our drive turned to a dirt road then turned to the highway. It seemed like a matter of seconds until Mason was pulling into a parking space in front of the courthouse.

"I don't think I can do this," I whispered.

His hands framed my face. "You can, and you will. You're the strongest person I've ever met."

Tears gathered in the corners of my eyes. "What if it's not what we're hoping?"

"Then we're taking Justin and Lyla, getting on Cain's plane, and flying to Vietnam."

"What?"

He pressed a kiss to my forehead. "Did you really think I wouldn't have a backup plan?"

"Mason. You can't leave your life behind."

He pulled back just a fraction. "Haven't you realized? You're my life now. And that's never going to change."

Heat flared to life in me, so much that it burned, like numb limbs waking up again after being frozen. "I love you, Mason."

"Never wanted to hear three words more. Love you to the ends of the Earth." His mouth met mine in a bruising kiss. Everything we'd been holding back poured into it. Nothing existed in that moment except for Mason and me.

I pulled away, breathless. "Let's get this over with so you can take me home."

He chuckled. "Now that's a plan I can get behind."

We climbed out of the SUV, seeing Keisha headed our way. She grinned at me. "You might want to fix your hair."

I scowled at Mason. "You could've warned me." I patted down the locks that he'd tangled and sent into disarray with his fingers.

Mason shrugged. "I think you look gorgeous."

"Aw," Keisha said. "Now, come on. Let's go get you those kids."

Mason's fingers wove with mine. "We're a team. Remember that."

It had been so long since I hadn't felt alone. Even with the friendships I'd formed in Sutter Lake, and reestablishing a relationship with Chelsea, I'd still felt as if I was going through life on my own. If things went up in flames, I was the only one who could put them out.

But over the past few months, I had slowly been making a family. The kind I'd always dreamed about but was too scared to reach for. I wasn't alone anymore.

I let that knowledge flow over and around me. Strengthen me. And with my hand in Mason's, I headed up the courthouse steps.

The doors to the courtroom were already open. My parents were seated on their side with their lawyer, but my father couldn't keep the sneer from his expression as we entered. I looked around, bracing myself to face Derek again, but breathed a sigh of relief when I saw he was absent. I was sure he could only leave his drug business for so long, even in an attempt to destroy his ex-girl-friend's life a second time.

Mason tugged me towards a bench behind the table Keisha would sit at. He tried to distract me with conversation about what movie I wanted to watch with Justin and Lyla later, and if I would finally try pineapple on pizza. But none of it worked. My gaze didn't stray from where the judge would appear.

A bailiff walked out. "All rise."

We did. I tried to read the judge's face as he entered, but like before, I couldn't catch a glimmer of anything. He sat, and we did, as well. He began speaking, some formal phrases, and I gripped Mason's hand tighter.

"In terms of the custody for the two minor children, Justin Foley and Lyla Foley, I order that physical and legal custody remain with their aunt, Anna Foley, and her husband, Mason Decker."

Blood roared in my ears. I could barely make out the judge's words as he said my parents would have zero visitation unless Justin and Lyla requested it. I was trembling. Shaking so hard that I took Mason with me.

He released his hold on my hand and wrapped an arm around me, pressing a kiss to my hair. "You did it. They're safe."

I burst into tears, big, heaving sobs that I couldn't hold in. I didn't hear the rest of the judge's words as I buried my face in Mason's chest. Soon, he lifted me, and the judge left the courtroom. Mason turned me towards him, kissing me. "They're safe."

"Thank you," I whispered against his lips.

"I'd do anything for you."

I sniffed. "I'm starting to see that."

"I wouldn't celebrate quite yet," my father barked from across the aisle. "We'll be appealing."

I stiffened as I turned to face him. Of course, he would appeal. My dad never took defeat lying down. My mother looked pale and shaken behind him. She likely knew he'd take his anger out on her later. Yet she stood by his side nonetheless.

Keisha stepped forward. "You're welcome to explore all of your legal options, Mr. Foley. But I think you'll find there aren't many left to you."

He glared at her and then turned his hateful gaze on me. "They should've left you to rot in that prison cell. Maybe then you would've learned your lesson or at least done us all a favor and died."

Mason lunged, but I grabbed hold of him and pushed him back. "Mase, no. That's what he wants," I cried.

Keisha helped me push him back farther. "She's right. This won't help. It'll only give him ammunition."

Mason blinked a few times before coming back to himself and no longer straining against us. "I want to kill him," he growled.

"I know." I patted his chest. "But, trust me, he's not worth the jail time." My father was a sad and pathetic man. He would die bitter and with only my mother under his thumb.

Mason's gaze flicked down to me. "You called me Mase."

My cheeks heated. "I think I kind of like it."

He pulled me into his arms, pressing his mouth to mine. "It sounds good on your lips."

CHAPTER
Thirty-Eight

Anna

"**A**RE YOU SURE YOU DON'T STILL FEEL SICK?" I FELT Justin's forehead.

"I'm fiiiiiine. Swear," he said, ducking out of my touch.

Mason chuckled. "He just ate one too many scoops of ice cream."

Justin dragged a duffle bag towards the front door. "It was a celebration."

My lips twitched. It had been the most epic of celebrations. Pizza, ice cream sundaes, two movies, and a fort that was still hung haphazardly in the living room. "I don't think you'll exactly be eating healthy on a camping trip. Maybe you should wait and go on the next one."

"No!" Lyla called, jumping down the final two stairs to the entryway, a backpack on. "Jensen said we might see the wild horses where we're going. *Please*? I really wanna go."

Mason held up both hands. "Don't look at me. This is all your aunt's decision."

I scowled in his direction. I loved that Justin and Noah were becoming fast friends, and that Lyla was so interested in Jensen's horses and everything she could teach her. But we'd just gotten the judge's ruling, and letting them out of my sight right now felt terrifying.

Mason crossed the space, pulling me into his arms. "You're going to have to let them go eventually. This is good. Normal. Friends and camping trips with people we trust."

Jensen's husband Tuck worked for the Forest Service, so I knew they'd be safe. "You're right. I know you are."

"But it's hard to let them go."

I nodded into his chest. "They'll be back tomorrow."

He pressed a kiss to my temple. "Just one night."

"Eeeewwww," Justin moaned. "No mushy stuff."

Mason chuckled against my hair. "I can't wait until he has his first crush. I'm going to throw this very moment in his face."

An SUV honked as it rounded the circular drive. Lyla jumped up and down. "We can go, right?"

"You can go," I agreed.

Justin and Lyla cheered and ran out the open front door. Mason shifted me and wrapped his arm around my shoulders. "You know, this means we'll have an empty house tonight."

Heat rose to my cheeks. "I don't hate that."

"Me, either. I'll pick up a bottle of that Riesling you like."

I brushed my lips against his. "We can take a soak in the hot tub."

Tuck let out a wolf whistle and covered Justin's eyes. "At least let the children leave before you start in on that."

Justin grabbed at Tuck's arms. "I told them to stop with the mushy stuff."

"It never works," Noah grumbled as he climbed out of the SUV. "My mom and dad are the *worst*." Drew followed, hitting the ground with an oomph.

"Did you hear that, Wilder? We're the *worst*," Tuck said with a devilish grin.

Jensen rolled her eyes. "He's hopeless."

"That's not what you said last night."

She smacked his shoulder. "Tuck!"

Mason barked out a laugh. "Well, we'll be happy to take Noah and Drew for a sleepover another time if you guys want a date night."

Tuck gave Mason a fist bump. "I knew I liked you."

Jensen pulled me in for a quick hug. "I'm so happy for you guys."

"Thanks. I feel like I can finally breathe."

"I'll bet. I don't want you to worry about them tonight. We've planned for every emergency under the sun and where we're going has cell phone service. I'll text you."

The tension between my shoulder blades released a fraction. "Thanks. I'm new at this whole thing. I don't want to screw up."

Jensen chuckled. "Oh, you will. There's no way to avoid it. But you'll fix whatever it is you messed up, and everyone will be fine."

"I hope you're right."

"I am."

Tuck let out another of those whistles. "All right, team, fall in. Let's get our camping on."

Justin and Lyla gave me and Mason quick hugs and then piled into the large SUV after Drew and Noah. Tuck gave us a salute, and Jensen waved her phone in the air. "Call anytime."

We watched them disappear down the lane, Mason's arm going around my shoulders again. I sniffed. "Why do I feel like I need to cry?"

He choked on a laugh. "Seriously?"

I gave him a light elbow to the ribs. "Not nice. It's emotional. Their first camping trip."

"We'll have to go on our own trip."

"I've never been camping."

Mason tugged me in closer. "Really?"

"Nope. But I could get behind some starry skies and s'mores over a fire. Just as long as you bring me one of those air mattress things."

"Noted." He checked his watch. "I have to get going, I have a meeting at nine."

"What time is it?"

"Eight forty-five."

"Shoot. I'm supposed to meet Kennedy at the bakery at nine for a breakfast meeting."

Mason gave me a little tap on the ass. "Better get going."

"I'm gonna get you back for that," I warned, heading for the house.

"Promises, promises."

I slid into a parking space a couple of blocks down from the bakery. The tourists were out early this morning. Trying to hold onto the last tendrils of summer, I guessed. In two weeks, Justin and Lyla would start school at Sutter Lake Elementary. And not long after that, the leaves would turn. The kids couldn't wait for the snow. They'd gotten a couple of inches here and there back home, but nothing like what we got in the mountains.

I bumped my door closed with my hip and beeped my locks before shoving my keys into my purse. "Late, late, late," I muttered as I hurried down the street.

My bag slipped from my shoulder, and as I moved to catch it, I knocked into someone. "I'm so sorry. I wasn't watching where I was going—" My words cut off as I took in Juliette's angry snarl.

"Of course, you weren't."

I straightened, doing my best to keep my expression neutral. "I'm sorry."

"You ruined my relationship with my brother. The only person I've ever had to count on. But you don't care about that."

The cup of coffee I'd had a few hours ago soured in my stomach. "I don't think it's ruined. Mason loves you."

She scoffed, but I saw the angry tears gathering in the corners of her eyes. "Not as much as he loves you, apparently."

"It isn't a contest."

Her eyes blazed now, a heat that looked as if it could burn anything in its path. "You have no idea what we went through. All you see when you look at him is dollar signs."

"I love him."

"Bullshit."

"I do. I know nothing I say will convince you of that, but maybe you'll see over time. I love him because he's the kindest man I've ever known. I know what mean feels like, and there isn't a speck of mean in him, Juliette. He's everything I was too scared to reach for, and now that I know what it's like to be loved by him, I'm never letting go."

Juliette's face turned the shade of a tomato. "I don't know what kind of con you're running, but—"

"Ladies," a deep voice cut in. "Everything all right?"

I looked up at Walker. "You have some convenient timing."

He grinned at me. "You never know what you might come across on patrol." He turned to Juliette. "It's nice to see you again, Juliette."

"Have you run this—this *crook* who has my brother bamboozled? Maybe you can talk some sense into him."

Walker arched a brow. "Bamboozled, huh? You got that kind of mojo, Anna?"

"If I did, I would've used it long before now."

Juliette let out a growl of frustration. "You people need help!"

My shoulders sagged as she hurried away. I wanted to hope that she would come around, but I didn't see how it was possible.

Walker placed a gentle hand on my shoulder. "You okay?"

I nodded, forcing a smile. "The worst is over. She'll come around eventually."

"I hope you're right."

CHAPTER
Thirty-Nine

Mason

I HIT SEND ON THE LATEST PROPOSAL FOR CAIN. I THOUGHT this newest incarnation covered all of our bases. And I had to admit, it was nice to be back in the flow at work. My mind had been elsewhere these past couple of months, and I could see that I hadn't given this project enough of my focus. But now that the custody case was settled, I could devote that time and attention again.

My cell phone buzzed on its dock, and Dante's name flashed across the screen. "Hey," I greeted.

"Mason," he returned. "I know everything's wrapped up in court, but I came across something I wanted you to know about that I'm going to pass along to the Las Vegas PD."

The earlier buzz of my project coming together faded. "Tell me."

"I ran financials on the Foleys. I was looking for big withdrawals, so this didn't pop right away."

My fingers tightened around the phone as I waited for Dante to continue.

"They were staying outside the Hoover Dam on their anniversary trip."

The trip they had been on when Chelsea died. The Hoover Dam was roughly thirty minutes from Vegas. "Is there any sign they were in Vegas proper? Anywhere near where she was killed?"

"Not that I can find. But thirty-minute miles is a little too close for comfort for me."

Me, too. "Did you find anything that made you think they might've known Chelsea was leaving Portland for good?" When Anna and I had talked about it, she'd said that Chelsea wanted to be fully settled before letting their parents know she was gone.

I'd met the woman once or twice, and I'd gotten to know her a lot better through her sister and children. She probably knew that if she told them about her plans, she'd cave when they pressured her to stay.

The sound of papers rustling came across the line. "That, I have no idea about." He was quiet for a moment. "I've been doing this job a long time. I've found that people who keep that much to themselves are hiding something. And it's usually not good."

I pictured Mr. Foley's face as he left court yesterday, the rage simmering just beneath the surface. I heard the words he spat at his one living daughter. And I knew he was capable of murder. Planning it to look like she'd succumbed to the same addiction her sister supposedly struggled with would've been his perfect twist of the knife.

I checked my watch. It was almost noon. Anna had to be done with her meeting by now. "I need to bring Anna up to speed."

"Okay. Do you want me to stay on this?"

"Yes. Anna needs to know the truth, and her sister deserves justice. Whatever that looks like."

"I'll call you when I know more."

"Thanks." I tapped end on my screen and stared at my phone. How did I tell her this? I didn't want to. What I wanted was to shield her from all of it. But that hadn't worked out well last time. Honesty was my only option.

I scrolled to her number, staring at it for a moment before I tapped. It rang twice before she answered.

"Hey, Mase."

I'd never get tired of hearing my nickname from her lips. "Hey."

"What's wrong?"

Of course, she could tell that something was amiss with a single word. "I really don't want to tell you this."

Anna was silent for a moment. "Sounds like it's something I need to know."

"It might mean nothing." God, I hoped it was just a coincidence.

"Tell me."

"Dante found records that your parents' vacation was to the Hoover Dam area. They were within thirty miles of Vegas when Chelsea died."

There was no sound in the background. No squeak of a desk chair or tap of a pen. I couldn't even hear Anna breathing.

"Anna?"

"What do we do with that information?"

"Dante is sharing what he found with the Las Vegas PD, and I'll loop Walker in, see what he thinks."

Her chair did squeak then, followed by footsteps on the tile floor of her office. "That's good. The police will know what to do."

I could feel the pain cut across the line. I pushed back from my desk and stood. "I'm coming to the shelter—"

"No, don't."

"Anna."

"Not because I don't want to see you, but if you come, I'll break. I need to finish this workday. Then I'll let myself fall apart."

I gripped the edge of my desk, fingers digging into the wood. "I don't like you hiding your pain from me."

"I'm not. I'm telling you I'm hurting. It's already been a shitty day, and I just need to get through the rest of it. I want you and that bottle of wine and our hot tub."

"What else happened today?"

She was quiet for a moment. "Nothing important, just stuff that gives me a headache."

"I'll rub your head as soon as you're home."

"Thanks, Mase," she whispered.

"I love you. You know that, right?"

"I love you, too."

"I'll see you in a few hours."

"See you."

I tapped end on my screen. It took everything in me to ignore my instincts to go to the shelter anyway, to force Anna to come home with me so I could take care of her. But I had to trust that she knew what she could handle.

I scrolled down to Walker's name and waited for the call to connect.

"Hey, man. You've been on my list to call today."

I sat back in my chair. "Oh, yeah, how come?"

"I hate to be the bearer of bad news, but I think you need to have another conversation with your sister."

"Shit. What did she do now?"

Juliette had texted and said that she was going to stay in town for another few days so we could have lunch. I'd thought there was a chance she might be coming to terms with the changes I had made.

"She had Anna cornered on the street this morning, spewing some pretty ugly shit."

"This morning?"

"Yup. Right outside the bakery when I was picking up breakfast."

I took a long, steadying breath. I'd just laid a heavy load on Anna's shoulders. She likely had forgotten all about that encounter with my sister. I glanced at my watch. Ten to noon. She'd had three hours to call and tell me. Hell, she could've just sent a text to give me a heads-up and say that we'd talk about it at home, but she hadn't. She'd made the conscious choice to keep it from me. Again. I could hear Anna promising that she would let me know if my sister approached her. But, apparently, that promise didn't mean much of anything to her at all.

I sat on the back patio watching the sun lower in the sky and took a pull from my beer. I'd heard from Anna but only to tell me that she'd be a little bit late coming home. Not a single word about her run-in with Juliette.

The knowledge made my skin feel too tight for my body. This person I'd fallen for, opened every locked door to, was still hiding things from me. It made me wonder if she wasn't sharing other things.

The back door opened, and footsteps sounded on the pavers. "Hey. I thought we were having wine. Changed your mind?"

I looked at Anna as she slid into the chair next to mine. God, she was beautiful. "Have you?"

"Have I what?"

"Changed your mind."

"About wine?"

There wasn't even a flicker of regret in her expression. That killed most of all. "I thought we were going with total honesty. Even when it was inconvenient."

Anna's brow furrowed into little wrinkles. "What are you talking about?"

"My sister."

She was quiet for a moment, her fingers curving around the wide-planked arms of the Adirondack chair. "It wasn't a big deal."

"You promised me you'd tell me if you had a run-in with her. Are our promises not a big deal to you, either?"

"Of course, they are. But we've been through a lot, and we finally caught a break with the ruling yesterday. I just wanted us to have a chance to breathe without some sort of drama raining down on our heads."

"You don't get to make that decision for me. Juliette is my sister, and I want to know if she's making trouble for you. And if you're not honest with me, it makes me question everything."

Anna looked as if I'd slapped her. "So, I'm exactly what she accused me of being because I didn't call you immediately? Because I wanted a night for just you and me to forget all the horrible stuff that's going on right now?"

I pushed to my feet and went to her. "I didn't mean it like that."

Anna stood and moved out of my grasp. "No? Is that what you think? That I'm a liar. A con artist. That I'm taking advantage of you?"

"Of course not. But I don't want to question whether I can trust you to keep your word."

Her eyes glistened in the amber light of the setting sun. "I'm not a liar because I didn't report to you immediately."

I snapped my mouth closed. This was getting us nowhere. "I think I need to take a walk and cool off."

"Probably not a bad idea." She turned on her heel and headed back inside.

I was alone again. And for the first time since Anna and the kids had moved in, I felt it.

CHAPTER
Fonty

Anna

I SAT ON THE STAIRS. LISTENING. UNABLE TO MOVE. ANYWHERE I could go held memories of Mason. They were burned into the walls, carved into the floors. So, I sat on the stairs. Not entering any room. Staying in the in-between.

My arms curled around my waist as I saw the hurt flashing across Mason's face. His words echoed in my mind. He questioned everything. He questioned me.

I should've been wiser. Known that if the person he loved most in this world were whispering doubts in his ear, those doubts would eventually take hold. But, instead, I'd held onto my reckless hope. And now, I was paying the price.

Footsteps sounded on the hardwood. The front door opened and then slammed closed. The sound reverberated in my chest, echoing through the empty space.

He hadn't taken his car or an overnight bag. He was coming back. The knowledge didn't ease anything in me. Because even if he came back, it wouldn't fix a damn thing.

Tears filled my eyes, spilling over and tracking down my cheeks. They dripped off my chin and onto the carpeted steps. I didn't do anything to stop them. I simply let them fall, one after the other.

My phone rang on the stair next to me. I wanted to ignore it, but it could've been Jensen. I swiped it up and looked at the screen. Clearing my throat, I answered. "Hey, Kenz."

"Oh, good. I completely forgot to give you the mockups for the new building we talked about this morning. I'm driving past your place on my way home. Can I swing by?"

"Sure. You know the code."

"See you in a few."

I pushed to my feet and headed for the half-bath downstairs. I turned on the faucet as cold as I could get it. Splashing water on my face, I soaked up the freezing burn. Welcomed it. I patted my face dry with the hand towel and looked in the mirror.

I looked like hell. My skin was shock-white. Eyes red and swollen. But as the doorbell rang, I knew there was nothing to be done about it now. Maybe the light was dim enough that Kennedy wouldn't notice.

I headed out of the bathroom and towards the entryway. Pulling open the door, I forced a smile. "Hey."

"Hey—" Kennedy's smile fell. "What is it? What's wrong? Are Justin and Lyla okay?"

"Everyone's fine."

She scowled at me, pushing her way inside. "Bullshit. Where's Mason?"

"He went for a walk."

Kennedy surveyed my face. "Did you guys have a fight?"

I bit my lip to keep from crying and nodded.

She pulled me into a tight hug. "It's going to be okay."

"I'm not so sure about that."

"Come on." Kenz guided me towards the kitchen, depositing me in the breakfast nook we rarely used. She bustled around the kitchen until she found a kettle and some tea. "Honey?" I pointed to the pantry, and she retrieved it. "Do you want milk?"

"No, thanks."

In a matter of minutes, she slid into the nook next to me and handed me a mug. "Have some of this. It'll help."

I stared down at the swirling liquid. God, I wished it held all the answers I needed. That when I finished it, everything would somehow be miraculously mended.

"Tell me what happened."

I placed a dollop of honey into the mug and swirled it around. "I had a run-in with Juliette this morning and didn't tell Mason. But he found out and was royally pissed."

"Because he wasn't there to protect you?"

"Because I promised I would tell him if I had a run-in with her."

Kennedy was quiet for a moment, taking a sip of her tea. "So, why didn't you?"

"Because it was already the day from hell. We were supposed to have tonight. Just the two of us. Wine, the hot tub…"

"Aaaaah."

"Instead, it ended up being a blowout fight." I rubbed at an invisible spot on the handle of my mug. "He said it made him question what else I was hiding from him."

Kennedy straightened on the banquette. "Excuse me?"

"I think maybe his sister's words got in his head."

"You mean her paranoid, selfish tantrums."

"Or you could call them that." I wanted to smile. Almost got my mouth to cooperate but couldn't quite get there.

"What a freaking idiot. And he just *left*?"

That was what hurt the most. After all of his talk about being a team, when things got hard, he walked away. Maybe we weren't as strong as I'd thought we were. "He said he needed to cool down."

Kennedy set her mug down with a thud. "Well, maybe he should just go jump in Sutter Lake, then."

That startled a laugh out of me. My sweet, kind, empathetic friend had a bit of a vengeful streak when someone hurt the people she cared about. "I love you, Kenz."

Her expression softened, and she laid a hand over mine. "Love you, too. And as much I'm pissed as all get out at Mase right now, he loves you, too."

My stomach cramped at her words, wanting to hold onto them as truth. "This won't work if every time I mess up, he thinks it's a sign I'm hiding a whole secret life."

"You guys moved really fast. And did things a little out of order." Kennedy held up a hand when I opened my mouth to say something. "I'm not asking the whys of it. I'm pretty sure I already know. But what I'm saying is that you both need to give yourselves some grace. Give yourselves time to catch up to where you catapulted yourselves to a couple of months ago."

She had a point. Mason and I had done everything backwards and upside down. We were still getting to know one another, how we operated, how we reacted in times of stress. Maybe the walk was exactly what Mason needed when things got heated. And if that was the case, I needed to give it to him.

"How'd you get so wise, anyway?"

Her eyes seemed to almost twinkle. "I went through the wringer with my broody bastard."

I barked out a laugh. "How would Cain feel if he knew you were calling him a broody bastard?"

"He'd probably be flattered."

"I think you're right."

She squeezed my hand and then released it. "There was a time when I thought there was no hope for me and Cain. He hurt me. Badly. But we made it through. And I've never been happier that I walked through that valley to get to the mountaintop. Just keep walking forward. You'll find your way."

I moved on instinct, pulling her into a hug. "I'm so lucky to have you."

"Right back at you, sister." When she released me, she glanced at her watch. "I should go before Cain calls in the National Guard. Unless you want me to stay? I can call him."

I waved her off. "No. I'm better now. Thanks for the talk."

She scooted out of the breakfast nook. "Anytime. And you know you can always stay with us for a few days if you need to."

I really hoped it wouldn't come to that, but I appreciated the gesture, nonetheless. "Thanks."

I walked Kennedy out to her SUV, watching as the taillights disappeared into the darkness. A chill skittered down my spine. Mason still wasn't back. I hoped he had his phone to use as a flashlight, at least.

I heard rustling on the side of the house. "Mase?" I started towards the sound. "Is that you?"

Nothing. My footsteps slowed. Crap. There were coyotes and cougars around here. This was dumb. I turned and headed back towards the light of the house. Every sound was amplified, from the crickets to the wind.

The crunch of gravel echoed in the night, and I whirled around, only to meet a blow. Pain and light bloomed bright. Then faded to nothingness. As I crumpled to the ground, it was Mason's name on my lips.

CHAPTER
Forty-One

Mason

I'D LOST TRACK OF TIME AS I WALKED. I'D MADE IT DOWN THE lane to my property and another few dirt roads until I found myself at the gate to Cain and Kennedy's. I stared at the call box.

I'd been lost in my head as I walked, running everything through, forward, backwards, and sideways. I still felt as if I had zero perspective. But I did know that I'd hurt Anna, and that was the last thing I ever wanted to do. Even when I was pissed as hell.

I hit the button on the call box. A few seconds later, Cain's voice came across the line. "Mason?"

"Hey."

"Did you walk here?"

"Uh, yeah." It now felt beyond ridiculous.

The gate buzzed and began to open. "Come on down."

I started down the road lined with trees. And by the time the lake house came into view, I no longer had any idea why I was even there. Cain stood on the front steps and handed me a glass of water. "Figured you might want that."

"Thanks." I took a healthy gulp.

"Come on in." He led me inside to the house that had massive windows overlooking the small lake beyond.

"Kenz around?"

"She was working late. Should be home soon, though." We eased onto the massive couch in the living space. "You want to tell me what has you walking miles to my house?"

"I didn't have a destination in mind. I just kind of ended up here."

"You know you're welcome anytime."

And I was grateful for that. The friendship Cain had given me was more like a brotherhood, and I'd never really had that before. "I got into it with Anna."

He raised a brow. "About?"

"She had a run-in with my sister and hid it from me."

"Hid it from you? Or delayed in telling you?"

I bit the inside of my cheek. She hadn't lied outright. Hadn't deceived, exactly. But it sure as hell felt like it. "Probably the latter."

"Probably?"

"She promised me that she'd tell me if Juliette caused any more trouble. She didn't."

Cain was quiet for a moment. "I told you this open and honest thing wouldn't come as easily for Anna. But it doesn't sound like it was malicious."

I set my glass on a coaster on the coffee table. "I don't think it was outright malicious. I just…"

"You feel like she's hiding things from you."

I nodded.

Cain sighed, leaning back on the sofa. "I lost it on Kennedy once."

The admission came as a shock. I'd never even seen Cain look annoyed at his wife, let alone raise his voice to her.

"I let my baggage completely color how I saw something. My fuse blew. I kicked her out of my house, said things I'll never be able to take back."

My gut soured, the look on Anna's face flashing in my mind. She'd been so hurt. "*Is that what you think? That I'm a liar. A con artist. That I'm taking advantage of you?*" Her words echoed in my mind.

"I take it from your silence that you might've done something similar."

I gripped a throw pillow, letting my fingers sink into the downy material. "She misinterpreted something I said."

"You hit a trigger you knew would hurt."

Had I? Maybe somewhere in my subconscious, I had known the accusation I tossed at her would cut deep. Because what she had done had cut me. But instead of saying that, owning my hurt, I'd lashed out. "Shit."

"You're seeing it now."

I scrubbed a hand over my jaw. "I didn't mean to."

Cain met my gaze. "You and I, we carry heavy histories. Things that happened to us that we'll never forget. When you let someone into that, show them some of that darkness, it makes us vulnerable."

"And if someone crosses a line after we let them in…"

"We might not react in the best way."

Understatement of the century. I pressed at that spot between my eyes. "I don't know how I'm going to make this right."

"By going home and not stopping until you find a way. Nothing's over until you give up."

He was damn right about that. And I'd do every form of groveling necessary if it meant that I could make this right. "Can you give me a ride?"

Cain gave me a shit-eating grin and slapped me on the shoulder. "Of course."

As we rose to head for the garage, the front door opened. Kennedy appeared. She strode over to me and smacked the back of my head. "What is wrong with you?"

"Shit," Cain muttered.

My gaze went from Kennedy to Cain and back again. "What did I do?"

"Made Anna cry. And she never cries."

Everything in me locked. "When was she crying?"

"Just now. I stopped by to give her some paperwork for Hope House. You were a real asshole to her, Mase. You need to fix that immediately. If I didn't like you so dang much, I'd bar you from the house."

Cain grinned at his wife. "You'd bar him from his own house?"

Her hands went to her waist. "Don't underestimate me. And don't annoy me right now. I'm so pissed at men and their idiocy, I'm tempted to make you sleep on the couch."

He couldn't hold in his chuckle. "There are like six guest rooms in this house."

"Nope. The couch. So don't mess with me right now."

Cain crossed to his wife, giving her a long, slow kiss. "Never."

She came away a little dazed. "Good. Now get Mase home so he can fix this."

I followed Cain in a sort of trance, climbing into the passenger side of his SUV. But all I could hear was Kennedy telling me that Anna had been crying. All I could see in my mind was her tear-streaked face. And I'd never felt lower in my life.

CHAPTER
Forty-Two

Anna

I GROANED AS I STRUGGLED TO OPEN MY EYES. EVERYTHING hurt. But the worst of it seemed to emanate from my head. The pulse through my skull felt like daggers.

"Finally waking up? It took you long enough."

That voice. The timbre of his tone had me jerking upright as if my body recognized danger before my mind could.

Everything came together in flashes. I was in a car. My hatchback. I couldn't move freely. My right hand was taped to the door handle. Derek.

"Uh, uh, uh," he said, pointing a gun in my direction. "Don't even think about it."

I itched to lash out. A punch. My nails. Whatever I could use. But my mind was still catching up with what my body knew. Trying to put the pieces together.

I looked around. We were parked on the dirt road at the edge of the lake. I could just make out the bench we'd put in place for Chelsea.

"Did you miss me at all, Anna?"

My gaze snapped back to Derek. "Did I miss you?" I only seemed capable of parroting his words.

He leaned against the driver's side door. "I did everything for you. You think you'd miss that dedication."

"You set me up to take the fall for you."

Anger flared in Derek's eyes, making the brown seem to glow amber in the dark. "You were fifteen. You got off easy. I needed to stay out so you had somewhere to go once you were released. You never understood that. What would've happened to you at your parents' house if I'd been locked up? Did you ever think about that?"

The same thing that always happened to me. My father knocking me around. I'd lived through it for fifteen years. I would've made it another two. I would've made it to freedom. Instead, that freedom was stolen from me. And I'd lost the only two people I'd cared about: my sister and Derek.

"I loved you," I whispered. "And you threw me to the wolves."

He lashed out in a flash, grabbing my hair and yanking it hard. "Watch your fucking mouth. I made a strategic decision. For both of us. But you wouldn't let me get a word in to explain it to you."

I didn't fight the pain. I let it take over. It made me more alert. And I didn't take my eyes off Derek. How had I not seen? He had the same rage and control issues my father did. Only the anger had never been directed at me before. Maybe because I'd always done what he said. I'd been young and so desperate to get out of the situation I was in. I'd thought I was walking into safety when, really, I was exchanging one prison for another.

"What do you want?" I spoke low, doing everything I could to keep my voice from shaking.

"How about a little respect for once? Some gratitude? That fucking cop took you away before I had a chance to explain myself. I should've put a bullet in him then. Maybe I'll go back and pay him a visit."

My mouth went dry, and I struggled to swallow. "Why?"

"Why? Because I gave you everything, you ungrateful bitch! And then there you were, spilling your guts to every cop who would listen, trying to get them to come for me."

Because he was the guilty one. He had been so eager to throw me under the bus to save his sorry self. It had nothing to do with me and everything to do with him.

He sneered at me. "I thought you were finally going to get what was coming to you. There was something poetic about it. Losing the only people you had left. Your sister. Those two kids."

And Derek had been determined to make sure I suffered. "Because I didn't want to take the fall for you?" He'd been willing to send Justin and Lyla to a hell he knew everything about just to make sure I hurt. The wave of rage that crested and roared through me took my breath away.

"You left. I was ready to give you the world when you got out, and you blew me off. Then your bitch of a sister came sniffing around—"

I froze, every muscle in my body tensing. "What?"

Derek smiled, but it was devoid of warmth. In fact, everything about him was empty. He lacked the ability to truly feel where another might be coming from. "I wondered for a while if she'd told you what she was up to. So, I dragged my ass to the middle of nowhere to watch. I stayed out of sight for a good while, just to see what you were doing."

"The texts."

He held up his phone, dancing it back and forth between his fingers. "It was fun to take a stroll down memory lane. I probably should've left when I realized you didn't know shit about what Chels was up to."

"What did she do?" My question came out in a whisper, each word a struggle to get past my lips.

Derek chuckled. "Can you believe she thought she could con me? Either that or get me to grow a conscience. She hired a freaking P.I. to track me down. Flew to L.A. to try to *talk* to me."

"About what?" I asked, but I already knew the answer.

"That bitch thought she could get your sentence overturned. Said she wanted to do it to make up for not sticking by you years ago."

I felt dizzy, as if the air wasn't fully reaching my lungs. "What did you do?"

That ugly grin was back. "Told her I had to think about it. And that I couldn't talk there. Got her to meet me in Vegas a week later."

The world dropped out from under me. My entire body felt weightless and fuzzy at the same time. As if I no longer truly existed. "You killed her."

"I got a charge out of turning her into what everyone thought you were. I knew that'd get your parents going, too. God, it was fun to watch all of that play out. Help in all of the little ways I could. Didn't hurt that I got paid for the trouble, either."

Tears burned the backs of my eyes as I stared straight ahead. Chelsea. Having her back in my life was enough. It didn't matter that other people might think the worst of me, as long as the people I loved knew the truth.

My gaze locked on my wrist secured to the door and the final pieces came into place. I hadn't been hurt enough for Derek's pleasure. He was going to end me altogether.

My breaths came faster as I tugged at the tape. As I clawed at the bindings, Derek laughed. "It won't do any good. Too many layers. It's unfortunate that mental illness runs in a family. First, one sister overdoses, and then the other dies by suicide. A shame."

"Don't do this. Please." I wasn't above begging. "I'll do whatever you want—"

"I don't want a fucking thing from you."

My free hand went to the horn, hoping someone would hear me. Maybe Mason was close. My chest constricted as his face filled my mind. I'd messed everything up, and now my last words to him would be ones of anger and hurt.

The butt of Derek's gun slammed down on my hand as I pressed the horn again. I cried out in pain, bringing my arm to my chest.

"Enough," he barked. "We're done."

"Don't," I whispered, tears of pain and desperation leaking out.

"Should've let you give me the world." He climbed out from behind the wheel.

I frantically searched for keys but there were none. My hatchback began rolling towards the water. I reached for the gear shift, but my fingers could barely grasp it. And when I tried to close around it, the pain was blinding. I couldn't. There had to be broken bones in my hand.

Water surged around the vehicle as Derek gave me a final push down the incline and into the lake. I yanked as hard as I could on my bound wrist but got nowhere. I pulled my feet up, kicking against the horn. Hoping against hope that someone would hear me. But if they did, no one came. And the water swallowed the vehicle whole.

CHAPTER
Forty-Three

Mason

CAIN ROLLED DOWN THE WINDOW AND PUNCHED IN THE code to my security system. As he did, a horn sounded. He glanced at me as the gates to the property swung open. "What the hell was that?"

"I have no idea."

He guided his SUV down the drive and left his window open. The horn sounded again, this time in rapid succession. Then there was silence.

The noise was too close to have been from a passing motorist or someone who'd been in an accident out on the main road. I rolled down my window. "I think it might be coming from that direction." I pointed towards the dirt road that led to the lake.

"I see a light," Cain said.

What looked like a flashlight beam glinted in the far-off distance. A chill slid down my spine. No one should be out there. I pulled out my phone. "I'm calling Walker. Something's off. Turn off your headlights."

A million different possibilities ran through my mind. All of them bad. But none of them made any sense.

Cain reached across and pressed a thumb to a lock on the glove box. It popped open, and he slid out a gun. "Just in case."

The phone rang three times before Walker answered. "Hey, man."

"I might have an intruder on my property. There's a vehicle by the lake."

"You have one of those ridiculous security systems. An alert didn't go off?"

He had a point with that. I pulled the phone away from my ear and hit the speaker button. "Hold on, I'm checking something."

Cain pulled to a stop so we could both look at the feed. I rewound until I saw myself on the video. Then I pressed play at two-times the normal speed. Kennedy came and went. And then nothing.

"Hold on. Go back. Play between when Kennedy arrives and leaves again," Cain said.

I did, this time at a normal speed. That's when I saw it—a shadow. Someone jumping over the fence and trying to avoid the cameras they likely knew I had. It wasn't the right shape for an animal. It had to be a person. My blood went cold. "Walker, get officers here now. Someone's on the property."

"Don't do anything stupid. Wait for us to get there—"

I hung up, cutting him off. I hit Anna's contact and said a silent prayer that she was in the house. It just kept ringing. I looked at Cain. "You try her." She was pissed at me. Maybe she simply wasn't answering because she was still mad.

Cain held his phone to his ear for what seemed like forever. "Voicemail."

A horn sounded again. "We go in the direction of the noise."

Cain jerked his chin in agreement and headed down the dirt road. It wasn't used often, so we bumped along it. The beam of light looked as if it were moving. Then it illuminated a car.

Anna's hatchback.

"Turn on your headlights. That's Anna's."

Cain flicked on his lights. They revealed someone watching as the vehicle sank into the water, but as the light came on, the person whirled. Derek. He took off running.

Cain screeched to a halt, the tires spitting up dirt and gravel. "I've got him. You make sure no one was in that car."

I was already moving, running for the water. Images flashed in front of me. Memories. The water swirling around our windows. Mom screaming. Juliette crying. My dad not saying a word. *"Get her out, Mason. Get Juliette out, please."*

I pushed my muscles harder as the hatchback disappeared beneath the surface. I ran into the water and then dove. The lake wasn't deep, but it was at least twenty feet. And the vehicle was sinking fast.

I kicked harder, water blurring my vision. I caught the edge of the passenger-side window. A partially open window. Anna thrashed against her seat, and my heart seized. Her hand was taped to the door handle.

The hatchback settled on the bottom of the lake, and I grappled with the door, finally getting it open. I tore at the tape but wasn't having any luck. My lungs burned, and I looked at Anna. She shook her head, pointing up. She wanted me to leave her? Wasn't going to happen. But I did need more air.

I kicked my way to the surface, sucked in a few deep breaths, and then dove again. It was less than a minute. Sixty seconds. As I swam, I pulled my keys out of my pocket, but when I reached Anna, she wasn't moving.

I didn't let myself think about her still body, the water invading her lungs. I sawed at the duct tape with my sharpest key. One layer. Then another. The metal cut into my fingers, but I didn't think about it. Once the final layer started to give way, I pulled. Bracing my feet against the car, I tugged with every ounce of my fading strength.

It gave way. I hooked my arm around Anna's body and maneuvered her from the vehicle. I kicked as hard as I could towards the surface. Everything burned, but I only pushed myself harder. As I broke the surface, I sucked in air. The breath hurt, but not nearly as much as not knowing if Anna was okay.

I swam to the lake's edge and dragged her onto the shore. I collapsed next to her, rolling over to check if she was breathing. Nothing. My hand shook as I felt for a pulse. There was no telltale fluttering against my fingertips.

I got to my knees and tipped Anna's head back. I centered my hands and began compressions. I counted to thirty and then breathed into her mouth twice. Nothing. I continued the pattern as sirens sounded in the distance.

"Don't do this to me, Anna." My voice didn't even sound like my own. "Breathe."

Shouts sounded, but I didn't move from my task.

"Step back, sir. Let us help her."

But I couldn't. "She's not breathing. I have to breathe for her."

A CPR mask covered her face. "We've got this."

Someone pulled me back. I struggled against the hold, but Walker's voice cut through the roaring in my ears. "They can help. Let them."

EMTs surrounded Anna. Her body looked so small. Then, I could no longer see most of her. Only her feet. She didn't have shoes on. When had she lost them? In the water? Before? I needed to get her socks. A blanket. She was probably cold.

"We need to move. Now!" an EMT shouted.

I could only stare at her feet and think of all the ways I'd failed her.

CHAPTER
Forty-Four

Mason

I FELT EVERYTHING AND NOTHING. THE HARD PLASTIC OF THE waiting room chair digging into my spine. The hum of the fluorescent lights vibrating my skin. Lyla pressed tight against my side. My arm resting on Justin's shoulders.

Yet I couldn't take in any of it. Not truly. The room was full of people. Cain and Kennedy. Taylor. Jensen and Tuck. The only reason Liam and Tessa weren't present was because they were watching everyone's kids.

I knew all of them were here, yet I couldn't make out any of their faces. Everything was just a bit blurry, as if what was happening wasn't real.

I didn't want it to be. Wished I could just shake myself and wake up from the nightmare. I blinked a few times. Everything in front of me remained the same.

The ambulance had rushed Anna to the hospital. Cain had driven behind, not letting up on his speed until we reached the emergency room. But they'd taken her away before I had a chance to see her. To know if she was breathing again.

A nurse had given me dry scrubs to change into and guided

Cain and me to a private waiting room. That had to mean it was bad. If she hadn't put us in with the general public, she thought we'd be getting bad news.

I struggled to breathe. My ribs felt too tight around my lungs— the air unable to get in.

This wasn't happening. I couldn't lose her. The last words I'd said to Anna had cut deep. A wound I needed the chance to make right.

Walker appeared in the doorway and motioned to me. I stiffened but gave Justin's shoulder a squeeze and pressed a kiss to the top of Lyla's head. "I'll be back in a few minutes."

"Promise?" Lyla asked, her eyes red.

"Promise."

Kennedy swooped in, wrapping an arm around Lyla. "I've got you, Lyla Bean."

Lyla burrowed into Kennedy's hold, and I mouthed *thank you* to her. She gave me a wavering smile. "We'll be fine. Take your time."

I glanced at Justin, Cain on his other side. He was trying to hold it together, but I knew he was dying inside. "You tell Cain if you need anything."

He nodded. "They got the bad guy?"

"They got him," I assured Justin. I didn't know the details, but I knew that Cain had taken Derek down in a tackle, and the police had cuffed him shortly after. Now, I needed to know everything I could. So when Anna woke up, I could assure her that everything was okay. That she was safe.

I headed into the hall where Walker was waiting.

"Any word from the doctors?" he asked.

"Nothing yet. What about you?"

A muscle in Walker's jaw ticked. "We found the mother lode in his hotel room."

"What?" I gritted out.

"He killed Chelsea."

I froze. That made no sense. "Why?"

Walker ran a hand through his hair. "It looks like she was trying to get him to confess to setting Anna up when they were teenagers. There was a small digital recorder in his possession with the conversation on tape. Once we had that, he told us everything."

"But why come for Anna? He'd gotten away with it."

"At first, he just wanted to see if she knew what her sister was doing. Then I think it burned that she was happy. Without him. The only thing I'm sure about is that Derek Raymond is a sick man."

"Tell me he's going away for this." There had to be justice. I had to be able to give that to Anna as soon as I saw her.

"For a long, long time. And he gave us the Foleys."

"Bribery?"

"Yup. I've got Portland PD picking up Jeff now because he took a bribe, too. Then, they'll get the Foleys. They're going down, Mase. It might not be for as long as they deserve, but I'm going to do everything I can to make sure they see the inside of a jail cell."

They deserved more. To feel each blow they'd leveled on their children. To never breathe free air again. But this would have to be enough. "Thank you, Walker."

"I'll do whatever I can to help."

I knew that. But the help we really needed wasn't something he could give. Only the doctors or a miracle could.

Heels sounded on the linoleum floor. "Mase!"

I looked up at the sound of Juliette's voice. She hurried down the hall, concern marring her features. "What happened? Walker wouldn't tell me—"

Walker winced. "Sorry, man, she came by your place as we were working the scene."

"Jules, I can't do this right now."

"Tell me what happened."

"Anna's ex-boyfriend tried to kill her!" I barked. "The same ex-boyfriend those parents you tried to help brought into town.

I have no idea if she'll make it, but I know you don't give a damn. So, please, just leave me the hell alone."

Juliette blanched. "Mase…"

"Juliette, why don't you go wait in the waiting room with everyone else?" Walker suggested. "I'll keep you updated."

"But Mason—"

"Later," Walker instructed, almost pushing her towards the waiting room.

She looked over her shoulder as she went, pain lacing her features, but I couldn't find it in me to care.

A Hispanic man in scrubs strode down the hallway towards us. My body locked as I tracked his movements. He nodded at Walker. "Are you Ms. Foley's family?"

"Yes." My voice broke as I said it, and I cleared my throat. "I'm her husband."

It was the first time I'd claimed the title. And right now, it felt as if I had no right to it.

The man nodded. "I'm Dr. Martín. I've been taking care of Ms. Foley. She's in serious but stable condition in our ICU."

"What does that mean?" The words *serious* and *stable* were polar opposites in my mind.

"It was touch and go. Her heart was stopped for some time, but we got it beating again. After some tests, it's evident she has hypoxia. Oxygen deficiency in the brain."

"But she's going to be okay." It wasn't a question. It was a demand.

"The next day or two will tell us more. Right now, she's in a coma. She has a ventilator breathing for her, and we're tracking her stats carefully. But I can take you to see her if you'd like."

"Yes." The word came out as a whisper.

Walker clapped me on the shoulder. "I'll update everyone else."

"Okay."

I could only manage these one-word answers because my brain was spiraling. Anna's heart stopping. Coma. Ventilator.

I followed the doctor down the hall to an elevator. "What are her chances?"

The doors opened, and we stepped inside. "Her chances for survival are good. Her brain function is in the normal range. But you need to be prepared. We have no way of knowing what damage has been done until Ms. Foley wakes up."

"Damage?" I rasped.

"She could have neurological impairments after this. Symptoms similar to a stroke. Or the reaction could be milder. Insomnia, short-term amnesia."

Endless possibilities circled in my mind as the doctor led me down another hall. We stopped at a hand sanitizer pump outside a set of double doors. Dr. Martín sprayed some into his hands, and I did the same. As he opened one of the doors, a cacophony of beeping sounds filled the air, punctuated by what almost sounded like gasps.

A number of rooms surrounded what appeared to be a nurses' station. Martín gestured to it. "Your wife will have 'round-the-clock monitoring."

I should've been relieved by the knowledge, but it made me sick. She needed that monitoring because I'd left her. Let her down in the worst way imaginable.

"She's right in here. Don't be put off by the machines, she's doing really well, all things considered."

"Thank you." I stepped through the open door, and all air left my lungs. Anna. She looked impossibly small in the bed. So many wires and tubes. Ones connected to electrodes on her head. Ones dipping beneath her hospital gown. To her mouth. Her arm. One hand had a splint.

Everything burned. My eyes. My chest. But I pushed forward. One step, and then another. I lowered myself into the chair beside her bed. The hand resting on top of the covers had only an oxygen monitor clamped to her finger.

I lifted it, holding it between both of my hands, then pressed it to my lips. "Anna. I'm so sorry."

Those words weren't even close to being enough. But I didn't know what would be. Tears filled my eyes, spilling over and landing on our joined hands. "I love you. Please don't leave me."

CHAPTER
Forty-Five

Anna

THE PERSISTENT TICKLE IN MY THROAT WOKE ME. A scratch that wouldn't go away, no matter how much I swallowed. That was when the pain hit. The thrumming through my skull and the ache in my muscles.

What the hell happened?

I tried to open my eyes, but they didn't seem to want to cooperate. The lids themselves were too heavy. I tried again, straining. This time, they fluttered.

The light in the room was low but still felt too bright. Each blink cemented a picture in my mind. Curtains. White walls. Machines. Mason.

His head lay on my bed, his face turned towards me. He looked…haggard. Scruff even longer than usual and dark circles under his eyes.

I reached out, running my fingers through his hair. Mason let out a little moan. Then his eyes popped open, and he jerked upright. "Anna?"

"Hi." The greeting came out as a croak.

"Are you okay? How do you feel? How long have you been awake?"

"What happened?" As I asked the question, things came back to me in flashes. Our fight. Waking up in the hatchback. Derek. My breaths started coming faster, panic closing in.

Mason moved in, taking my hand in his. "It's okay. You're safe."

"Derek?" I whispered.

"He's in jail."

A nurse bustled in. "I thought there was a little spike in the heart monitor activity. Welcome back, Ms. Foley. Your young man has been quite worried about you."

I held it together while she checked lines and tubes and asked me a few questions. She explained that my throat was sore because I'd been on a ventilator until a few hours ago and assured us that the doctor would be in soon to check me over. Then, she left.

As soon as she did, the tears fell. Mason didn't wait. He slid onto the bed next to me, careful to avoid my IV line and arm brace. He pulled me gently into him. "You're okay," he whispered, almost as if he were telling himself as much as reassuring me.

"He killed Chelsea."

"I know. Walker found evidence in his hotel room. He's going to jail for the rest of his life."

I burrowed into Mason's chest. "Why did she do it? She knew he was dangerous."

"Because she loved you. And she wanted to make things right."

The tears fell faster. "All I needed was her."

"I know." Mason pressed his lips to the top of my head. "I'm so sorry. For Chelsea. For what I said. I let my baggage get the best of me."

My hand fisted in his t-shirt. "I should've told you about Juliette."

"I should've given you time to get there." He brushed the hair away from my face so he could see my eyes. "I love you so much it scares me sometimes."

I pressed my palm against his chest. "I know." Because I felt that same fear at times. "I think it's the price we have to pay for loving so deeply. And I'll pay it every day for the rest of my life. If you'll be in it with me."

Mason brushed his lips across mine. "I only want to be where you are."

"Mase," I whispered.

"I'll love you forever."

Footsteps sounded on the linoleum. "I got more flowers. And I printed out those pictures from your phone. I read that if someone is having memory issues, it's good to have photos of familiar things around them and—" Juliette's words cut off as she took me in. "Oh, God, you're awake." Tears filled her eyes. "Is she okay? No brain damage?"

Mason smiled against my temple. "So far, things are looking good. We're waiting for the doctor."

"Well, where is he?" she demanded. "He should've been up here the second she woke up."

"What's happening right now?" I whispered to Mason. "Am I in the Twilight Zone?"

Mason chuckled. "Jules stepped up. Bringing me food and clothes. Dropping off meals to the kids, Cain, and Kennedy. And pretty much holding the medical staff hostage."

Juliette rolled her eyes. "I'm not that bad."

"I'm pretty sure Dr. Martín is terrified of you."

"Wait, how long was I out?" I asked.

Pain, stark and raw, flashed across Mason's expression. "Three days."

"Three?"

He pulled me in a little closer as if assuring himself that I was still there. "Never been more scared in my life."

"I'm here." I pressed a kiss to the underside of his jaw. "I'm not going anywhere."

"Damn straight."

Juliette shifted on her feet. "I'm going to go track down that doctor. And I'll call Kennedy so she can bring Lyla and Justin."

"Thanks, sis."

She nodded and charged out of the room.

"That was…"

"Jules?" Mason finished for me.

"Does this mean she doesn't hate me anymore?"

He toyed with a strand of my hair. "I think seeing me at my wits' end was a wake-up call for her. She went into fix-it mode. She'll have an apology for you eventually. She just needs to work up to it."

I didn't care. I didn't need it. All I needed was Mason. The family we were building. The knowledge that no one could break us apart. And when Justin and Lyla showed up forty-five minutes later, I felt a sense of completion I'd never felt before. All of us piled on the bed.

I looked around at each of their faces. "Love you guys so much."

Lyla's eyes were still a little red. "Love you, too, Anna."

"Yeah," Justin agreed.

Mason brushed his lips against mine. "Never been happier than when I'm with you."

CHAPTER
Fonty Six

Mason

I LOOKED OVER AT KENNEDY. "WHAT DO YOU THINK?"

Tears brimmed in her eyes. "I think she'll love it."

I stared down at the glimmering diamond on the black velvet. The oval stone set in rose gold would be perfect against Anna's skin. We'd had simple bands all this time, but she deserved more. She deserved everything.

I looked up at the jeweler. "I'll take it."

"Wonderful, sir."

I handed over my credit card and checked my watch. I'd made up some lame excuse about needing to get the house ready for Anna's return. She'd looked at me a little oddly when I'd said it. Probably because I hadn't left her side in the five days she'd been in the hospital.

I'd asked Taylor and Tessa to keep her company while I flew to Portland with Kennedy in Cain's jet. The flight itself was only thirty minutes or so, but I'd wanted to take my time picking out a ring, making sure it was perfect.

"This is so romantic," Kennedy said, sniffling.

"I hope Anna thinks so."

It was a little weird. Proposing to a woman I was already married to. But we'd skipped so many steps. The first date. Stolen kisses. Introducing each other to our families. I didn't want to miss this one. Even if we had to go backwards to get it.

"I know she will."

The jeweler handed me my card and a small bag. "Come back and see me if you need anything at all."

I stifled a laugh. With the amount of money I'd just dropped in his store, I had no doubt he'd love for me to return. And maybe I would. Adding a piece of jewelry at each anniversary. Something that marked Anna's and my time together. "Thank you. I will."

Kennedy hustled me out the door to our waiting SUV, the driver opening the door for her. "We have to hurry. Taylor just texted and said they're discharging Anna in an hour."

"Shit." I hoped there weren't any holdups at the small private airport we'd flown into.

Luckily, there weren't. But I still drummed my fingers on the armrest the whole flight. As we landed, I switched on my phone. A series of texts hit my screen.

Justin: *We're done with the banners. Cain and Walker are hanging them. Lyla wants to see the ring.*

Taylor: *We're leaving the hospital in fifteen minutes. I hope you're home.*

I shot her a quick text back.

Me: *Just landed.*

Taylor: *I'm walking out to pull the car around now. But I'll try to drive slowly.*

Me: *Thanks.*

Kennedy grinned at me, and we headed off the jet. "Nervous?"

I felt like I might vomit. "I'm fine."

"Then why do you look a little green?"

"Shut up," I muttered.

She giggled as she climbed into the passenger side of my SUV. "Being nervous just means you care."

I'd never cared more in my life. And I was ready to cement who Anna and I were to each other—without any false pretenses.

I did my best to keep just above the posted speed limits as I headed back to my house, but once I hit the two-lane road outside of town, my foot pressed down on the accelerator. Everything was taking too long. When we stopped at my gates, they were the worst of all, seeming to take eons to open.

Kennedy gripped the door handle. "Don't crash into a tree less than a mile from home, please."

"I'm a good driver."

"Maybe when you're not half out of your mind with anxiety, you are."

I made a conscious effort not to speed down the lane. "See?"

She arched a brow in my direction. "I'm amazed by your restraint."

I parked in front of the house, leaving plenty of room for Taylor to pull in behind me so Anna wouldn't have to walk far. The front door opened, and Justin and Lyla bounded down the stairs.

"I wanna see," Lyla cried.

I laughed as I climbed out of my SUV. "All right." I pulled the ring box out of the bag and opened it so Lyla could see.

She gasped. "It's like for a princess. So sparkly."

I glanced at Kennedy. "I think that means she likes it."

"I'd say so."

Justin peeked into the box. "It's sick."

That was all I was getting from the kid who needed to keep his cool factor. I snapped the ring box closed. "Show me the banners."

Lyla took my hand and tugged me up the steps. "We made them really pretty."

Cain and Walker both gave me slaps on the back as I entered the house and took in the two massive banners hung in the entryway. One read *Welcome Home*. And the second read *Marry Me? Again*. They were a mishmash of colors, and Lyla had drawn lopsided hearts over the marry-me one. They were exactly right. A symbol of our life now—all over the place but perfect in its disarray.

"You guys did an amazing job."

Lyla beamed. "Do you like my hearts?"

"Love them."

My phone dinged with an alert, and my gut lurched. It was the gate. I hit the icon to open it. "They're here."

Kennedy clasped her hands together as tears spilled over. "Here we go."

Cain wrapped an arm around his wife, guiding her to the side of the entryway where Walker stood. "Don't start in on that now. He hasn't even asked her yet."

She smacked his stomach. "She's one of my best friends. I'm allowed to be emotional."

"All right." He brushed his lips across her temple. "Love you."

Justin and Lyla hurried to stand with me, Lyla shushing everyone. We listened as the voices got closer. My hand tightened around the ring box as the door opened.

"Welcome home!" Justin and Lyla cheered.

Anna's eyes widened as she took in the group waiting for her. I watched as she read the first banner and then the second. I stepped forward, moving in close. I didn't drop to one knee—I didn't want that kind of distance between us. "Anna."

"Mase," she whispered.

"I think I loved you from the moment I saw you. Something in me recognized a person who could make my life so much *more*. You amaze me every single day. Your strength and your empathy. Your beauty and kindness. I love you more than I thought possible. Will you make a life with me?"

I opened the ring box. She didn't even look at it. Her eyes were only on mine. "Nothing would make me happier."

I slid the ring onto her finger as my lips met hers. "I love you, Anna."

"I love you, too. You gave me a family I never thought I'd have again."

Her words burned in my chest, etching themselves into my ribs. "It's more than I ever could've hoped for."

Epilogue

Anna

THE LATE-SPRING BREEZE KICKED UP, LIFTING MY HAIR around me as I stared out at the water. Some people would probably think it weird that I found peace here. The same place where I'd almost lost my life nine months ago. But I did.

On this bench that honored my sister. At this lake, where I'd gotten a second chance at life.

"Miss you, Chels. Justin and Lyla are doing so good. Justin's killing it on the soccer team. He has good friends and loves science. Lyla is this little bundle of energy, hopping from activity to activity. But she loves helping Jensen at her wild horse sanctuary. She's over there at least three times a week."

I watched as the wind rippled the water and wanted to believe that it was Chelsea telling me that she was listening. "I'm getting married tomorrow."

I grinned down at my lap. "I mean, I'm already married, but we're doing it for real."

We hadn't rushed this time. We'd taken our time to make sure the ceremony and celebration would be ours. We'd also taken the time to make Justin and Lyla a part of it all. And to let Juliette come around to the idea.

She wasn't my best friend by any stretch, but she'd made peace with the fact that her brother and I loved each other. And she was wonderful with Justin and Lyla. That was enough for me.

"There's something else." My hand rested on my still-flat belly. "I'm gonna have a baby."

I still couldn't quite believe it. Even after three pregnancy tests and a trip to my doctor. But here we were. I'd gone off birth control two months ago, thinking it would take some time to get pregnant. But, apparently, Mason's sperm was determined.

"I wish you were here." A couple of stray tears crested my lids and trailed over my cheeks. "For all of it. To stand up with me tomorrow. To be in the delivery room with me." I hated that Derek had robbed us of that. But Justin and Lyla were little pieces of her that I'd have with me every step of the way.

I turned at the sound of footsteps on gravel. Mason's broad form stood silhouetted against the sky. "Hi." I wiped at my cheeks.

He was next to me in a flash, sinking down onto the bench and pulling me against him. "Hey, what's with the tears?"

"Just talking to Chelsea."

He pressed his lips to my temple. "I wish she was here for you tomorrow."

"Me, too."

"You going to be okay?"

I nodded against his chest. "There's so much to be grateful for."

"That doesn't mean you can't miss your sister and want her with you. You have to let yourself feel the hurt. If you don't, you'll cut yourself off from the good."

And there was so much good all around for us to experience. I didn't want to miss an ounce of it. "I can't wait to marry you tomorrow."

"Me, either."

I pressed my palm to his chest. "I have something to tell you."

He tipped his head down to meet my gaze. "I'm listening."

"I'm pregnant," I whispered.

His body gave a little jolt. "What?"

"I didn't think it would happen so quickly. I thought for sure the test was wrong. But then I took three and saw my doctor."

Mason's hand went to my stomach as wonder filled his gaze. "We made a baby."

"Happy?"

His mouth met mine in a long kiss that made me wish we were somewhere a little more private. "Best wedding present ever." I smiled against his lips. "Are you happy? This is a little quicker than we'd planned."

I leaned back into his hold, my hand joining his on my stomach. "I love him or her so much already. It's wild. But I'm scared, too."

"Scared?"

"Mase, I had the worst example of parents you could possibly have. I don't know what I'm doing. It's terrifying."

His thumb swept across my stomach. "Anna. You mother every single person that comes through those shelter doors. Even if they're seventy years old. You've gone through the hardships and triumphs with them, been encourager and disciplinarian. You're raising Justin and Lyla. It's in your bones. You're going to be amazing."

My heart stuttered and rolled at his words. "You're already the best dad. I can't wait to see you in action from day one."

Mason framed my face in his hands. "That life we've been building is taking root."

And as those roots dug deep, we'd get to watch new life sprout and cycle. We'd share the winters and springs. But through each hardship, those roots would only grow stronger. It would allow us to enjoy every single bloom. And I'd want no one else by my side through it all.

He brushed his lips across mine. "Ready to celebrate that?"

I smiled against his mouth. "Ready."

Mason stood, tugging me to my feet. As we headed down the dirt road back towards the house, laughter and voices lifted on the breeze, punctuated by the occasional shout from one of the children. It was exactly the background music I wanted for our rehearsal dinner. This perfectly chaotic melody of the family Mason and I had created for ourselves.

Juliette caught sight of us approaching and made a beeline in our direction. "Oh, good, you're here. The caterers didn't bring enough champagne. I told them how many bottles, but they clearly didn't listen. I should've triple-checked—"

"Jules," Mason cut her off. "It's fine. Raid my wine cellar if we're running low."

"It might not be the same vintage."

He chuckled. "If you haven't noticed, we're not worried about that around here."

I looked around. Lyla and Justin ran in some sort of game with the other kids. Lyla burst out in a fit of giggles as Cooper Cole dove into a sort of somersault. The kids were all in play clothes, and the adults were casually dressed. We had lawn games set out, along with more food than we'd ever be able to finish. This wasn't a fancy crowd, and it was exactly how we liked it. Juliette just hadn't quite figured that out yet.

I met her gaze. "Thank you for wanting to make sure this is so special for us."

She blinked a few times as if surprised I would compliment her. "You're welcome." Juliette looked up at Mason. "It isn't every day your brother gets hitched." She rolled her eyes at me. "At least he told me he was doing it this time."

I couldn't hold in my laughter, glancing at Mason. "She does have a point there. You could've called her."

Mason rubbed the back of my neck. "So, I might've flubbed that piece of things last time. But you were in on all the planning this time."

"I wish you would've let me plan the bachelorette party," Irma said as she walked up with Jensen.

"Gran…Anna didn't want strippers," Jensen reminded her.

Irma harumphed. "What good is a bachelorette party without strippers?"

Juliette held out a hand for a high-five. "Amen, sister."

Irma pointed a finger in her direction. "I knew I liked you. What do you say we go get some champagne?"

Juliette looped an arm through Irma's. "I'll show you the way."

"Should I be worried about that developing friendship?" Jensen asked.

"Definitely," Mason answered.

"I better keep an eye on them." She started to follow the two women, but Tuck pulled her into his arms, laying a sizzling kiss on her lips. Jensen swatted at his shoulder, but the blush on her cheeks told me they might be sneaking away from the party early.

Her and Walker's parents were hosting a slumber party for all the kids at their ranch tonight so the parents could have a night to themselves. And if I knew anything about Tuck, it was that he wouldn't waste a night alone with his wife.

A soft strain of notes floated through the air, and I turned to see Liam helping Noah with a song on the guitar. Tessa looked on, so much love in her eyes. As Noah picked up the tune, Liam straightened, wrapping his arms around her from behind and resting his hands on her stomach.

The way he caressed her belly had me looking up at Mason. "Do you think Tessa's pregnant, too?"

He looked in their direction, studying the couple. "I have no idea. But it wouldn't surprise me."

No, it wouldn't. Tessa had always wanted the biggest family possible, and Liam would give anything to keep his wife happy. Mason wrapped an arm around my shoulders. "Why don't we get you something to drink?"

I nodded, a smile curving my lips. "Maybe a ginger ale."

"Have you been feeling sick? Maybe you should sit. Rest. God, I have no idea what you should or shouldn't be doing. I need to get some books—"

I cut Mason off with a kiss. "I'm fine. A little nauseous here and there, but the ginger ale will help cut it off before it starts."

"You're sure?"

"Positive."

We headed for the bar. Mason asked for a beer and a ginger ale. He handed me the soda, and as we turned to head back to our small party, Taylor and Walker were there. Taylor's gaze zeroed in on the soda bottle the bartender tossed in the recycling and then at my glass. "Oh my God. Are you pregnant?"

Walker pulled his wife into his side with one arm while the other balanced his daughter. "If she is, she might not want the entire world to know, Shortstack."

"Sorry," Taylor whispered but then beamed at me. "Are you?"

I couldn't hold in my laugh. "We are. But it's really early."

Taylor squealed, pulling me into a hug. "I'm so happy for you. You've earned every bit of this joy."

Something about the sentiment had tears burning the backs of my eyes. That so many people wanted so desperately for Mason and me to be happy. "Thank you, Tay."

She released me, wiping under her eyes. "Well, I'm just going to have to drink some champagne for you."

"I think that's a great plan."

Taylor looked up at Walker. "I think we should make another one."

His eyes widened a fraction as he bounced his daughter in his hold. "This one's still in diapers."

She shrugged. "Then what's one more set?"

Walker leaned into his wife and gave her a slow kiss. "I'll give you a baby."

Mason chuckled as we stepped away from the couple lost in

their own world. "Tonight might singlehandedly be responsible for a baby boom."

I linked my fingers with Mason's, leaning into his side. "I like that idea."

He pressed a kiss to my temple. "Me, too."

"Anna," Kennedy called as she hurried over to me and pulled me into a hug. "Happy almost-wedding day."

"Thanks, Kenz." When I pulled back, I studied my friend's face. She was glowing. "What is it?"

She stepped back into Cain's hold, grinning up at him. "Should we tell them?"

"Up to you."

"Tell me, or I won't give you any champagne," I argued.

Kennedy beamed. "We've got a new foster placement coming next week. Our social worker says she thinks he'll be eligible for adoption in another month."

"Kenz." My throat clogged as I looked at my friend. This was what she'd been waiting for. "I'm so happy for you." I pulled her into another hug. "Looks like we're going to be raising kiddos together."

She jerked, pulling back but holding onto my shoulders. "Are you?"

I nodded.

She bounced up and down. "This is the best day ever."

I looked back at Mason, who gazed at me tenderly. This man had given me a family I'd never even dared to dream of. We had built a life that was loud and chaotic, warm and loving, and above all, steadfast. I never doubted how Mason felt about me. I always felt safe and cherished. And that life was only growing.

I stepped into his arms. "Thank you."

He brushed his lips against mine. "For what?"

"Everything."

ACKNOWLEDGMENTS

So many people have supported me as I worked on this Sutter Lake project, and I'm grateful for every single one. An extra-special thank you to Emma, Grahame, Kelly, Laura, Sam, and Willow. Your friendships mean the world to me.

To all my family and friends. Thank you for supporting me on this crazy journey, even if you don't read "kissing books."

To my fearless beta readers: Crystal and Anelise, thank you for reading this book in its roughest form and helping me to make it the best it could possibly be!

The crew that helps bring my words to life and gets them out into the world is pretty darn epic. Thank you to Susan, Chelle, Janice, Julie, Hang, Stacey, Jenn, and the rest of my team at Social Butterfly. Your hard work is so appreciated!

To all the bloggers who have taken a chance on my words… THANK YOU! Your championing of my stories means more than I can say. To my launch and ARC teams, thank you for your kindness, support, and sharing my books with the world. And an extra special thank you to Crystal for wrangling it all.

Ladies of Catherine Cowles Reader Group, you're my favorite place to hang out on the internet! Thank you for your support, encouragement, and willingness to always dish about your latest book boyfriends. You're the freaking best!

Lastly, thank YOU! Yes, YOU. I'm so grateful you're reading this book and making my author dreams come true. I love you for that. A whole lot!

ALSO AVAILABLE FROM
CATHERINE COWLES

The Tattered & Torn Series
Tattered Stars
Falling Embers
Hidden Waters
Shattered Sea
Fractured Sky

The Wrecked Series
Reckless Memories
Perfect Wreckage
Wrecked Palace
Reckless Refuge
Beneath the Wreckage

The Sutter Lake Series
Beautifully Broken Pieces
Beautifully Broken Life
Beautifully Broken Spirit
Beautifully Broken Control

Stand-alone Novels
Further To Fall

For a full list of up-to-date Catherine Cowles titles please visit
www.catherinecowles.com.

ABOUT
CATHERINE COWLES

Writer of words. Drinker of Diet Cokes. Lover of all things cute and furry, especially her dog. Catherine has had her nose in a book since the time she could read and finally decided to write down some of her own stories. When she's not writing, she can be found exploring her home state of Oregon, listening to true crime podcasts, or searching for her next book boyfriend.

STAY CONNECTED

You can find Catherine in all the usual bookish places…

Website: catherinecowles.com

Facebook: facebook.com/catherinecowlesauthor

Catherine Cowles Facebook Reader Group: bit.ly/ccReaderGroup

Instagram: instagram.com/catherinecowlesauthor

Goodreads: goodreads.com/catherinecowlesauthor

BookBub: bookbub.com/profile/catherine-cowles

Amazon: https://www.amazon.com/author/catherinecowles

Twitter: twitter.com/catherinecowles

Pinterest: pinterest.com/catherinecowlesauthor

Printed in Great Britain
by Amazon